John Fulghum Mysteries

Vol. II

E.W. Farnsworth

Also by E.W. Farnsworth

John Fulghum Mysteries
Engaging Rachel
Pirate Tales

Coming Soon

Love in the Time of Baro Xaimos

John Fulghum Mysteries Vol. II

E.W. Farnsworth

For permission requests, write to the publisher at the address below:
Attention: Permissions Coordinator
Zimbell House Publishing, LLC
PO Box 1172
Union Lake, Michigan 48387
emailto: info@zimbellhousepublishing.com

Published in the United States by Zimbell House Publishing, LLC
http://www.ZimbellHousePublishing.com

Print ISBN: 9781942818663
Kindle Electronic ISBN: 9781942818670
Library of Congress Control Number: 2016902488

Dedication

For Ev, Maggs and Rita

CONTENTS

Hammer

I never knew him by any other name but Hammer, but I knew him well from his bloody legacy and I was decidedly not his friend. I grew to know increasingly more about him after the police found the pieces of his chainsaw-ripped body mixed with two others in an otherwise empty oil drum in the back of a stolen Ford truck, wiped clean of prints, down near the docks.

Word has it if you wanted someone hurt bad or worse, you made the call to a man named Sharpie over at the pool hall and he became the conduit to Hammer and for the cash. Sharpie was Hammer's choice as a front because he kept his mouth shut and his dealings mostly clean though he skimmed ten percent off every transaction in cash that was never reported. I found a cardboard box full of twenties with rubber bands around them, fifteen thousand dollars in all, in the loft of the pool hall right where Sharpie must have hidden it. Sharpie's body was also in that barrel with Hammer's, unhinged by a chainsaw just like his.

What Dolores Bleacher was doing with those two no one has discovered, and making her was somewhat difficult because her fingers and toes had been removed before the heavy work began. No fingers, no toes, no prints. The coroner believed that she had been alive through most of the cutting though he could not gauge the pain levels she must have experienced. He told me that at some point the woman must have passed out, and then, of course, she had died.

Dolores had gone missing at roughly the time when all three in the barrel had been executed, and yours truly demanded that the woman's DNA be checked against the database. At this point, they identified her as a high-end prostitute with a criminal record for extortion and murder-for-hire. I was not convinced that I could eliminate any of her priors from this case. I only know that nothing is more intimate than a ménage `a trois, mingling one brunette broad with two dead male bodies in a drum with blood as the binder.

An anonymous tip received the night they were found supplied the location of the abattoir where they had been slaughtered. A tip that was buried by the flurry of other emergencies that night including a robbery in progress and a drug network raid that involved half the force, the DEA, the FBI, the ATF and other sundry alphabet agencies. Long after finding the truck, when I asked that they check the record of incoming calls, they found a partial transcription of the anonymous call with the address and sent a squad car out to the warehouse. There inside on the floor, the two officers found blood everywhere and three still-working chainsaws caked with the same. They roped off the entire building and called in homicide to make the link to the barrel of fun with Hammer and the others. When forensics did their job, no prints were found, but the blood from the warehouse matched the blood in the barrel with no exceptions. The warehouse was where Hammer, Sharpie, and Dolores had been murdered in cold blood. Homicide believed that at least three perps did the executions, and others may have been present also. Maybe it was 'theater in the round'. Who knows? Unless I could break the case or the police get another tip from the anonymous caller, we were stuck.

I checked on Dolores through informers and cold interviews with working girls in her district. Dolores, they all said, was a stuck-up chick who kept to herself. She worked hard, and she did business with johns some of the others had turned down even when a lot of money had been offered. If Dolores did what those men wanted, they said, it served her right. She would even have those bearded, uncircumcised weirdoes who wore smock gowns and beat their women and their prostitutes with canes. The last anyone knew of Dolores was the night before she had disappeared when one of those bearded men had been seen departing from her little apartment room on the street. The man had been twirling his worry beads over in his hand and whistling as he walked with a swagger.

I usually avoid making direct contact with the Imams at the mosques, but under the circumstances, I decided to call on a couple of informants in the community and discovered that Dolores was the prostitute of choice for the Imams. They bragged to each other about having the woman first and then caning her for being an infidel and sinner afterward. One Imam, in particular, was a regular, once a week at least. Sometimes he took friends along to participate or just to watch. Shortly before Dorothy disappeared, the Imam took a hard-looking man with a scarred face along for an evening's entertainment.

I made an appointment to talk with this Imam, and he chose to come to my second-floor office where I had tidied up my racing forms in neat piles on the floor by the wall and shuffled my stack of unpaid bills as if they were important papers in my inbox. I dusted the visitor chair across my desk, even emptied and polished my ashtray but worked hard to fill it again with butts and ashes before he arrived. When he knocked on my door, I thought the smoky den was almost presentable. After he had entered, it was clear that he felt the place was unclean and unfit for someone of his stature, spiritual leader that he was. I had to admit the man had presence, with eyes that probed and insinuated. When he sat down uncomfortably in the wooden armchair I had dusted for him, he obviously avoided making contact with its arms and launched into a defensive battery of objections about being questioned in regards to an infidel slut and whore. He asked whether I knew that Muslims do not frequent prostitutes because the Quran forbade it, and when I stated coolly that I had witnesses with times and dates of his weekly assignations with Dolores Bleacher, he changed tactics to accuse his flock of occasional indiscretions. When I described the Imam's companion voyeur at his last encounter with Dolores, the Imam jumped at the chance to fob off the blame to him, by talking very fast, ending in a diatribe against radical Islam.

The upshot of the Imam's vituperation was that a fellow Muslim visiting from a foreign land had asked to be taken to a clean prostitute, and the Imam had taken him to Dolores. The Imam confessed that he had witnessed the coitus of the man with the prostitute, but that he had beaten both parties with a cane for their sinful behavior. Righteously, the Imam said that the foreigner had remained for two weeks in the city and then flew with his associates back to their country. Questioning his account, I learned that the foreigner and the five men who were with him during his stay at the Mosque were Iranian. The six Iranians had been in the city on business that involved buying and selling, and the Imam, a fellow Shiite, had been recommended as the right contact for them by the people who know such things in Iran.

When I asked the Imam about the leader among the Iranians, he said that the man was a former member of the Iranian Quds Force—a great warrior who had suffered many wounds, including a gash on his face, in support of just causes, Allah be praised. He had come up from South America via a ground route. After the six had completed their business, they had all flown back to Iran. I thanked the Imam for being forthright in answering my questions, but I wanted to ask one additional question, "What business, do you suppose, these Iranians had in this city?" The Imam said that he had no idea.

I sat at my desk thinking and chain smoking for at least an hour after the Imam departed. I felt like taking a bath for having been in his presence, and I did wipe the seat in which he had sat to be sure that he left no cooties behind. I thought I knew a lot about hypocrisy, but I had never seen such a slimy wiggler of a hypocrite baldly lying about everything because, for him, it is obligatory to lie to me, the infidel. I took a friend, Jack Daniels, with me, and slipped my .38 caliber revolver in my belt just in case.

Kenneth Mander and I went way back, but I cannot tell how because that would be a violation of national security secrets. After he had arrived at my motel room in the late afternoon, I poured us three fingers each of JD and launched into my hour-long account of the Hammer case and the Imam's interview. When I had finished my narrative, Mander poured us each another three inches of JD, and he began, in his cryptic way, to tell me what at first seemed to be an unrelated tale.

Mander said that a group of six Iranian spies had landed in Caracas, Venezuela after a flight from Iran. They were led by a current member of the Iranian Quds Force, an assassin, and dirty tricks villain, with a list of nefarious exploits too long to enumerate. His A-team had resumes that made Capote's *In Cold Blood* read like *A Child's Garden of Verses*. For these animals disguised as humans, he said, their own word halal must have had no meaning because they made an abattoir everywhere they went. They left mutilated corpses, many dismembered by chainsaws, to cover their movements through each country they passed. Fatalities stretching from Panama through Mexico, along with the latest example of their work—the slaughter of Hammer, Sharpie, and Dolores. It was characteristic for these Islamists to consort with prostitutes and cut-outs where they did business, killing them all just before they departed for home with their mission accomplished. Mander, taking another long drink from his glass, contended that the Quds Force was up to something much nastier than their blood lust slaughtering of a few no longer useful tools. Theirs was no longer a case for law enforcement, but one for the shadowy operational world of the CIA. In fact, Mander confided, a classified Presidential Finding had been issued to assassinate the six Iranians who had killed so wantonly whenever the opportunity should arise. I told Mander that I appreciated the intel and that I felt as if I wanted to help in some way.

Ken Mander shook his head, "John Fulghum, you are a true patriot, and I know that you will tell us if anything further turns up that might interest the Agency. For example, if the leader of the group turns up in the city again. I warn you that talking with the Imam has put you in the danger zone. Watch your Six, if you'll pardon the pun."

We parted with a handshake, and I knew that I no longer had a case. The Agency would chalk up the three murders to the list of accounts for which the six Iranians would atone. Knowing Mander, I felt that he would make the kills himself if he could do so.

****

I forgot about the entire affair insofar as expunging memories of the repellant blood, body parts and scents of putrefaction can be accomplished. Five weeks later, under the office door, a postcard appeared. On the picture side was a photo reproduction of a painting by Soutine, and on the message side was a greeting with the valediction, "Six Down!" I took a thumbtack from my desk drawer and pinned the Soutine postcard to the poster board behind my desk. I do love knowing what I cannot ever really know. So far, I have not seen the Imam again, but the thought of him makes me regret that he was not included in the atonement.

I returned to my captain's chair with two racing forms and dumped the contents of my overflowing ashtray into the trashcan under my desk. I then lit up a Marlboro and watched the smoke curl up into the dingy area of the ceiling. Something was definitely missing. I pulled out the second desk drawer on the right. There it was, right where I had left it - an unopened bottle of Jack Daniels whiskey and a glass. I raised the bottle and opened it. Having taken out the glass and polished it with my handkerchief, I poured two fingers of the brown elixir. For good measure, I poured a third finger.

The image of the abattoir would not go away. I thought about the things that kept me in the game. Helping the good guys win was at the top of my list. I took a long drag on my Marlboro, raised the glass of JD and gazed at the rich brown color. I thought a toast was in order.

"Here's to the agents who took down the six!" I said aloud. I drank and felt the warmth run down to my stomach, yet somehow that did not seem sufficient. I tried again.

"Here's to the good guys whoever they are!" I drank again. This time, I felt much better.

I picked up the racing form and with a pencil ran down the names of horses until I found the one I was looking for—Hammersmith. It was surely worth a try.

Crop Duster

The two boys' bodies were found along a red clay road, not five minutes from the local airport, and from the way the bullets had entered their craniums from the top rear indicated execution-style slayings. The location of the corpses was not where the boys had been murdered because no sign of their blood or brains was found anywhere near the bodies. Additionally, the color and consistency of the clay dust on their clothing did not match the ground where they lay. The two .38 caliber slugs that had done the fatal damage may have been fired by two police weapons, but it would have been dangerous to speculate in that direction so no one did so.

Public outrage about the killings was limited to the boys' mothers because the boys had often run afoul of the authorities. By the time the corpses had been buried, the case was rapidly becoming cold and would have been erased from memory except that Jean Sturral, the comely elder sister of Ben Sturral, the older of the two slain boys, brought in the outside help of John Fulghum, PI, to find the murderers and bring them to justice. Jean Sturral was an equestrienne and friend of a former client of John Fulghum. Fulghum was frankly tired of doing pro bono work, but Ms. Sturral and his former client were importunate and his interest deepened when Jean told him what she thought her brother Ben and his friend Stew were doing on the night they died.

Fulghum was intrigued by the idea that the teenage boys wanted to observe a crop duster's landing and handling way past the middle of the night while remaining out of sight. He was also intrigued by the speed with which the local police wanted to shelve any inquiry into the murders, which had been proclaimed unsolvable for no good reason. Something about this Arkansas homicide case smelled even more pungently than the reek of the solvent that had been found on both the murdered boys' shoes. In fact, it smelled like a mix of Little Rock, Arkansas, and Washington, DC, black politics. Fulghum, knowing about black ops from his military service, suspected the root of the matter went fairly high up in both the state and federal governments.

Fulghum was a patriot as his combat record with three Bronze Stars and a Purple Heart clearly showed, but he could not abide the cold-blooded murder of two innocent children or the cover-up of a heinous crime that had huge implications. When Fulghum arrived in Arkansas, he had no trouble laying his hands on the coroner's reports or viewing the area where the bodies had been found. He interviewed Jean Sturral for three hours, and she put him in touch with her friend Lucy Moran, the girlfriend of Stew Burrage. With the help of Jean and Lucy, Fulghum pieced together a pattern that stretched back over a year to the first time when Ben had stayed out all night to shoot raccoons out by the airport. Jean said that Ben had observed a lone crop duster land on the runway of the airport around two o'clock in the morning. That was anomalous and suspicious, but what happened next was a mystery.

A group of three men met the plane on the ground and watched it taxi to the wash-down area where the pilot climbed down and pulled on a slicker and boots that were provided to him so that he matched all the others' dress. With hoses and brushes, the four men washed the plane from stem to stern, with particular attention to the undercarriage and wheel assemblies. After the plane was clean, they pushed it into a special hangar, closed and locked the hangar door, and then hosed down the entire wash-down area. A particularly rank-smelling solution was applied to it, then brushed off the tarmac with push brooms. Then the four men took off their slickers and boots, put them into an upright barrel, applied kerosene and burned them. Ben watched the process without being seen and he wrote down everything he could recall about it in his diary when he returned home. After sharing what he had seen with his friend Stew, the two decided to penetrate the mystery represented by the plane.

Jean told Fulghum that the two boys became obsessed. They went on early morning observation raids regularly before they discerned a pattern of takeoffs and landings that focused their surveillance in two windows of time on one day of the week. They recorded how the plane was loaded prior to takeoff and how it was scrubbed with the same elaborate care each time when it returned. The boys could not find evidence of any night crop dusting that occurred anywhere in Arkansas or within two hundred miles of the airport. Then Stew began to draw range rings for the maximum possible round trip of the plane, and he reached the absurd-seeming breakthrough that the plane, which always headed south right after takeoff and came from the south on its return, must be flying regular missions offshore to Cuba and back again.

Fulghum asked the girls about the location of Ben's diary, but they both shook their heads as Jean told him that it had been seized by the police as evidence without leaving a receipt for it. On a wild guess, Fulghum asked whether either of them kept diaries, and they both said that they did but that their contents were very personal. Fulghum asked Jean whether she had made any record of her brother's quest in her diary, and when Jean said she had, he asked if she would transcribe only those records with their dates and give the transcript to him. After she agreed to do that, Fulghum then asked Stew's girlfriend to peruse her diary for any mention of the boys' activities and provide a transcript. He told both girls to keep a copy of their transcripts in a safe place because he did not know how dangerous it was for them to have any records regarding the boys' activities. He told them that the boys had been executed, for knowing what no one outside a few designated persons should know, and it made sense that whoever killed the boys would also kill others who were in a position to make trouble.

Fulghum studied the girls' diary transcripts and discovered that the boys had observed the crop duster's landing and clean-up operations on the same day every week for seven months. In Jean's transcript was the date when Cuba was first recorded as the possible destination for the flights. In Lucy's transcript was the mention of the Governor of Arkansas observing a wash down in his blue jeans and coveralls one early morning in July. In August, Jean's transcript mentioned that the boys' truck had been ticketed by the state police while the boys were on surveillance. Fulghum realized that would have been the boys' visibility point for the authorities. In September on the same night of the week that they did their observations, both boys had been killed. Fulghum thought that the boys were found in their hiding place, taken to a site where they were questioned, killed and then repositioned at the location where their bodies had been found. Fulghum put the chances at 50/50 that law enforcement officers had pulled the triggers, but he put the likelihood of his proving that at zero. He thought it more likely black ops personnel had used the .38 as a weapon because it had a police signature.

John Fulghum, a former Special Forces tracker, decided to find the place near the airport tarmac where the boys had hidden to watch the plane. The airport had so little use that Fulghum had no company when he searched the woods, and he found his setting right where he would have staged an operation just like theirs. In a natural enclosure made with honeysuckle vines, they could have lain on the ground and seen the wash down area, the special hangar, and any vehicles coming into or out of the operational area.

Fulghum did a box search around the hideaway, and he found a place where a half-dozen people had trampled the ground. Carefully combing the place on his hands and knees, he found two spent shell cases for a .38 caliber weapon. Fulghum picked up the casings with the point of his ballpoint pen so as not to disturb any fingerprints on the shells. He also found what might have been pieces of skull along with heel marks where the bodies had been dragged a distance to a place where the woods met the airport tarmac. He said to himself, "Bingo!"

When Fulghum returned to his motel, he called a friend at the FBI for an urgent meeting without explaining why. Without prying, his friend told Fulghum to fly to National Airport where he would be met upon arrival. Fulghum was greeted by a female agent, who drove him to an unmarked FBI office in Rosslyn, Virginia. Fulghum met Special Agent Fulbright in the office and motioned with a spinning finger and a shake of the head that he wanted to talk where no microphones were present.

Without a further word, Fulbright escorted Fulghum out of the building and into the multi-story public garage down the street. They climbed into Fulbright's personal automobile, and Fulghum put his friend in the picture, showing him the diary transcripts plus the shells that he had harvested in the woods.

Fulbright whistled when he was fully briefed, and suggested that he would discover what he could from the shells if Fulghum would take a receipt for his taking custody of them. Fulghum agreed and gave Fulbright the baggie with the shells in return for a signed, handwritten receipt.

On a hard-copy map, Fulghum had indicated the precise location of the hide he had found, the location of the probable scene of execution, the place where he had found the two shells and where the authorities could find evidence of blood and brain that could be DNA matched to the boys' bodies. He also told Fulbright he would provide copies of the girls' diary transcripts and the coroner's records if he could use Fulbright's Xerox machine to do the copying.

Before the two left the car, Fulbright said that Fulghum surely had a tiger by the tail. The FBI could provide intelligence, he said, but the Bureau could not take control of the two murder cases unless a Federal angle was discovered, which may not be possible when the perpetrators themselves might be Federal. He told Fulghum that black ops against Cuba were occurring every night from many locations along the Gulf of Mexico. He explained that all of those clandestine operations were covered with special protocols and caveats because they were technically illegal.

The involvement of the Governor of Arkansas—if it could be proven—could create a sensation, but it might not help solving the double murder case. He also warned Fulghum that once the two shells went to forensics, he could not guarantee that the chain of custody would be maintained. "Hell, Jack, depending on how high up this goes, the shells might just disappear, along with you, me and the two girls that provided the transcripts."

Fulghum asked his friend to provide whatever intel he could, and then the two returned to Fulbright's office where he made the copies and handed them to Fulbright as promised. Fulghum then flew back to Arkansas, watching his back carefully, and began to plan his own surveillance of the airport on the night of the next scheduled Cuban flight operation.

Fulghum was not a teenager on a lark, but a trained reconnaissance expert and at one time had been a certified assassin. By night, he infiltrated to his own hide near the hide that the boys used. He wore a black ninja costume and took night vision binoculars equipped with a high-tech camera feature that melded views taken by multiple means. He recorded the entire sequence of events in a combination of IR and optical, luckily capturing the Governor of Arkansas, his arms flying, his fists threatening and his anger clear. When the plane had been moved into its hangar, the Governor's assistant gesticulated at the woods where the old hide lay. The four operators fanned out and enclosed the old hide in a very professional manner. They moved into position quietly, and advanced in a rush from four directions into the honeysuckle, finding nothing. Frustrated, they went back to the tarmac and told the Governor's assistant that the hide had been found empty with no evidence of having been used in the recent past. All of this action was recorded by Fulghum, who ex-filtrated stealthily when the men had departed. *You can run, but you cannot hide,* Fulghum thought.

Fulghum flew back to Washington again, crashed another meeting with Fulbright, showed him the recording and provided him a copy, complete with a signed affidavit as to its authenticity. The date and time stamps, together with the GPS locational data affixed, were solid evidence, but Fulghum's name added credibility of intent. Fulbright gave

Fulghum a run down on the findings of his ballistics and forensics teams. The weapons were stolen police .38s. No prints were on the shells. Fulbright explained that Fulghum had shaken the tree, and those who guarded the guards were now going to be a problem. Fulghum returned to Arkansas, spending his week waiting like a tourist visiting the sights, savoring the tastes and hearing the sounds for which Arkansas was famous. When the week was up, he returned to the woods dressed like a ninja and carrying his weapon.

This time, Fulghum discovered that a bulldozer had been through the woods on a mission to destroy all the evidence that he had found. The old honeysuckle hide had been destroyed, the area where he had found the shells had been cleared to two inches below the ground, the area where the bodies had been dragged had also been razed, and the small hangar had been flattened. The crop duster was nowhere to be seen. Through his night vision device, Fulghum saw where four men were situated watching for an intruder; he had been expected to return this night.

Consequently, he swung wide so that he would not be ensnared in a trap and screwed on the silencer for his weapon. Reliving his SF days, he circled silently to the back of each of the four watchers and put a bullet through his skull—downwards from the rear, execution-style in the precise manner that they had used on Ben and Stew. After he had executed each man, he searched him but discovered no identification, so he took fingerprints of each man with a kit he carried with him on such missions. He did not attempt to move the dead bodies. Fulghum wanted them to remain as his personal message.

Instead of returning to his motel, Fulghum took off his ninja costume and deposited it in a convenient dumpster.

Pulling on a T-shirt that read, "New Orleans Here I Come," he drove to Louisiana, stopping only for refueling.

At a local FedEx Office Print shop, he faxed the fingerprints with no explanation whatsoever to Fulbright's office. Then at the first airport having such a service, Fulghum paid for a ticket with cash and took a direct flight back to his home city. He called Jean and pretended to be a representative of an exterminator business looking to clean out any remaining pests from her properties. His phrasing made her smile, "If you have any further extermination needs, do not hesitate to call us. You have our number."

Fulghum never did hear anything further from his friend Fulbright, but through his other Bureau connections, he learned that Fulbright had been promoted and reposted to the West Coast as a special agent for counterintelligence.

He learned from sources he knew on the Hill that a formal Congressional inquiry had been launched into alleged long-term, illegal operations against Cuba from all along the US mainland. Nothing was ever reported in the news about four men killed execution-style in the woods near a small airport in Arkansas. Though another friend wrote that in a training accident in Arkansas four men had been killed. This friend was taking up a collection for the unfortunate men's families, but Fulghum wrote back that he was fresh out of cash and besides had been considering taking up a collection of his own to fund his JD habit.

Fulghum put his feet up on his dusty desk, dragged on his Marlboro and watched the smoke twirl and the dust motes dance in the sunlight that streamed through the dirty windows high above the back of his desk. He picked up a racing form from the pile on his desk and began strategizing where to place his bets when he was interrupted by a fist pounding hard on his glazed office door.

Fulghum had excellent reactions, so he hit the floor beside his desk, his revolver cocked and loaded, as he peered around his desk to gauge what was happening. A one-page note slid under the door. The person who had knocked and slid the note just walked away and stomped noisily down the stairs.

Relieved, he stood up, holstered his weapon and picked up the note, which read:

Thank you. If you come by this way again, you will need to stay at a new motel because the one you liked burned to the ground the night you disappeared. Don't worry, we are both okay here. Y'all take care now. Love, Jean.

Looking around his office, Fulghum thought it might have been hit with a crop duster, but then he pulled open his lower desk drawer, hauled out his old friend Jack Daniels and poured three inches of brown velvet delight. Then he lighted up another Marlboro, took a drag on the cigarette, and with the look of someone who was trying to remember something important began to rummage through his racing forms.

Gypsy Traveler

To the sounds of bells, Zara Rapello stepped inside the second-story office of John Fulghum, PI, and espied in the smoke around his desk, the detective hunched over his racing forms. For a moment, she was uncertain what to do, but a gruff voice told her to sit down and say what was on her mind. She sat in the captain's chair across the desk from the detective with her bracelets and bells making an unsubtle music. She wore a brilliant orange kerchief tied over her head and tucked her curly black hair behind her ears before putting her hands in her lap.

"Mr. Fulghum, I am Zara Rapello. A mutual acquaintance, Joe Pounce, recommended you. My brother, Marcello Rapello, has been arrested for a murder he did not commit. No one will listen to me because everyone thinks he's guilty. Can you help me? Please." She was on the verge of tears, but she was also curious about the figure who sat across from her.

John Fulghum raised his eyes from his racing form when he heard the name of the gifted son of his friend Officer Pounce of Boston Homicide. Through the smoke from his lighted Marlboro, he saw a beautiful gypsy girl in a long, dark green dress. She had raven black hair, onyx eyes, and an olive complexion. She looked as if she were from central casting to audition for the part of the devious fortune-teller in a Sherlock Holmes film.

"Miss Rapello, how do you know Joseph Pounce?"

"That is a long story. The short version is that we were classmates at the Boston English School before he went up to Harvard. He gave me his cell phone number in case I should ever run into trouble. I'm fine, but my brother was arrested, so I called Joe. He told me to get in touch with you right away." The girl leaned forward in her chair, her eyes flashing with expectation.

John Fulghum sat up in his chair and chain lit another Marlboro. "Do you smoke?"

"Yes, I do. Would you mind if I smoked here?"

"Be my guest. Here, have one of mine." Fulghum lit a Marlboro from the one he was smoking and handed it to the girl. She took the cigarette between her thumb and index finger and inhaled deeply. Fulghum saw that each of her fingernails had been decorated individually. The girl did not relax but shifted her position now that he had made a kindly gesture. She set the hand with the cigarette on the arm of her chair and re-engaged on another tack.

"Mr. Fulghum, what do you know about gypsies?" she asked, squinting her eyes and pursing her vermillion lips.

"Miss Rapello, I have known a few gypsies and I've read enough to know not to believe in the Hollywood stereotypes. I'm sure that not all gypsies are thieves, fortune tellers, and bear baiters. I'd hazard a guess that you are derived from gypsies. You must be special because Joe asked you to call me. What else would you like me to say?"

"Yes, I am a gypsy and proud of it. Two generations ago, my people came to America from Europe to escape the Nazis. My grandmother told fortunes for a living. My grandfather brought his bear from Europe and people paid him to see the bear. We had family in this country, so we had support and food. We traveled whenever we felt unwelcome. We now live on a small farm in Reading."

"How did you get to Boston English School?"

"When I was very little, I was forced to go to school in Portsmouth, Virginia. A teacher there saw that I needed glasses to read, so she paid for them. She also gave me two books—a Bible and the complete works of Shakespeare. In return, she only wanted me to study hard and achieve whatever I could. I felt very grateful, though soon afterward, my family moved because a theft at a dry goods store went badly for us." She stopped for a moment to take a long pull on her cigarette.

"Please go on," the detective urged, now fully engaged.

"I went to school when I could, but we never stayed long enough in one place for me to have good records. When we arrived in Reading, my mother set up shop as a reader-advisor. My father was off trying to find work in Virginia. While he was away, the headmaster of the Boston English School became one of my mother's steady customers. In lieu of payment for her services, my mother asked the headmaster to admit me to his school. At first, the man was reluctant but he finally agreed to see me. After an interview, he invited me to apply for a scholarship. I won the scholarship."

"Good for you."

"Thank you. Fortunately, my family has not had to move lately. I've been attending classes and doing as well as I can. Joe and I became friends at school because we were both in the debate club. He was my partner in the debate competitions with other schools. We always won. Now Joe has moved on, and because of my brother's troubles, my family might be moving on as well." She stubbed out her cigarette in the heaping ashtray and sat back looking at the detective as if her situation was hopeless.

"Now tell me as much as you like about your brother's situation."

"My brother has a police record for theft. He is very fast with his hands, but sometimes not fast enough. Since he never steals anything large, he has gotten jail time for breaking and entering and petty theft. He has never been violent. He would not kill anyone unless honor was at stake. He would kill anyone who harmed me, or my mother. Three weeks ago, a man whom my brother knew was found dead in his kitchen with his throat slit ear to ear. On the floor, by the body, was the knife used for the killing. It was my brother's knife and his fingerprints were on the handle. The police came to the farm where we live in Reading and took him away." Again, she seemed to be on the verge of tears.

"I don't know which to offer you, a handkerchief or a cigarette. Which will help the most?"

"I'd like a tissue, please, and then another cigarette." She accepted Fulghum's handkerchief, with which she dried her eyes and blew her nose. She balled the kerchief up in her left hand. She then accepted another lighted Marlboro in her right hand.

"Thank you."

"Tell me why you think your brother is innocent."

"My brother would never kill a person he loved for any reason."

"Are you telling me that your brother Marcello loved the man who was found murdered?"

"Yes. I know it for a fact. Standish Howling was the son of our family's benefactor."

"What do you mean by that?"

"When gypsies came to America from abroad in those days, we needed someone to vouch for us. Whoever did that had to pledge to support us. Charles Howling, Standish's grandfather, made that pledge for my grandfather and grandmother. My grandfather told me our family owed him everything. Without his help, we never would have escaped the Nazi death camps. His son, Charles, Jr., continued to support us after his father died, and the torch passed to his eldest son, Standish."

"Was Standish Howling responsible for your family's coming to Reading?"

"My mother told me that Standish Howling arranged for our welcome in Massachusetts and our temporary lodging at the farm in Reading."

"When you say that your brother Marcello loved Standish Howling, did you mean that he was grateful, or something else?"

"Mr. Fulghum, Standish Howling was gay. So is my brother Marcello. They were lovers. Does that surprise you?"

"Miss Rapello, nothing surprises me. Were your brother and this man a couple, or did they have an open relationship?"

"Marcello always talked as if they were a couple. He looked forward to being formally married when the law permitted that."

"Your brother never mentioned being jealous?"

"No. Everything he said implied that their feelings were mutual."

"How widely known was their relationship among your family?"

"It was a secret. I knew because Marcello told me in confidence. I've only told you because the fact is material to his defense and because Joe told me you'd keep everything I said between us."

"I will keep that matter confidential, but you aren't my client yet."

"Does that mean that you won't help me?"

"I didn't say that I won't help. Why don't we agree to meet again tomorrow at the same time as today? I'd like to check on a few things before I agree to take your case."

"I can get you money if that's what you need."

"If I take your case, all I'll need is one dollar. I just don't want to waste your money and time—and my time if nothing can be done."

"I'll be here tomorrow then." She rose and extended her hand across the desk. Fulghum stood and shook it. With a faint smile, she gave him back his handkerchief.

"What is the address of the farm where your family stays?" Fulghum asked her.

"Here is a map with the location indicated by an 'X,'" she answered as she rummaged in her enormous handbag, fetched out a folded sheet and handed it to him. "At the entrance to the farm is a small building with my mother's place of business. You can't miss it. The sign reads, 'Reader, Advisor,' in bold red letters."

The girl did a pirouette and walked out his door and down the stairs to the street.

John Fulghum called Officer Pounce to get the inside story about the arrest of Marcello Rapello.

"John, it looks like an open-and-shut case of murder one. The weapon belongs to Rapello. He has no alibi."

"Has Rapello confessed to the murder?"

"No, but we're working on it."

"What's the motive?"

"We don't have one yet. Are you working this case on the outside?"

"Not officially, no."

"The Chief wants this case to be simple. The Howlings are a blue-blood family with enormous wealth and influence. If you decide to get involved, you'll have to work miracles to stop the moving freight train that will convict this young man. Just read the morning papers, and you'll see why. Anything else now? I've got to get back to the grindstone. You won't believe how many victims we saw in the last twenty-four hours. You'd think this was New York City from the carnage."

John Fulghum decided that he desperately needed to see the future clearly and not through the smoke of his dingy office. To help with his clairvoyance, he would drive to Reading and consult a certain reader-advisor. The drive through the red and gold landscape that Indian summer afternoon put him in a good mood. The fields of the Reading farm were all tilled over and lined with maple forest in full color. Outside the farm among the trees, was the shack with the mystical sign of a fortune-teller named Rosa. Fulghum parked and walked straight through the door into a dimly lighted, incense-filled area where a fifty-something tattooed woman in a dun red dress sat smoking a cigarette while she played solitaire. She sat back in her chair to appraise the detective.

"Come right in and take a seat. You don't need an appointment, and we can get started right away, whatever you need." Fulghum took the only seat available, adjacent to the fortune-teller at her table, which was cluttered with the accouterments of her trade. He saw a Tarot deck, worry beads, an Ouija board, assorted feathers and a small brass censer with smoke curling from it.

"I don't suppose you can guess why I'm here."

"Looking at your eyes and your posture, I'd say you were a gumshoe, formerly a soldier. You've been smoking. You like drinking. You need a shave. You don't like to put on airs. Since my son is now in jail, I'd have to say you're here about him somehow. Since my daughter has been missing from school since noon, I'd say she came to you to get help with her brother's case. There's something else, but I can't quite place it. Let's see. Games of chance might be the ticket. From your dress, you don't look like a lounge lizard or a casino man. You can't be a successful gamer. So I'd say you play the horses, off-track. Could it be that you're looking for the name of a winning steed?"

"Rosa, you are a fair gumshoe. Maybe you can tell me why your son Marcello is in jail for murder."

"You probably know his knife was found next to the victim's body. That will probably be enough to convict him what with all his priors. I knew that my son and the deceased had a relationship though I was never clear about what that meant. I knew that my son was frantic about finding his knife. It had been missing for a week before the murder. From what I've heard, my son does not have an alibi for the night when the murder was committed. Pardon me while I light up."

"Have one of mine. I'll join you." Fulghum lit two cigarettes and gave one to the fortune-teller. He watched her shake her head and heard the tinkle of her enormous earrings. He saw how her black hair, black eyes, and olive skin were all passed down to her daughter.

"You and your daughter might be sisters."

"Once upon a time people said we were ringers for each other. Now dye helps, but my wrinkles are a dead giveaway. Look, detective, my son did not kill Standish Howling. It wasn't written in the stars. I don't have a lot of money, but I'd give everything I have to find the person who did kill Standish so my son can come home."

"How many close friends does your son have?"

"He has exactly two friends, Thomas Porro, and Ollie Strong. They are both no good. They got Marcello in trouble with their thieving ways but they aren't killers."

"You said your son and the victim had a relationship. Can you explain what that was?"

"It wasn't like with Thomas and Ollie. Marcello spent a lot of time with Standish. They would go all over New England together, with Standish paying for everything. Marcello would often spend the night at his house."

"Did you know Standish?"

"I knew him, and I knew his father and grandfather before him. That family sponsored my family, and we owe the Howlings more than we could ever repay."

"Tell me about Standish."

"He was handsome, smart, generous, kindly, and enormously rich. He might have been a lady's man."

"Was he a lady's man?"

"Not like his grandfather and father were. Hahaha. Those gentlemen never tired of finding new women."

"Did the Howlings ever ask for anything in return for having sponsored your family?"

"Never once did they ask for a penny. They did not want praise or recognition. Naturally, my own mother provided services as a fortune teller, and so did I for a while."

"You didn't provide Standish with your services?"

"No. That ended with his father, Charles, Jr."

"That would mean that you did not know much about Standish's private life."

"I only knew what Marcello told me about that."

"What did Marcello say?"

"He told me that Standish was a major player not only in New England but also in the country."

"In what sense was he a major player?"

"He had connections with very rich and powerful people—senators, sports team owners, media figures, company presidents, those sorts. Marcello said that he did not like to remain in the limelight. Instead, he played in the shadows."

"Do you know what he meant by that?"

"No, but I can guess."

"Please do so."

"Standish liked to be everything his father was not. His father ran for office on numerous occasions. He was always getting his name in the newspaper. For that matter, his grandfather was the same sort. Life wasn't interesting for those men if they were not doing something grand."

"Something like sponsoring a gypsy family from Europe."

"Exactly so. In contrast, Standish wanted to keep his name out of the papers entirely. He had people at the Globe who made sure that nothing made the papers about what he did."

"Do you know any specifics about what he did?"

"Marcello told me that Standish was a spy."

"Did Marcello say anything about Standish in the week or two before the murder?"

"He only said that Standish was up to his old tricks again. He said the man was in danger up to his neck but paid no heed to warnings."

"When your grandfather and grandmother came to America, were there other gypsies from your family in this country?"

"Yes, both here in Massachusetts and in Virginia. Both places were—and still are—tolerant of Roma like us. We connected with our family immediately after arriving here."

"Are they all with you on the farm?"

"Not hardly. Aside from three families—ours, Thomas's and Ollie's, they've spread out across the nation."

"I read somewhere about gypsy leadership. In Europe wasn't there a king of gypsies?"

"You'll read about gypsy kings and queens, but that really refers to the head man or head woman in a group. The airs that the current so-called king puts on in Moldova are the laughing stock of real gypsies."

"How are infractions handled within the families?"

"We keep a close eye on our own."

"And if a young person wants to be married?"

"Permission must be granted, naturally."

"If a match is not considered suitable?"

"Hahaha. If a gypsy's heart wants a match, it would be very hard to combat."

"What about jealousy? Or honor?"

"Those are settled in the gypsy way. Outsiders would have no visibility into that."

"Do you have any thoughts about why anyone would want to murder Standish Howling?"

"Jealousy might be a motive, but I could not divine the nature of it."

"Not honor?"

"That would depend on matters beyond my ken."

"For a moment, let's have a professional relationship." Fulghum placed a hundred-dollar bill on the table and waited for the woman's response. She looked at the bill for a moment. She stubbed out her cigarette. She lit another cone of incense in the brass censer. Then she folded the hundred and placed it in a box on the side of the table. She laid her hands face down on the table and closed her eyes. The smell of sandalwood and musk filled the room.

"Standish had many friends he could not acknowledge. One of those was Marcello. He knows of two others. As for the Saturday races, none of those favored to win will be in the winner's circle. The rest is cloudy and our time is up." The woman's closed eyes streamed with tears.

Fulghum left Rosa sitting at her dark table with her secrets and her grief. He drove onto the farm and found what he was looking for in a copse of trees by a stream running through an otherwise open field in view of the farmhouse. He parked next to an ancient Jeep without wheels that was being used as a jungle gym by a group of gypsy children. Young women were using clothespins to hang out colorful clothing that had been washed in tubs. Two young men with long hair and mustaches in sweatshirts and blue jeans came out to greet him.

"Hello. My name is John Fulghum. I'm looking for two men named Thomas and Ollie. Do you know where I can find them?" The men laughed mirthlessly. One went to the right side of Fulghum's car, the other to the left. The children left the rusty Jeep and thronged around out of curiosity to see the show.

"Nice car, mister. He's Ollie. I'm Thomas. Are you from the law?"

"That depends. Your friend Marcello is sitting in jail on a murder charge. Do you know anything about what happened?"

"We know nothing. Isn't that so, Ollie?"

"Nothing. You need to have your windshield wipers changed, mister? The winter's coming. It's going to snow."

"That's good advice, Ollie. Did you know Standish Howling?"

"Stuck up bastard, that's what he was."

"Yeah. He was always looking down his nose at the likes of us." Thomas muttered.

"When did you last see him?"

"It must have been a month ago, wasn't it Thomas?"

"Roundabout. I asked him about his needing new windshield wipers. He said he'd think about it. Then suddenly, he really did need new wipers."

"Hahaha. He did at that," Ollie smirked.

"I'd appreciate it if you left my wipers alone."

"Sure, mister. Is that all you wanted to know?" Thomas inquired.

"Do you think your friend Marcello killed Standish Howling?"

"No way. I'd have believed it if Howlings killed Rapello though."

"What do you mean by that, Thomas?"

"Howling hated being with gypsies like us. He treated us like scum—as if we were beneath him. One day, we thought Howling would take his gun and shoot Marcello. It was only a matter of time."

"Why would he want to do that?"

"Because of what Marcello knew about him."

"And what was that?"

"That's for us to know and you to think about knowing."

"And for twenty dollars, what would you say about sharing your knowledge?"

"For twenty each, maybe."

"If what you have to tell me is solid gold, it's a deal, provided I keep my wipers in place."

The two men became very serious. They put the wipers back down against Fulghum's windshield. They then shooed the children away because they were now conducting serious business. They waved the girls at the clotheslines to get back to their work. Then they closed on Fulghum like two thugs about to roll a victim. They stopped on either side of the detective.

"We know that Marcello was doing secret things for Standish. Terrible things. Howling told Marcello that he would be killed if he ever said anything. Marcello would not listen to his threats. He only wanted the glory."

"Glory?"

"Yeah, glory. It's funny, mister. The more Marcello did, the more Howling asked him to do. We had no part in any of it."

"Can you be more specific?"

"This is the most I can say—Marcello was Howling's patsy. If anything was ever to go wrong, Marcello would be the fall guy."

"Fall guy for what?"

"You're the guy asking questions. Figure it out. It seems Howling was right. Marcello will be the patsy for his own death."

"And this is supposed to be worth twenty dollars?"

"That's forty dollars. One bill for each. Then no messing with your wipers." Thomas folded his arms. Ollie imitated Thomas. The two smirked and then, like automatons, extended their right hands for the cash.

Fulghum had another thought, "So which of you was Howlings's lover?"

Thomas made the very bad mistake of grabbing for his knife. Fulghum caught his wrist and snapped it like a rotten branch. Ollie would have pulled his own knife, but he saw what was likely to happen to his wrist at the hands of this warrior. He backed off and waved his hands to indicate that he was not looking for trouble. Thomas was now writhing on the ground. Fulghum kicked his knife away from him and picked it up. He pulled out two twenty dollar bills and threw one at each man. Then he walked back to his car.

As Fulghum backed out of the grove, he observed the eyes of the gypsy children and the girls on him. They were soulless, ominously hostile and without any of the intelligence that informed the eyes of Rosa and her daughter. Fulghum thought to himself, *They might all be from the same gypsy family, but there is a chasm between those who are animated and those who have been beaten by whatever formed their lives.*

As he drove out the entrance to the farm, he decided to stop by the reader-advisor's shack again. He found the woman tidying up after her day's work. She beckoned him to sit down. He did so and placed Thomas's knife on the table in front of him.

"Tell me, Rosa, is this knife like the one your son owned?"

"It is identical to it. Where did you get it?"

"Thomas tried to slice me with it, so I disarmed him."

"Marcello, Thomas, and Ollie were given knives from the same batch. They were proud of them."

"Who gave them the knives?"

"Standish Howling, of course."

"Why did he give them the knives?"

"He told them that they needed the knives for self-defense."

"That knife just cost Thomas a broken wrist. After I have my forensics people work on it, I'm going to give it to you. You can then give it back to him or not as you like. Is there a chance that Thomas is gay?"

"I've always wondered about that. He could very well be gay. You should ask my daughter. She might know."

"Speaking of your daughter, she told me that you once were the reader-advisor for the headmaster of the Boston English School. That was the way that she got her chance for education. Is that true?"

"I'm still his reader-advisor, and, yes, it's true but it's not what you're probably thinking. I never have slept with the man though I was tempted on account of my husband being away."

"Your husband is looking for work in Virginia?"

"Wherever he is, he's probably not looking for work."

"What do you mean?"

"My husband is asked to do things by many people. They need his services for a while. When he completes a job, another comes almost immediately. It's always been that way."

"What does your husband do that puts him in such demand?"

"He's never told me. I've never asked since the first time."

"What happened then?"

"He beat me senseless and left me for dead."

"Is that an old gypsy custom?"

"It has nothing to do with being a gypsy. It has everything to do with my husband's penchant for secrecy. Marcello's a lot like his father."

"Thomas and Ollie informed me that Marcello did secret work for Standish Howling. They also said that Marcello told them he was in danger."

"That does not surprise me, Mr. Fulghum. Men have secrets. You, for example, have secrets. I can see it in your eyes."

"All people have secrets, Rosa. Some secrets make us human. Others make us inhuman. What kind of secrets do you harbor?"

"Mr. Fulghum, my fortunes don't trespass on people's secrets. They unearth the guilt and deception, not the secrets."

"A profound thought, Rosa. Now if you'll pardon me, I must be going."

"More racing forms to consult with your new knowledge?"

"Yes and a late afternoon meeting with a friend."

"Would your friend's initials be J and D, perhaps?"

"Rosa, hold that thought. I might be back with other questions for you."

Rosa reached into her box and withdrew the hundred-dollar bill. She tucked it into her bosom and smiled at Fulghum.

"You have a running tab any time you like. Goodbye, Mr. Fulghum. Please give my regards to Mr. Jack Daniels. We are old friends."

What with its being rush hour, Fulghum arrived in his office at dusk. He turned on his desk light and pulled open the second drawer on the right side of his desk to fetch out his bottle of Jack Daniels and his dirty glass. He polished the glass with a tissue. Then he poured himself three fingers of the velvety brown nectar. As he imbibed, he thought over the afternoon's work. He still had not decided to take the case, but something about his encounter with Thomas and Ollie was nudging him to be favorable. He lit a Marlboro and watched the cigarette's smoke curl as it rose to the ceiling.

The next day was gray, drizzly and foggy. It was an excellent day to summon a ghost from the past, so Fulghum telephoned his old friend Ken Mander of the Central

Intelligence Agency with a simple question—did the Agency have any association with the Howling family of Greater Boston? Mander told Fulghum he would check on that, and tell him what he found.

Fulghum then went to the Boston Globe archives to research references to gypsies who had passed through the area. He made a list of names and arrest records. He began to associate those on his own but soon realized that he still had an account with Rosa so he drove out to ask the fortune-teller about his findings. She was alone in her office without appointments scheduled for the rest of the morning.

"Rosa, when your husband is out of the area, how do you get in touch with him?"

"I call him on his cell phone. What else would I do in these modern times?"

"Will you please call him and let me speak with him when you reach him?"

"Do you want me to call him right now?"

"Yes, please call him now. Your son's life might depend on it."

Rosa dialed her husband's number, and the gypsy answered after the first ring. Rosa put the cell phone on speaker mode and introduced John Fulghum to Roberto Rapello.

"Mr. Rapello, I am a private investigator working to find evidence that will free your son Marcello from suspicion of murdering Standish Howling. Will you help me with that?"

"I would very much like to help you, but to do that I will need to talk with you face to face. Right now, I am very busy where I am so I cannot fly to Boston. Is it possible that you can fly down to meet me in Norfolk, Virginia?"

"Will you provide the airfare for me to do that? If so, I'll fly down tomorrow and meet you at the airport at three o'clock in the afternoon."

"I will reimburse you in cash for your round trip flight and your time. Thank you for taking the initiative. I am worried about my son. I know he did not commit this crime."

"Mr. Rapello, can you tell me anything that can help me right now?"

"Mr. Fulghum, this is an open line. It would be a severe breach of security for me to elaborate any more than I already have done. Already we have talked too much. We'll talk tomorrow when you arrive here. Goodbye." Rapello terminated the call. Fulghum looked at Rosa, who only shrugged.

Fulghum drove back to his office and found Ken Mander in a trench coat waiting for him at his door at the top of the stairwell. Instead of entering the office, Mander asked that they drive around and talk in Fulghum's car. When they reached the 128, Mander began talking shop.

"John, for three generations, the Howling family has been connected to the Office of Strategic Services in World War II and to the CIA from its founding until young Howling died. The family members, Charles, Charles, Jr., and Standish, were never agents on our books. They helped out in difficult matters, often using their own funds to support missions inside and outside the country."

"What is the gypsy connection?"

"I'm coming to that. This will take some meandering, so bear with me. In the meantime, just drive around in the miserable drizzle and listen. Keep an eye out for followers."

Fulghum nodded and lighted a Marlboro. Mander lit up also, and they cracked their windows while Fulghum turned on the defogger full-blast.

"Wild Bill Donovan personally asked Charles Sr., to sponsor the Rapello family, as a reward for their work for us against the Nazi threat before we entered the war. The gypsies were under threat, but some, like the Rapellos, wanted to fight back at the risk of their lives. They helped us take key agents out of Germany, and they supported agents we infiltrated. They asked for nothing in return. It was enough for them that they were striking hard at the Nazis. Donovan saw an opportunity in using the gypsies when they came to the US in a variety of missions. He made sure that the Rapellos and others were settled and connected to their relatives who were already in this country."

"That all makes sense, Ken. There had to be advantages in having a group outside the mainstream that could do odd jobs. So, the Rapellos became fellow travelers, so to speak. How did their cooperation get extended through the Cold War? Isn't it true that even the USSR had a gypsy king throughout the Cold War?"

"It is interesting that you mention that little-known fact. Even more secret than that, what the USSR had fashioned, we also fashioned from the same fabric. We even copied each other's methods in using gypsies within our separate spheres. That allowed both sides to control a potentially disruptive group while protecting it at the same time and using the gypsy community as a talent pool to draw upon generally."

"That also makes good strategic sense. I'll guess that certain families were more susceptible to playing 'nice in the sandbox' than others. Further, I'll bet that the Rapellos were especially loyal. The granddaughter I met has all the earmarks of having been groomed to the trade."

"It's even better than you guessed. Because of their dispersion throughout the country, the gypsies became a mobile intelligence force without portfolio. They could be deployed at our will when they were needed, and they were self-sufficient. No records were necessary and no payments. The Rapello family knit the whole plan together by their own movements and their willingness to visit the other families all over the nation."

"That would mean that Roberto was an Agency stringer?"

"Yes, he was and still is. We have been grooming his son and daughter to follow in his footsteps as well though they are not aware of this." Mander looked at Fulghum to gauge his response. Fulghum took another long drag on his cigarette and nodded his understanding.

"Now a major monkey wrench has been thrown into the works with the murder of the man whose family is connected to the Rapellos."

"Yes and no."

"Please explain."

"This is where things get complicated. We discovered that the Rapellos not only had an intelligence potential but they also had counterintelligence potential. They could monitor attempts of the opposition to exploit the networks we had created. So, as the USSR and then the Russians tried to infiltrate the gypsy families in America with their own gypsy agents, we picked up, turned their spies and made them our own. Are you with me so far?"

"I follow you. Go on."

"Since the Russian Federation did a duck dive after the end of the Cold War, the gypsies were wide open territory for them to exploit—or so they figured. The sponsors and supporters of our gypsy network were also targeted in the name of the New World Order. Some of the sponsors, like the young Howling, fell for the Russian ruse hook, line, and sinker."

"You're telling me that blue-blooded Howling was turned by the opposition? How did that happen?"

"When they discovered that the man was a closet homosexual, it was very easy. They worked on him from that angle with a succession of agents who became his intimate companions. He sang like a canary. He gave up the Rapello family, for example. When the Agency discovered what had happened, the Deputy Director of Operations decided on a plan to turn the Russian operation inside-out."

"I assume that the gypsies were still off the reservation."

"That's right. They were, in effect, unacknowledged assets on American soil. We couldn't make the Russians' actions visible because the network of gypsies technically did not exist and because we could not be seen as acting outside our charter, which clearly forbids our operating against the enemy on our own shores. Consider the firestorm that would have occurred if we turned over what we had to the FBI, which is now the proper venue for domestic counterintelligence."

"I see what you mean. I also understand why the young Howling's death may have been expedient."

"We didn't kill the young man."

"You didn't, so who did?"

"I'm coming to that. Is there a Dunkin' Donuts around so we can get some coffee? I need my caffeine fix, and I suspect you do also."

"I'll find the nearest D&D if you'll tell me what the Agency plans to do next. I hope your plan has an angle that will work to free young Rapello."

"That's where we're going to need your help, John."

"Why did I see that one coming a mile off?"

"Hahaha. Bear with me a little longer, pal. A little bird tells me that you will be visiting Roberto Rapello in Norfolk, Virginia tomorrow afternoon."

"Now I see why Roberto was so anxious about our talking on his cell phone."

"Relax, John. You'll see that everything works for the good. Right now, we don't know where we stand with the Rapello family. We'd like to keep them working for us, but we're aware they are actively working with the opposition in ways that are difficult for us to penetrate for a variety of reasons."

"Okay, let me say this back at you to see whether I understand the state of play. You have a rogue gypsy family that is off the books of both our Agency and the Russian Federation. You need to realign those assets so that they are really working for us while they pretend to work for the Russians."

"You have it."

"But, Ken, I'm not finished. No matter who killed the young Howling, his death was the opportunity for the Agency to hold the young Rapello hostage under the credible threat of a conviction for murder one while you move heaven and earth to do the realignment. What dangerous symmetry! So the Agency benefits no matter what the outcome. I wonder why the bureaucrats aren't just taking the easy way out by sacrificing the one for the many. What does the life of the young Rapello mean in the context of the great game of intelligence?"

"John, I know you are being cynical now. The Agency wants to keep the young Rapello in play. To do that, we have to come up with what you are already looking for—the real murderer."

"Come clean, Ken, you tell me who murdered Standish Howling."

"That brings me to the last part of your briefing, which of course never occurred. We believe that Howling's handler for the Russians killed him because they thought him a security risk—their profiling department reached the same conclusion as our own. The man was deemed to be wholly unreliable and unpredictable. The Russian handler, a ruthless operative code-named Boris Nevsky, is openly gay and reports directly to the Russian resident in Boston. We have broken the message from Moscow Center that ordered Howling's assassination. The message was addressed to the Boston resident. We believe he issued the order to Nevsky. Within one week, Howling was found with his throat slit."

"That kind of evidence is Black Chamber stuff, Ken. Why don't you just pull the trigger on the scumbag and tell the local authorities to release their prisoner?"

"Think it through, John. If we make a move against Nevsky, we blow the fact that we're reading the Russian encrypted traffic. That is why we need you."

"Okay. You can't tell the truth. I can't tell anyone what you just told me. I'm supposed to find the murderer that I've already found and deliver cogent evidence that the Russian agent committed the crime within the next week to the Boston authorities. I'm seeing Zara this afternoon in my office and flying to Norfolk tomorrow to see Roberto. Can you give me any hints about what I'm to do to help you out of this FUBAR mess?"

"I never thought you'd ask. Will you tell Zara this afternoon that you'll take the case and help her brother out of his mess?"

"Gladly. I was going to do that anyway."

"Good. Tomorrow when you see Roberto, will you tell him that you are on the case officially and that you will find the murder without fail?"

"How can I do that when you've given me an impossible situation to deal with? I'm not going to lie. That's your business, not mine!"

"John, after all we've been through together, that's a low blow. Think for a moment that you are back in Afghanistan taking out the tangos in their lairs."

"I can relate to that. I repeat, though, what can you give me that will help me?"

"Let's order our coffees and I'll tell you. Make mine a regular with an extra two shots."

"You'll be flying all the way back to my office. Come to think of it, that's a good idea. We'll make it two of the same."

When John and Ken had their coffees and were back on the road, they both lit up cigarettes.

"Okay, Ken, this had better be good."

"Do you remember the man Thomas whose wrist you broke yesterday?"

"I do. What of him?"

"He is definitely gay."

"I figured as much, but what has that got to do with the situation?"

"Thomas is romantically involved with Boris Nevsky."

"What?"

"Thomas provided Marcello's knife to Nevsky so he could plant it next to the corpse. Nevsky used Thomas's knife to do the killing so he could avoid getting his own prints on that planted knife."

"How do you people know these things? No, don't tell me. I don't have the need to know. In any case, Thomas is, therefore, an accessory before the fact."

"True, but not sufficient because we can't use any of that information in a court of law."

"We are stuck and up the proverbial creek."

"Not quite. Think through what I just told you and tell me how you can use the information when you see Roberto tomorrow."

"I let on to Roberto that I know that a man named Boris Nevsky killed Howling. I further state that Thomas gave Nevsky the knife that was planted near the corpse of the victim. I let him know that I coincidentally took possession of Thomas's own knife and was having police forensics work on it to link the weapon to the murder and the murderer."

"Excellent. What do you think will happen next?"

"Roberto, being a good gypsy and knowing he has revenge to accomplish will want to kill both Thomas and Boris. That will remove any chance of our freeing young Rapello and bring Roberto to two counts of murder one."

"You're forgetting one thing—Roberto has a Russian controller who is not Boris Nevsky. Roberto will report the matter to his controller before he takes any independent action."

"You're sure of that?"

"I am certain of it."

"Why are you so sure?"

"Because the man Roberto thinks is his Russian controller is actually an officer of the CIA."

"Why do you need me in this mix? Oh, wait. I see it now. You need a credible third party to tell Roberto the pieces of the truth without showing him the evidence. Roberto will report everything to his Russian controller. Then his controller will tell Roberto to wait while he sends a message to Russia for instructions. Then what do you suppose will happen?"

"Moscow Center will realize that their man Nevsky is in hot water. They will order his resident to clean up the mess pronto and get Nevsky back to Moscow soonest."

"What will they do with Roberto? He will be aching to take revenge."

"No matter what they send as his orders, the Russians will be sure to keep him clear of Boston while the mess is fixed. They want to keep their organization intact, and he is the lynchpin now."

"Tell me how we get the young Rapello out of jail."

"Thomas will get him out."

"How will he do that?"

"Zara will convince him to confess to stealing her brother's knife. That will take the key piece of evidence right out of the prosecutor's hands. Where will their case be then?"

"The Chief of Police and the whole chain of command above him including the Mayor and the Governor are already beating the drums that they have an open and shut case."

"They'll have to live with the consequences of their premature closure."

"Okay, Ken. I'll play along, but I've seen plans that were far less complex than this one blow up in my face."

"In those cases, you didn't have me watching your back."

"That's true. Let's get back to my office. I have just enough time to reach my desk before Zara comes to call. I'll drop you by your car."

Fulghum dropped off Mander and made it to his desk just before Zara Rapello's footsteps sounded in the stairwell leading up to his office. The detective had lit a cigarette just before she knocked.

"You just turn the knob and push. Come right in and have a seat."

Zara Rapello entered in a blue dress but her rings, earrings, toe bells, and bangles sounded her entry theme. In her hair today was a bright peach bandana. Her black ringlets showed around her radiant face. She took the cigarette that Fulghum offered her and sat down in the captain's chair as she had before.

"Well, will you help me?"

"Yes, Zara, I will. But I have one condition, and it is an absolute requirement." He said this in the stern tones of a judge on the bench. She was duly alarmed.

"What do I have to do? Sleep with you? You know I haven't any money."

"No, Zara. All I want is for you to convince Thomas that the police know that he stole your brother's knife. He must confess to that and to what he did with the knife, or he will be charged with first-degree murder."

"Did he steal my brother's knife?"

"Yes, he did. Today I took this knife from him when he tried to kill me with it." Fulghum drew her attention to the knife that lay on his desk. "I know that your brother and his two friends were given the same style of knife. I know that Thomas stole your brother's knife without harming the fingerprints that were on it. I know that the knife that killed Standish Howling belonged to Thomas. Police forensics will prove that without a shadow of a doubt."

"Did Thomas murder Howling?"

"I don't think so. He knows who killed the man. By coming forward now with what he knows, he will shield himself from suspicion of murder." Fulghum let that thought sink in. "His evidence will crush the case against your brother. Your brother will be set free. You want that to happen, don't you?"

"Yes. It's why I came to you in the first place."

"Tomorrow I'm going to see your father in Norfolk, Virginia. I'm going to tell him the same things I just told you. I caution you both—if Thomas were to die, we'd lose any chance of freeing your brother. We must have Thomas' confession, preferably tonight or tomorrow morning."

"I have an idea—let's have Thomas visit my mother in her shop right away. She'll reveal what you've said in a séance. I won't have to say a thing. Thomas will be singing like a bird before she's done with him. We'll have to get moving. Here, I'll call her right now."

Zara first called her mother and filled her in. Then she called Thomas and asked him to meet her at her mother's shack outside the farm in an hour. When he began complaining about his broken wrist, Zara cut him off.

"Thomas, I can help you if you'll meet me at Rosa's right away. If you don't come, it will be the worse for you. Will you be there, or not?"

Thomas evidently agreed to attend the séance, and Zara hung up with a smile at Fulghum. She drove to her mother's shack in her car with Fulghum following her. Fulghum explained to Rosa what he wanted. She told him to stand behind a tapestry located near the small table where the séance would be held. He had only just hidden when Thomas entered the shop. Zara and Rosa made room for him at the table. He protested but they forced him to be quiet for his own good. The session began.

"Thomas, close your eyes. Don't fall asleep. Empty your head of all thoughts. Listen to me carefully. I am calling the spirit of a dead man to exonerate you from his murder. I feel his spirit coming now. My feeling is strong. The spirit is here in this room right now." To Fulghum, Rosa sounded very convincing.

"Tell me, spirit, whether the man Thomas, who is seated here killed you." She waited as if hearing what the spirit said.

"That's good. I'm glad Thomas did not kill you. Someone with a Russian name killed you? Wait. Why are you troubled?" She again waited as if hearing what the spirit was saying.

"The knife that killed you belonged to Thomas? The knife on the floor by your dead body was Marcello's?" She listened with her eyes closed.

"Thomas, tell the spirit about the knives. Tell him now. The spirit is very angry. He is threatening to tell others that you killed him if you don't speak."

According to Zara later, Thomas became extremely uneasy now. He was sweating. His face was contorted but his eyes remained closed.

"I did not kill you. I loved you. It is true, I stole the knife from Marcello and I made sure his fingerprints were not harmed. I gave mine away. I didn't know what was going to become of either knife. I later learned that Marcello's was found by your body. I was given my own knife by the man I gave it to."

"Thomas, tell the spirit the name of the man you gave the knives to."

"I gave the knives to Boris Nevsky because I love him."

"Thomas, the spirit is very angry. He is jealous of your love for this man Boris Nevsky. The spirit wonders whether you are trying to deceive him."

"I'm telling the truth. Why won't you believe me?"

"The spirit says in good faith you must sign a paper stating that you stole Marcello's knife and write in that statement the date when you stole it. You must then sign the statement and Zara and I will witness it. Will you do this so that the spirit can be released and so that you can go away from this table without harm?" Rosa was scarily intent at this point. Thomas was conflicted to the breaking point. He was on the edge of making his confession. Zara took Thomas's right hand and put a ballpoint pen in it. She placed a clean sheet of white paper on the table.

"Thomas, you have a pen in your hand. You have paper on the table. Write what the spirit requires. Open your eyes and do so now. When you are done, sign the paper and close your eyes again."

Thomas said, "My wrist is broken. I don't know whether I can write at all much less sign my name."

"Do your best, Thomas. Or better, I will write the statement. All you need to do is sign afterward. Even an 'X' will do. We'll witness it. Tell me what I should write."

"I stole Marcello's knife about six days prior to the murder. He searched everywhere for the knife but could not find it because I gave it to another man. That man's name is Boris Nevsky. I also gave that man my own knife, which is identical to Marcello's."

"Okay, Thomas, I've written exactly what you just recited to me. I've dated the statement today and made a line where you need to sign right now. So sign it on the line, or make an 'X'!"

"I'm signing. Hahaha. It's crooked. Can you read it?"

"Yes. We'll now witness your signature."

Zara and Rosa signed as witnesses. Zara folded the paper three times and hid it in her bosom. Rosa told Thomas to close his eyes again.

"Spirit, are you satisfied now? Will you leave us in peace and not disturb us again? I feel the spirit receding. It is releasing us. It is now gone. Whew. Everyone open your eyes. The séance is over."

"What do I do now?" Thomas asked.

"You go with the police to the station to deliver your statement, Thomas." Fulghum said this as he stepped from behind the tapestry with his pistol pointed right at Thomas's heart. "Do not resist me. You know what I can do to you, and I assure you I will take great pleasure in killing you for what you have done to implicate Marcello in murder. Turn around slowly. Put your hands behind you. I am putting a cuff on your left wrist. I am now putting a cuff on your broken right wrist. I am trying to do so without hurting you. Now, Thomas, please sit down gently. Rosa, please dial 911."

While the police were on the way, Fulghum called Officer Pounce and informed him of what had happened.

He told Pounce, "Whether the statement holds up in court or not, it is enough for the police to release Marcello Rapello from jail. It is also enough to incarcerate Thomas Porro as an accessory before the fact and, with proper questioning, to focus on arresting the man named Boris Nevsky for murder one. I have in my possession a knife belonging to Thomas Porro. Forensics should be able to prove that it is the real murder weapon."

"I'll set everything in motion, John. Will you be coming to the station tomorrow to help sort everything out?"

"I'll be flying to Norfolk, Virginia, tomorrow to sort out something related to this case. I should be back the day after, but I expect you'll have made the progress you need to make with your internal resources."

"Detective, you continue to amaze me. Believe that everyone is going to be upset by your revelations."

"All the politicians almost condemned an innocent man—and it's not the first time."

"No, and it won't be the last time. I suspect there's a story lying back of what I've just learned."

"Probably, there is, but we'll have to be in good company to have it told just right. I think you'll agree that Jack Daniels should be there."

"Hahaha. Good work, John. We'll make a date for that meeting. Goodnight."

The black and white arrived with lights flashing and siren blaring. Thomas Porro was taken into custody and escorted to the police station. When the police had left, Fulghum said goodnight to Rosa and Zara. Both women kissed him on the cheek, and Zara hugged him. Fulghum then drove away in the drizzle. He lit up a Marlboro and rolled down his left window a crack so the smoke would escape.

Darkness was falling like a black cape over the beautiful fall countryside. Rain was accelerating the leaf fall. Tomorrow it would be cloudy with a sixty percent chance of more rain throughout New England. Fulghum reckoned that in Virginia he would see the sunshine. He had more work to do, but his new role was to convey information to a man conflicted.

Perhaps, he thought, *the man will listen to me now that Marcello is going to be set free. That is another beginning to a long story that will continue, except for this small interval, to play out in the shadows.*

Gypsy Noir

John Fulghum, PI, flew out of the New England fog into the Virginia Tidewater sunshine to meet Roberto Rapello, his gypsy contact, at the Patrick Henry International Airport in Newport News. He arrived early in the afternoon and expected to do his business in a matter of two hours so that he could return the same day to make his important appointment with Jack Daniels in his office late that evening. After all, the detective, with the help of Roberto's wife and daughter, had elicited the confession from Thomas Porro that sprang Roberto's son from jail and removed the threat of his formerly almost certain conviction for the first-degree murder of Boston blue blood Standish Howling. The morning Boston Globe had trumpeted the latest turn of events in a fanfare, and the political fallout from the reversal of expectations was only just beginning.

Fulghum was confident that, on one level, his job was done—Zara Rapello had asked him to free her brother and he had done that. The trouble that remained was not on the public or the personal level. To free Marcello Rapello, Fulghum had been constrained to consult with his friend, CIA agent Kenneth Mander. Through Mander, Fulghum had learned that the Rapello family was deeply involved with sensitive, off-books intelligence matters that connected to a half century of conflicting American and Russian operations within the continental United States. Because Mander had provided the back-story to free the young gypsy Marcello

Rapello, the detective owed his intelligence friend the return favor. At a minimum, he had to deliver a message to Roberto Rapello that would tip the balance of his loyalties towards America and effectively shut down the Russian attempt to co-opt the decades-old gypsy connection with the CIA.

Even if Fulghum had not seen a recent picture of Roberto Rapello, he would certainly have recognized this bear of a man standing by the baggage claim area holding the sign that read, "Gypsy Noir." The olive-complexioned man stood five-feet-eleven and was built strong as an ox with long, curly black hair and a weeping mustache. He wore dark aviator glasses but Fulghum could see in the way his body moved that the man radiated both energy and impatience.

Immediately Fulghum thought Gypsy King, and he was not wrong about that. They made contact and the burly gypsy threw his arms around the detective and hugged him tight for having saved his son. He then escorted Fulghum to his waiting Saab and began to drive south talking at a fast clip about a torrent of issues, chiefly surrounding his son Marcello.

Fifteen minutes into Roberto's nonstop reasons for not being in Boston to protect his son, he alluded to his role in resolving inheritance disputes, soothing family quarrels, and working both with police and political figures to keep his larger family out of jail as well as media figures to keep the lid on potentially inflammatory stories that might defame gypsies. Rapello was a force to be reckoned with, waving his arms and bellowing as he drove across the Hampton Roads Bridge-Tunnel. Fulghum let his loquacious companion complete his lengthy self-introduction before he launched into a succinct situation report about the latest developments in the case against Marcello.

"Thanks to your wife and daughter, Thomas Porro wrote out and signed a confession that he stole your son's knife a week before the murder. That confession redirected the murder case and freed your son."

"Detective Fulghum, again I am delighted that my son is free. Rosa and Zara called me to tell me everything that happened. We owe you a debt that cannot be repaid. You are now part of my greater family. How much have you discovered about the real killer and his motive to implicate my son in this heinous crime?"

"The key connections will be proven by Boston police forensics, but everything points to a Russian citizen named Boris Nevsky. Thomas Porro's confession and his knife, which was the murder weapon, are the basis for the murder case now. Porro is in jail. Nevsky has been picked up for questioning. It's only a matter of time before the police will elicit what they need to indict Nevsky for murder and Porro for complicity."

"With my bare hands, I will sort out Thomas Porro, that viper in my nest. I will also find and use my knife to get revenge on this man Nevsky."

"I understand your desire for revenge. Remember, though, that Porro must live to substantiate his allegation that he stole your son's knife. If he dies, Marcello may go back to jail. Nevsky is well connected politically. He is likely to use political means to escape this country. If he does that, the whole story will never be known and the murderer may not come to justice."

"Gypsy justice is better than the judges and courts and lawyers of the legal system. It's clean, fast and sure."

"Gypsy justice may also be your ticket to a murder rap. Do you want to die or spend the rest of your life in prison for those characters? Your son is free now. Why not let the wheels turn and watch what happens?"

"How long can you stay here in Virginia?"

"I can leave almost immediately. I've given you the information I came with. Additionally, I've also advised you to be cautious about how you proceed. Your daughter came to me with a request to free her brother from jail and I've done that. Once you pay me for my trip and time, I have no further obligation to fulfill."

"As a detective, don't you want to know the truth about the murder?"

"Mr. Rapello, I have learned that truth and justice rarely coincide. That's because truth is evanescent and justice is often arbitrary."

"Pfft. Words! Mr. Fulghum, spend a day or two with me and learn a few things about the gypsy ways. I'll pay your hourly rate for every hour, waking or sleeping. When you know the whole story from me, you'll realize that your work for my family has only begun. Let me put this in the form of a business proposition. Will you give me forty-eight hours of your professional time?"

"I do have an important meeting at my office tonight, but I suppose I could defer it."

"Rosa, my wife, told me about your special friend Jack Daniels. If you reach over the seat to the floor behind us, you will find I have brought your friend with me. You can meet him whenever you like while you remain here. So what do you think?"

"Where will I stay?"

"You'll stay with me in my trailer at the gypsy camp in Portsmouth. You'll dine with my greater family and me for breakfast, lunch and dinner."

"How can I refuse your hospitality?"

"Don't even think about refusal. We need to know each other better because we have many things to do together."

"I'll agree to stay for forty-eight hours—unless emerging developments of the murder case in Boston require my immediate departure."

"Detective, we have a deal. Let's shake hands on it." Roberto offered his right hand and Fulghum shook it with a firm grip. Roberto hit his steering wheel with the flat of his hand and smiled.

"We'll arrive at the camp in about forty minutes. While I drive, I'll tell you a few stories about what I do for my greater family. If you have questions as I ramble on, just ask. If you'd like to smoke, go right ahead. I'll join you. On Rosa's advice, I bought a carton of Marlboros for you."

The two men lit their cigarettes, and Roberto began to spin his tales.

"We gypsies have a hard time earning trust. The legends about our petty thievery and other crimes follow us wherever we go. It's true we live off the land and outside the normal social boundaries. Not all of us are scoundrels and knaves. Some of us, my immediate family included, are pure in our bloodlines back into antiquity. Rosa and I come from pure stock though we have to watch over many who are of mixed blood, like Thomas Porro and his friend Ollie Strong. Often men and women like them cause trouble for us all." He let Fulghum digest this generality as they descended into the tunnel. On the Norfolk side, he launched into the story of a strong man named Ruggiero.

"Some of the gypsy families are circus people. My cousin Ruggiero was such a man. Ruggiero, a circus strong man, had a beautiful sister Bianca who was a circus performer. She stood on a bounding bareback horse while it ran around the ring. She was very good with balance. She was also beautiful. One night after her day's performance, Bianca came to Ruggiero weeping with her clothes torn. She was bleeding. She said that the circus master had raped her in his quarters. Ruggiero told her to go to her van, to clean herself and to say nothing. The circus master was found dead with an iron bar twisted around his throat the next morning. When interrogated by the police, Ruggiero denied any involvement and suggested that the circus master might have committed suicide. Why would he have done that? The reason was his unrequited love for the gypsy Bianca. Hahaha."

"And the police bought this story?"

"They had two choices. They might have taken the easy road and arrested Ruggiero for murder, or they might treat the death as a suicide and tell the circus to move on to the next town. I had a talk with the men from homicide. The list of men and women who hated the circus master encompassed the entire circus crew and many backers from the outside. Three people had threatened to kill him in front of witnesses. All three had motives where Ruggiero seemed to have no motive. I told them nothing about the man's rape of Bianca, and they asked no questions that might have brought that fact to light. The upshot was a determination of suicide. The circus packed up and, with a new circus master, moved on to the next town."

"Were you satisfied with this gypsy justice?"

"The circus master got off too easy. Other than that, I was satisfied. Bianca was devastated. After the rape, she was never quite the same person. She finally married another distant cousin, who was a juggler in a circus. She's now in Arkansas raising a family and still riding bareback. Her three children are growing up in the circus. They will know nothing about the night of the rape or what followed afterward."

"We all have our secrets," Fulghum said as he chain lit another cigarette. The detective was trying to steer Roberto towards the big secret that he was harboring. The gypsy was not yet ready to talk about that matter. Instead, he spun another story.

"I had another cousin named Ned. He was a brainy person who went to college and majored in anthropology. He liked the work of a man named Levi Strauss. His anthropology professor advised him to write about his gypsy family, but Ned was not going to divulge the family secrets. Instead, he began to explore the underworld off campus with his cameras. Ned filmed lost women. His films were not erotic, merely similar to Diane Arbus, sad. Some people said his pictures were exploitative. Ned's women posed for money, and he paid them well. The Mob bought Ned's films and sold them to sadists. Then Ned's top heroines began to disappear. When he was arrested for pornography, he hired a Mob lawyer and was acquitted. Now he owes the Mob. Ned never got his degree, but he is making good money in New York City. I can do nothing for him because of his Mob relationship. He is beyond wanting help now." Roberto paused for effect and glanced at Fulghum to gauge his reaction.

"I know about the hold that the Mob can exert on people. The Mob is not the only such organization that can do that."

"We gypsies know a little about how society can strangulate freedom and co-opt the souls of its citizens."

"Yet gypsies have served honorably in the US armed forces, some winning the highest medals for bravery."

"I'm told you were a warrior, Fulghum. From what Rosa told me, you beat Thomas in a knife fight and broke his wrist in the process. Thomas was a viper, but he was one of the fastest men with a knife I have ever known. How did you manage to beat him?"

"I thought ahead. That's all. By the time he got out his knife, I was already reaching for his wrist and stepping to the side. I've been in the same situation before. I got lucky—again." Fulghum squinted as he reflected on his Afghanistan experience with knife-wielding terrorists. "One of my fellow soldiers was a gypsy. He knew knives well. He taught me a few tricks about hand movements. He would go out alone in the night yet when he returned in the morning, he would be silent and smile. I knew he had killed many terrorists when he got that look. I'm very grateful I was never his enemy."

"Hahaha. Gypsies learn sleight of hand in the cradle. Slow hands mean a slow mind. Boys and men especially, but girls, and women too need both agility and practice. Ordinary people don't have the timing or the speed of recognition. Pickpockets and lifters can't afford to be caught too many times. Jail is a lousy place to ply your trade."

"You said you were too busy to come to Boston when your son was in jail. What was so important that you could not leave?"

"I came down to the Tidewater to resolve a dispute between two half-breed families, the Kings, and the Strongs. Those are the family names, but don't let the symbolism fool you. The Kings have no power and the Strongs have no strength. It happened that one of the King men insulted one of the Strong men in the parking lot of a supermarket at Janaf Shopping Center."

"What was the insult?"

"He accused one of the Strong women of liking a Scot in the area."

"How is that an insult?"

"Hahaha. Gypsies and Scots don't mix. So the Strongs decided they would take revenge on the Kings. They challenged the Kings to do battle the next morning and they accepted the challenge. Later that night the Strongs had a second thought. They gathered their weapons—knives mostly, but also a machete and a gun—and attacked the Kings in their homes. The attack was a total surprise. Two of the King men were killed and one was the man who had issued the insult. None of the Strong men were injured."

"It's hard to cover up a murder."

"What you say is too true. The next day the authorities got involved. They arrested seven of the Strong men and confiscated their weapons. That's when I received the call to come down and help."

"With an open-and-shut murder case, what could you possibly do to help?"

"I could stop another round of revenge. Sure, seven of the Strongs were in jail, but the Kings wanted revenge. The slaughter was going to continue unless arbitration occurred. So I've been here sorting out the mess and keeping the peace. I can only do so much because we gypsies have a refined view of revenge. Blood feuds can go down through the generations. I managed to head off an immediate attack. I also redirected the authorities' attention on one of the Strong men instead of seven. Things are fairly calm now, but if I had departed, I don't know that the peace would have held."

"Isn't someone in this area capable of settling disputes as you can?"

"The gypsy queen cannot interfere in affairs of honor among men. She can help when women quarrel, and she can judge when marriages are to be arranged."

"Does that mean that you are, essentially, the gypsy king?"

"I'm nothing as grand as that. I'm just the convenient peacemaker on this occasion. The timing was bad on account of what happened to Marcello. I suspect after another three weeks, I'll be able to go back to Massachusetts."

"Are you resented on account of your being in charge?"

"Of course, I am. What can I do? No one has dared to come against me. Unless I become sick or injured, no one will. Of course, I might die. Then all bets are off. So far, my people's need for me outweighs their resentment of what I do." Roberto took a long drag on his cigarette and chain lit its successor.

"Do you travel only between Massachusetts and Virginia?"

"No. I travel all over the country—wherever I am called."

"You have no deputy or surrogate?"

"No one can help me. This is just as it was for my father and his father before. Anyone who becomes powerful enough to challenge me will have to be very capable. Marcello, my son, may not have what it takes to be my successor. We shall see. He'll have to live long enough, and he'll have to be lucky."

"What sort of luck are you thinking about?"

"We have always been protected by an invisible hand."

"You're talking about someone or some organization that lies behind you?" Fulghum thought Roberto might be ready to talk about the Agency.

"It's something like that, detective. Let me tell you the story of my great-great-grandmother, whose name was Celestina, who became queen of gypsies in Europe. She was sponsored by a wealthy man because she was naturally graceful as a dancer. So she became the consummate, beautiful ballerina. She was lithe and small with exquisite legs. Celestina bettered what was done by petite contenders for the prima ballerina role. Her sponsor wanted to marry her and give her a title. That was the fortunate part of her life. Then things changed."

"How so?" Fulghum was fascinated by the fantastic, Cinderella story.

"One day outside the Parliament building a terrorist's bomb took off both of Celestina's shapely legs. She struggled to live though she despaired because she would never dance again. She learned to use prosthetic devices that allowed her to function, barely. Her sponsor abandoned her leaving her with a small pouch of gold. She worked as a freak prostitute in a high-class hotel, not for the money but to find the bomber. He found her in the hotel bar and carried her upstairs to her room to have his pleasure. She squeezed him to death with her iron legs. The authorities ruled that the man had died from his exertions and besides he was a known terrorist."

"What happened next?"

"My great-great-grandmother went back to her family and wed someone who, I'm told, looked like me. They raised goats and for money, Celestina posed for portraits made from the waist up. The bombs had not destroyed her beauty."

"Roberto, you have a colorful family."

"I haven't told you about our most famous present-day hero. His name is John. You'll be able to guess his last name when I tell you his story."

"Give it a shot."

"My cousin John did not like the traveling life. He was brilliant with computers, so he settled down and found a small company that hired him to do odd jobs. He became a computer expert and wrote software at night. Later with a friend's money, he started a small software company that grew so rapidly that it could not keep up with demand and so failed. John then segued into writing for a living, but success did not come easily. He had married a fellow gypsy at the height of his software success, and she stuck with him after his firm collapsed. His wife reminded him that his best creative work reflected what happened in his life. John then worked for two years on a Broadway musical about his small startup's failure. He juxtaposed personal romance with business comedy. Broadway loved it. Now John is working on a second romance about the gypsy life."

"I'd think that Celestina's story would make a smash hit."

"No one wants to watch a play about a woman who has lost her legs to a suicide bomber!"

"What is your cousin's new play about?"

"It's about a gypsy falling in love with a woman who is not a gypsy."

"How does that story connect to John's life?"

"The characters are not promoted as gypsies. Instead, Jim, the hero, is a programmer and Martha, the heroine, is an avatar. It goes something like this—Jim had never dated an avatar before. Martha was edgy, sarcastic and witty. She laughed and changed her expression with every word. In fact, Jim saw blue-eyed Martha as an anthology of personas like a crowded vase of flowers. Jim's rule was to give as much as he got. So as Martha changed, Jim modulated in syncopation with Martha's moods. Halfway through their two-hour appointment, Martha hesitated, shrugged and then shook her head and forced a crooked smile. 'Jim, are you for real?' Jim's hand gently squeezed hers. 'Maybe we should start again.' This time, they took things slowly. So what do you think?"

"I'd have to know how the plot develops, but the premise is interesting."

"I have a lot of trouble with it because I know the play is really about the gypsy experience from the inside. A female outsider, however malleable and willful, can never entirely adapt to the gypsy life. John's romance could never have a happily ever after ending." Roberto paused in his storytelling to reflect on what he had just said. He chain lit another cigarette while Fulghum did the same. Silently, Fulghum thought the "happily ever after" idea catalyzed Roberto's next reflection.

"No matter how you hope for things to remain stable and good, fate intrudes. Like Bianca's rape or the blast that took off Celestina's legs."

"I've found that to be true as well. Change is the only constant."

"Well put, detective. Now I'm going to tell you what you need to hear. We have a few minutes before we arrive at the camp. Once we are there, I won't be able to talk about this in plain terms. So listen carefully."

Fulghum nodded and took a pull of his cigarette.

"My family was brought to America from Europe during the period when the Nazi's rose to power. My grandfather and grandmother did service for the anti-Nazi intelligence forces. They were about to be exposed when the OSS made arrangements for them to leave Europe and immigrate to America. We already had distant relatives living here. This country paid my ancestors well for their service, but they required further assistance once we arrived here. Those services were performed by my father and mother throughout the Cold War then by my Rosa and me in the time after that. I cannot talk about the specifics for security reasons. Do you understand what I've told you so far?"

"Yes, I do. Please continue."

"What I say next must remain between us. It would be very dangerous for anyone else to know. I am taking a great risk telling you, but I consider you family now. Please do not violate this confidentiality."

Fulghum nodded indicating he could be trusted.

"When the Cold War ended, things changed with respect to our relationship with the intelligence organization in this country. It was as if a major part of our lives had changed overnight. Things were no different for our family members who managed to survive the historical events in Europe. The family that had brought us from Europe no longer had the same views as before, particularly the man who was murdered. Howling's friends introduced us to Russians, who had new ideas about what we should do for them now that the old rivalry between East and West was over. At first, we thought this was an impossibility, but our Agency contacts grew cold and disinterested. They wanted nothing from us anymore. So we began to work increasingly with the Russians—for money. This seemed to be strange at first, but the more we worked with them, the more the money made a difference."

"Please clarify that for me."

"Of course. We gypsies were always self-sufficient from the time we reached America. We made our own way, and our intelligence minders gave us very little by way of financial reward for what we did for them. We felt we were paying back a favor that was priceless. It was entirely otherwise with the Russians. For them, everything had its price. There was no honor. There was no memory. You must know that the USSR helped crush the Nazi menace, and the gypsies were given some degree of autonomy across the Iron Curtain. The Russians argued that gypsies should continue to be free throughout the world. They wanted those in America to make common cause with gypsies in Russia after the Cold War. Blood being thicker than water, we sympathized with that view."

"You're saying that you and your greater family worked for the Russians for money. Did your Agency friends know this was happening?"

"Yes, and no. The CIA is very powerful, but it is not omniscient. Some in the Agency knew that our resources were being neglected. Most did not. One agent told me that we were on the ash heap of history along with the Soviet Union. Another told me just to wait and watch because one day the Russians would change their character. Then, he said, the Agency would need the gypsies as never before. I did not know who to believe."

"A lot of propaganda was directed at convincing Americans and the world that the Cold War was dead and gone. Over the last twenty-five years, this country worked very hard to reshape minds and hearts."

"Well, detective, during the last ten years the Russians have changed. Standish Howling was an example of that change. I had a hard time dealing with what Howling was doing. He worked against everything that his father and grandfather believed. It became apparent to me that he was in bed with the Russians, literally as well as figuratively. Hahaha. He was hell bent on turning my son against his mother and me and against everything his family had done for the last fifty years."

"Did you bring this to the attention of the Agency?"

"Yes, I did, on many occasions. The response was always the same. I was, they said, showing that I was a useless old Cold Warrior trying to see ghosts of the past everywhere. Meanwhile, the Russians were playing blackmail games and making overt threats."

"Can you give me an example?"

"Yes. They told me that if I did not work with them exclusively, they would see that my son and daughter would be disgraced or killed. Because I resisted them, they tried to kill me twice."

"Did you tell your Agency contacts about this?"

"I did. They laughed at me. They said I had an overactive imagination. They said I knew nothing that would warrant the Russians to assassinate me. They placed no importance on what I have always done in my community."

"When Marcello was implicated in Howling's murder, you must have thought it was a trap the Russians had set for you."

"Detective, I know it was a trap. This was not a matter of my intuition but fact."

"Can you clarify the situation for me as you saw it?"

"At his estate over two bottles of wine that I took there to share with him, I confronted Standish Howling about what he and his controllers were doing to Marcello and to the relationship that had been created by his ancestors. We talked earnestly, long into the night. I believe he was beginning to see where his machinations had taken us. He even told me that he would have to think about what to do about our situation. He said that the Russians had so complicated his life that he did not know any way out but death. He said he had contemplated suicide on many occasions. I told him he had too much left to live for. I said he should not waste the chance. He then broke out two Montecristo cigars and said we should smoke them for old time's sake. We did that and continued our discussions. Finally, he confessed to me that he had been wrong. He said he would break off with the Russians, and he advised me to break off as well. That was the last time I saw him."

"Did you consider that the Russians may have bugged his estate?"

"Yes. In fact, I counted on that. I wanted to let them know the score."

"You also set Howling up for death. So let me ask an off-the-wall question. Did you intend to implicate your son in the inevitable assassination of Howling? Further, did you do the assassination yourself?"

"You are every bit as smart as Rosa said you'd be. I'll take your questions seriously. The answer to both is no. I never intended to implicate Marcello and I did not kill Howling. I'm glad that my son is free of that charge. I don't know who killed Howling."

"You cannot be entirely unhappy that Standish Howling is dead. You cannot be unhappy that your son has been shaken by his murder."

"You are right, detective. I hated Howling for what he was and for what he did to our families' relationship. I had the motive to kill him. I thought many times how I would manage to do that and fix the blame on others."

"Do you have an alibi for the time of the murder?"

"You'll meet her when we arrive at the camp. She's one of the reasons that I suggested that you spend the extra time with me."

"As for Thomas and the theft of Marcello's knife, did you have a role in that theft?"

"No, detective, I did not."

"Can you explain how Thomas would have managed to steal Marcello's knife without someone in your family helping him?"

"I cannot."

"Did you ever meet the Russian Boris Nevsky?"

"Yes, I met him at a Dunkin' Donuts shop in Lexington two weeks before the murder of Standish Howling."

"What was the purpose of that meeting?"

"He had a bulging envelope of cash for me on the condition that I would kill Howling. He said he would be making the same offer to others if I refused. He also said that Howling was already a dead man because he was unreliable."

"And you refused to do the job?"

"I told Nevsky I'd think about his proposition."

"Did you discuss Nevsky's offer with your own Russian connections or with the CIA?"

"I discussed it with both intelligence contacts."

"And what did they say?"

"The Russian said he would relay what I said to Moscow. The Agency man said that I was just imagining things again. He told me to stop finding demons under my bed and he implied that I was just trying to get attention."

"Did you tell Standish Howling about the threat to his life?"

"I called him on my cell phone just before I left to come here. I told him that a large cash payment was being offered to anyone who would kill him."

"How did he react to that news?"

"He laughed at me. He asked me to tell him something he did not already know. He called me an old superannuated fool. He even said that perhaps Marcello would take the challenge if I wouldn't. I thought he sounded ludicrous. I told him he was talking like a dead man. That's when he hung up on me. After that, I figured it was only a matter of time."

"Roberto, we've both got to get back to Boston as soon as possible. I won't mind meeting with your lady friend and hearing what she has to say, but I won't be able to stay with you. Instead, I have to insist that we fly immediately after our meeting."

"Why the urgency?"

"Thomas Porro may have stolen Marcello's knife, but he knew nothing about what happened to that knife or his own knife once he turned them over to Boris Nevsky. That's what his confession implied. Everything about the actual murder formerly depended on forensics alone. With your statement about the solicitation to murder, we have another clear line of defense for Marcello."

"Do you have the forensic evidence, or not?"

"The Boston police have the murder weapon and their forensics team will find the evidence we need."

"Do you mind if I pull over and make a short, private phone call?"

"I have no objection to that. In fact, I have my own private call to make."

Roberto pulled the Saab to the side of the highway. He walked ahead of the car while Fulghum walked to the rear of it. Fulghum saw Roberto excitedly talking on his cell phone and waving his hands while he did so. He then called Officer Pounce of Boston Homicide to get an update on the state of play.

"Hi John, I thought you'd be calling. Where the hell are you?"

"I'm in the company of Roberto Rapello, the father of Marcello, by the side of the road leading to Portsmouth, Virginia. Listen, he just told me that he was solicited to kill Standish Howling by Boris Nevsky. I'm planning to fly back there ASAP with him to clarify any details on that. So what's going on there?"

"Thomas Porro is trying to weasel out of his signed confession, but he is clearly implicated in the murder before and after the fact. We're still holding Boris Nevsky, but he may not be with us much longer because he's a Russian citizen and the wheels of the Russian Federation's bureaucracy have begun to turn. We'll need that deposition from Roberto Rapello in any event ASAP."

"I have a recording of my conversation with Roberto if you want the gist."

"Email what you've got. We still lack details, but we had enough to free Marcello. All members in the chain of command from the D.A. right up to the Governor are feeling cheated of a simple, open-and-shut murder one. The press is having us for breakfast and lunch. Do you have anything else for me now? If not, I gotta go."

"That's all I have now. Your recording is on the way now."

Fulghum noticed that Roberto was still heatedly talking on his cell phone, so the detective called Ken Mander but had to leave a voicemail message.

"Hi Ken, this is Fulghum, in Virginia. I'm sending you a recording of a conversation I've been having with Roberto Rapello. You'll get the drift. I hope to be back in New England tonight with Roberto in tow. I'll let you know when I touch down." Fulghum then emailed his voice recording to Mander. As he walked back to the Saab, he saw that Roberto was finishing his call as well. As the two men converged on the car, a very fast car in the right lane of the highway swerved and hit the Saab with a bang. It continued right towards Roberto, who faked right, then dove left off the macadam into the ditch. Fulghum ran, drawing his weapon. The car laid rubber and sped away. Roberto brushed himself off, waved that he was all right and climbed back towards the damaged car.

"That was damned close. It's a good thing I drive a Saab. It's built like a tank. Before you get inside, let's see if I can start it."

Roberto had no trouble starting the car, and its frame seemed intact. So he gesticulated for Fulghum to hop in. He lit a cigarette and Fulghum did the same.

"What do you make of that incident?" Fulghum asked.

"Well, it's either Wednesday afternoon drunken driving or the third attempt on my life in the last month."

"It certainly wasn't aiming at me."

"We're almost to the camp."

"Will we be pivoting and heading back to the airport?"

"Would you object to our leaving from the Norfolk side?"

"Not at all, why?"

"I have scheduled a quick meeting at the airport before we leave."

"I've got no problem with that."

It took Roberto another ten minutes to reach the gypsy camp pitched in a grove in the middle of freshly plowed open farmland. When he arrived, the gypsies approached his car from all sides to admire the damage that the Saab had suffered.

"Where is Maria?" he asked a teenage girl in tights with a long blue dress over them and a flower in her hair.

"She's back by the pens, milking the goats." The girl eyed Fulghum and smiled while she pointed towards the pens with a crooked finger.

"Come on back, Fulghum. She's not going to be happy about my having to leave, but what can you do?"

They walked through the grove, which was beginning to turn from the rich Virginia green to the yellow of autumn. New England was already in full color, but it would be another three weeks until Virginia followed suit. Maria was sitting on a three-legged stool, working a goat's udders expertly.

"You're late, Roberto!"

"Hi, Maria. I'm lucky to be here at all. A maniac struck my car while my friend and I were walking on the side of the road. The car nearly ran me over as it sped away from the scene." He hesitated while she finished her milking. When she rose with the wooden bucket of fresh milk, he continued.

"I'm afraid we won't be staying as I had planned. We're flying back to Boston this evening."

"Too bad you'll miss the feast. Well, there'll be more for the rest of us, I suppose. You must be the detective who helped free Marcello. I'm Maria Strong."

"Hello. I'm John Fulghum. Rosa and Zara did all the work freeing Marcello. You aren't from the same Strong family that has been feuding with the Kings, are you?"

Maria glared darkly at Roberto for having aired the family laundry. "As a matter of fact, I am. I'm the one who called Roberto down here to help patch things up after the men went haywire."

"I understand that he's been working around the clock to make the peace."

"That he has done. I don't know what I would have done without him."

"So he's been here for the last ten days, or so, without a break?"

"He's been here for the last twelve days, to be precise."

"I'm sorry to be taking him away in your time of need, but he is the key to a murder mystery we have in New England. Without his statement, we might not have a case."

"I see. How long until you can come back here, Roberto?"

"What do you think, detective?"

"I don't think you'll be away more than two or three days. We'll be arriving tonight in Boston. Tomorrow we'll have a full slate, after that we'll just have to see."

"Do you have time for a glass of fresh goat milk before you drive away?"

"We'll have some milk. I'm going to pack a few things then we'll be going. You two walk together, I'll run forward to take care of a few things."

Roberto loped ahead while Fulghum and the Strong woman followed. Fulghum would have offered to carry the milk bucket, but he did not know the gypsy protocol. Maria was clearly self-sufficient and, as her name implied, strong.

"You're probably wondering why we need Roberto in our times of travail. Well, he's all we've got. He comes whenever we call and never complains. He always knows just what to do. My husband is in jail, and things don't look good after the ruckus. We'll sort things out somehow. I don't know what I'd have done without Roberto. The way you were asking about how long he was here, I suppose he is a suspect in the murder up north. Well, you may have guessed already, but Roberto and I go a long way back. His wife and my husband know how close we are, and they don't care. If I had been pure gypsy-like Rosa, I'd have had him as my husband. Ever since the evil Nazis made the purity issue a matter of life and death, we've all been sensitive. I don't blame Roberto for opting for safety. We both have good families separately. Just the same, sometimes I wonder what it would have been like if things had worked out otherwise."

Maria raised her beautiful face to smile at Fulghum. Then she shook her head and concentrated on getting her bucket to her back porch. She went inside to get three glasses and a scupper to pour the goat milk. She handed one full glass to Fulghum and watched approvingly as he drank it down.

"That warm milk is perfect. Thank you. The girl in the blue dress resembles you. Is she your daughter, perhaps?"

"Yes, that's May Bell Strong. She's a looker. She is head over heels about Marcello and he feels the same way about her if the truth were known. I fear it will be the same old story—she's impure by someone's lights just as I am."

"Love will out, Maria."

"I hope so. Things have not been good, and it's a long way to Massachusetts. Here comes Roberto with his traveling bag. Roberto, here's your glass of goat's milk." The way she gave Roberto his glass and gazed into his eyes, Fulghum saw that she loved him. The detective had a sudden intuition that May Bell was their child. If so, the girl had her father's eyes and her mother's looks. When he had finished the milk, Roberto gave the empty glass back to Maria. She pecked a kiss on his cheek and blushed. He chucked her under the chin and looked into her eyes. Then he broke away and strode to the Saab with Fulghum following. May Bell fell in with the men and climbed into the back seat with the Jack Daniels and the Marlboros. She was evidently going to drive the car back to the gypsy camp from the airport.

On the drive, Roberto talked about life in a gypsy camp and the traveling life. May Bell remained silent as he rambled. When the men climbed out of the car, Roberto insisted that Fulghum include the bottles of Jack Daniels and the carton of Marlboros in his carry on. As he did this, May Bell shifted from the back seat to the driver's position. She kissed Roberto perfunctorily on the cheek, lightly shook Fulghum's hand, and drove away without looking back.

When they arrived at the counter, first class tickets were waiting for them. During the flight, Fulghum outlined the plan for the next day's activities, starting with a meeting at the police station at nine o'clock. They arrived at Logan Airport where Fulghum drove his car to his office while Roberto met Rosa and Zara to drive home together.

John Fulghum walked up the stairs to his second-story office and was not surprised to find that Ken Mander was waiting for him outside his office door.

"Hi, John. I thought we'd catch up on the state of play if you think our friend JD is ready for us."

After unlocking his door, Fulghum gestured for Mander to precede him and take a seat. He then went to the other side of his desk to unload the treasures from his carry-on bag. From the second desk drawer on the right, he pulled three glasses and polished them with his handkerchief. Rather than pouring from his half-empty bottle of JD, Fulghum opened one of the new bottles and poured three fingers of the velvety brown nectar into each glass. He gave one to Mander and struck it with his as a toast before he sat down. The third glass sat alone like a signal. They both imbibed and waited for the initial sensation to hit them. Then Fulghum sat and lit up a cigarette. He gestured for Mander to do the same.

"It's your nickel, Ken."

"That was some storytelling that you emailed earlier today. Sorry, I was unavailable to take your call. I was in the SCIF. Roberto flew back with you and tonight will be with his family. That's good. Did you have a close call today, or what?"

"It was very close. The car would have been totaled if it were not a Saab. Roberto would have been killed if he hadn't been agile and vigilant."

"You think it was an assassination attempt?"

"I surely do. If you listened to the recording, you know that was the third attempt on Roberto's life in a month."

"Roberto is in a red sector right now. He is vulnerable for all the reasons you can surmise. You were both lucky. It was a good play to get him back to Boston ASAP."

"Were you folks monitoring his cell phone conversations today?"

"Yes, we were. He called his Russian control just as we guessed he would. He told the control everything you told him, and he wanted permission to kill Thomas and Boris at the earliest opportunity. The control said to kill no one until Moscow Center relayed instructions."

"Was there any indication that Roberto was implicated in the murder of Howling?"

"Not a thing he said pointed to that, but keep an open mind."

"I'm glad to hear there was nothing explicit. The reason we've returned to Boston is to get Roberto's signed deposition about the contract Nevsky was putting out on Howling's life."

"I thought as much."

A knock on the office door interrupted their conversation.

"Officer Pounce of Boston Homicide, I presume. Come right in. Your glass of JD is waiting for you. Have a seat on the edge of the desk."

"Hi, John. Hi, Ken. John, you've certainly turned this Howling case on its head."

"The fun has only just begun, my friend. Roberto Rapello and I will be coming down to the station at nine o'clock so he can write and sign a deposition about Boris Nevsky's attempt to make a murder for hire deal with him well before the actual murder occurred."

"Do you think Roberto killed Howling?"

"No, but I'm keeping my mind open to that possibility. I just don't think the man would have put his only son in danger of being convicted of first-degree murder. That was clearly the murderer's intent. Have you managed to keep custody of Boris Nevsky?"

"Yes. We're cautiously optimistic about keeping him on ice for the next two days. Ken, your being here means that there's an Agency connection to this case. Can you tell me anything about that?"

"Officer, the Agency has an interest, but it does not conflict with the normal processes of Federal, State and Local law enforcement. We are keeping a respectful eye on the situation, particularly in regards to the international implications."

"Did the Agency have any involvement in the killing of Standish Howling?"

"No, it did not."

"Thank you. I suspect you and Fulghum will collaborate on all matters not strictly impacting on my murder case and that you will share anything germane as you go forward." For legal reasons Officer Pounce had to be entirely clear of Agency operations, and all three men knew the boundaries of his jurisdictional rights. He knew that admissibility of evidence was a key issue. The policeman's hands were tied with warrant procedures and chain of custody of evidence. The CIA had different rules.

"So John, what else did you learn on your jaunt to Virginia?"

"Roberto Rapello is a big man among the gypsies. He is the father figure for many and the peacemaker for all. Marcello may be his father's heir. So framing his heir for murder might be in someone's interest. I don't think that has anything to do with the Howling case, but we should keep the fact in mind. The key, for now, is getting his deposition and keeping both Porro and Nevsky under lock and key. Whatever you can do to support those aims would benefit your case. How are things going with the forensic examination of Thomas Porro's knife?"

"Our team has been over that weapon with a fine tooth comb. Naturally, Porro's own prints are on the knife, yet we also have a partial print that matches Nevsky and minute traces of DNA that matches Howling."

"That should be conclusive evidence if Porro's confession holds up."

"Yes, we definitely have a case now. Our only remaining obstacle is putting the whole picture together for the D.A.'s office. Working with what we have, we've concluded that a fourth person could have been involved in the slaying."

"We agree. The facts do not support Marcello being in the picture, and that's been my primary focus. I have not ruled out a fourth player besides Porro, Nevsky, and the victim. In fact, I have not definitively ruled out Porro having been the murderer. The way he lunged at me with his knife suggested that he is capable. His complicated love interests make jealousy a major motive."

"John, please review your thoughts on that." Mander was sitting straight up and listening intently.

"During his confession, which I recorded while I stood behind the arras in Rosa's office, Thomas said that he loved both Marcello and Howling. What he meant by that he did not say. Let's assume that they were involved in a love triangle. Porro's motive for framing Marcello might be his jealousy both of the young man's power as his father's heir and of his hold on Howling's affections. Porro might have been so incensed by Howling's preference for Marcello over himself that he killed the man. By planting Marcello's knife near the corpse, he killed both his lover and his rival."

"Do we know for a fact that Marcello is gay?" asked Officer Pounce.

"Does that really matter?" riposted Mander.

"Let's reconstruct the murder with what we know," Fulghum advised.

"Okay, John. From the recording of Roberto I heard today, Nevsky was looking for a hit man to kill Howling. Roberto said he did not provide the service even though the money for the job was significant. Let's assume that Roberto was telling the truth and his alibi with the Strong woman holds. In any case, either Nevsky or someone he hired killed Howling and planted Marcello's knife by the body. The murderer, or Nevsky if he was not the murderer, managed to return the knife to Porro. Discovery of the murder weapon was purely accidental. John obtained it with a lucky break."

"That's a sick pun."

"It's getting late, and it's been a long day," Pounce retorted. "With Roberto's deposition, we have conspiracy to commit murder against Nevsky. With Thomas's confession, we have accessory to murder before and possibly after the fact."

Mander interposed, "Is there any way to question Nevsky and get the truth about his role?"

"I'm hoping to do that with Roberto's deposition."

"Jack Daniels is telling us that we need to look to tomorrow and reconvene tomorrow night for a recap," Fulghum concluded. The three men agreed, finished their drinks and departed.

At nine o'clock the next morning, Fulghum and Roberto Rapello met Officer Pounce at the police station.

Roberto wrote out his statement and signed it. Officer Pounce took a copy of the statement to Boris Nevsky and read it to him. Nevsky insisted on seeing a representative of his country. He refused to confirm that he had any role in Standish Howling's murder. At eleven o'clock, a representative of the Consulate of the Russian Federation along with a lawyer funded by the Consulate arrived to free Boris Nevsky. On the basis of the gravity of the crime plus the evidence given in the deposition of Roberto Rapello and the confession of Thomas Porro, the D.A. and Officer Pounce were able to keep both men behind bars pending the results of tortuous bureaucratic and legal maneuvers. The Chief of Police, the Mayor, and the Governor lined up in support of the D.A.

At noon, Fulghum and Roberto Rapello went to lunch at Dalia's Restaurant on Route 4 in Bedford. There they were met by Marcello Rapello, who wanted to thank Fulghum personally for his services. The young man was the image of his father though twenty years his junior. He was tall, big and strong. His olive complexion, long, curly black hair, and weeping mustache were identical to his father's. Even his disposition was like a chip off the old block—confident and proud, a tintype of the masculine gypsy leader figure. Fulghum saw right away why May Bell had been smitten by him.

"Mr. Fulghum, I am glad to meet you. I owe you a debt I can never repay. Thank you." Marcello's handshake was firm and steady. Fulghum wondered why Roberto doubted that his son would be able to fill his shoes.

"Marcello, you can thank your sister and your mother for setting you free. Zara contacted me while your mother conducted the séance that gave us the insight and proof we needed. I have a couple of questions if you don't mind."

"Anything you want, just ask for it."

"Marcello, are you gay?" When Fulghum asked this, Roberto rose to his feet and looked indignant. Fulghum ignored the father and kept his eyes riveted on the son. The son's eyes did not flinch from Fulghum's gaze. His pupils did not dilate.

"No, Mr. Fulghum, I am not gay. What gave you that idea?"

"Bear with me for a moment while I follow up on that question. Is Thomas Porro gay?"

"Yes, sir, he is. He will admit the fact openly."

"What was the relationship of Mr. Standish Howling to Thomas Porro?"

"I don't know all the details, but I know that Thomas and Standish were lovers. They both made moves on me, but I am straight. In fact, I am very much in love with my girlfriend down in Virginia. We plan to get married if my father and mother will approve."

"Do you mean May Bell Strong?"

"Yes, sir, I do."

"Thank you. Do you know anyone who might have wanted Standish Howling dead?"

"I have numerous candidates because, though he was rich as Croesus, he was a hateful, spiteful man. He was playing games with unscrupulous people. It was only a matter of time before someone cleaned his clock."

"Can you be specific about that?"

"For one thing, Standish was always trying to play the spy. He thought of himself as James Bond in America. He had midnight meetings with sketchy figures like his friend Boris Nevsky. That man was always scheming."

"You did a lot of traveling with Standish."

"Yes, I did and I can account for every trip. We always booked separate rooms. I did not care about the rumors that floated about our being an item. A couple of times I heard him bragging about his supposed relationship with me. Probably I should have cut him off entirely, but, as Dad has probably told you, our families go way back. I just happened to be the connection to this generation's scion."

"Did you wish Standish Howling dead?"

"No."

"Were you happy when he was found dead?"

"I was not happy yet I was not surprised either. Actually, I felt a profound relief."

"Why was that?"

"I wouldn't have to continue a charade that no longer had any meaning."

"Marcello, you know how important our connection to the Howlings has been," interposed the father.

"Yes, Dad, but things changed. Then they changed again. Now we are roughly back where we started in the first place—another Cold War."

"Marcello, your father is worried that you won't be able to fill his shoes as a gypsy leader."

"I could never fill his shoes. He is a genuine hero. Our people would be lost without him. He is a great man—just look at us. I could never compare. I would not be accepted by the other gypsies. Besides, we have differences. One difference in particular."

Getting nervous, Roberto shifted in his chair. "Marcello, you know I don't like airing our family's differences in public."

"Dad, last night you told me that Mr. Fulghum is part of our extended family now. Was that not true?"

"It is true, Marcello. Continue if you must."

"I love and intend to marry a woman who is not a pure gypsy."

"But you must marry a pure gypsy. We have always done so." Roberto was pleading with his son. Marcello shifted against his chair back.

"You see, Mr. Fulghum, we do have differences. One in particular."

"And about the Russians, do you have differences there as well?"

"I'm afraid we do, but those are more subtle and complex."

"Roberto, can you untangle this riddle for me?" asked Fulghum.

"During the last fifteen years, I have felt cut off from the contacts I once enjoyed in the intelligence community of this country. I gravitated to the Russians because they appeared to be the only game for gypsies once the Berlin Wall fell. Marcello and I have a fundamental difference about this approach."

"Yes we do, Dad. I have always been an American first and a gypsy second. I used to argue with Standish about his connections with the Russians and with Dad about the same thing. I may be old-fashioned, but I like a consistent view. I hate vacillation about anything, especially fundamental issues."

"Son, you remind me of the man I used to be," Roberto gruffly uttered, his voice choking a little as his eyes began watering. Fulghum saw an opportunity.

"As an honorary member of your family, I must say that I see a way to bridge the chasms between you. Roberto, you are the peacemaker. Can you help me mend the rift between you and your son?"

"Mr. Fulghum, please leave us and let us talk things through. You've done us another service, but it is time for us to work together now without you." The bull of a man stood and so did his son. Fulghum shook both their hands and drove to his office. He figured he had done what he could, and now he had other things to do.

In his second-story office up the stairs above the ice cream shop, he pored over the racing forms and chain-smoked his Marlboros. He was about to pour his first glass of JD for the day when he noticed that the light through his dingy window high above his desk was dimming. A cloud had passed in front of the sun. Fulghum heard light steps on the stairs and thought he heard a slight knock on his door.

"Come right in. You know the drill."

Zara pushed open the door and sat in the chair across the desk from his. Today she was wearing a brown outfit that might have been a hundred years old. In her hair was a bright red bow. Her vitality made the outfit seem brand new.

"Why hello, Zara."

"My mother wanted to come because she has a message for you. She had a customer suddenly but she knew her message must be delivered this afternoon so you could use it."

"All right. What is her message for me?"

"Two words, 'Thunder Road.'"

"That's all?"

"Yes, that's all. Oh, yes, and thank you. She said, 'Thank you from the bottom of my heart.'"

"Tell her she is very welcome. I am touched. While you're here, I have a question for you."

"For me?"

"What do you think about your brother being in love with May Bell Strong?"

"I think that love will find a way. If only I had such a love, my world would be complete."

"You said it—love will find a way. Be safe getting home. I'll be right here if you ever need me again. Till then, goodbye."

"Goodbye, Mr. Fulghum." She rose and went out the door and down the stairs. At the bottom of the stairs, she almost collided with Ken Mander, who took the stairs two at a time, came into Fulghum's office and shut the door behind him.

Fulghum was about to raise JD from his second desk drawer on the right but Mander, grinning widely, waved him off.

"We got a few intercepts I thought I wouldn't share with you."

"Okay. I can live with that."

"The first is that Roberto Rapello called his Russian contact and told him, 'Go to hell.'"

"That's great news."

"The second is that Marcello Rapello has called his girlfriend May Bell Strong and informed her that his parents have blessed their match."

"This is also great news."

"Now for the best news of all—the Agency is going to recruit Marcello with all the bells and whistles. I need to know right now if you will vouch for him."

"That's three for three, Ken. I will definitely vouch for the young man. He is most impressive. Of course, this breaks all the traditions of the CIA's strategy of keeping the gypsies at arm's length."

"The Deputy Director of Operations made a command decision, endorsed by the Director himself. Some things can change."

"And about the murder of Standish Howling—where does that stand?"

"My guess is that the truth will never be known unless Boris Nevsky undergoes implemented interrogation. He's likely to be released from jail and deported, but that may give us an opportunity. As for justice, Thomas Porro may be the best you'll get—as the accessory, but not the murderer. Well, that's all the time I have for this business today. I'm off on another assignment starting this evening. I'll see you when I see you."

"Thanks, Ken."

"Later, John. Say hello to Jack Daniels for me." Then the spook was down the stairs and gone.

Fulghum thought for a moment and went to the piles of racing forms that lined the walls of this office. He found the form he was looking for and took it to his desk. Before he opened the paper, he lit a cigarette to establish the proper aura. Then he opened the form, looking for a specific name as he ran his thumb down the page. His prodigious memory had not failed him—Thunder Road. Should he bet her to Place or Show?

With the kind of insight I am relying on, he thought, *What the hell. Go for broke!* Then he had a second thought and decided, *I'll split the bet for win, place and show in equal thirds.* He felt it was time for a celebration. Now he sat back in his captain's chair and pulled open the second desk drawer on his right. There lay two and a half bottles of Jack Daniels whiskey. He pulled up the half-bottle and a dusty glass. He wiped the glass carefully and set it in front of him. He opened the bottle and poured out three fingers of the velvety brown elixir. He deliberated how he should frame his toast.

"To Thunder Road," he toasted out loud, thinking of the reference to the dangerous traveling life of gypsies and the one big break that could change their game forever.

Gypsy War

John Fulghum, PI, could not believe his luck. Thunder Road had won its race, and the detective had collected the winnings for his equal bets as win, place and show. He sat in his second-story office above Joe's Ice Cream Shop and chain-smoked Marlboros while he counted his cash. The source of his luck was a tip from the gypsy fortuneteller and reader-advisor Rosa Rapello, whose son Marcello he had helped extricate from a complicated murder case. The Standish Howling murder case was still grinding on, but its complications were compounding.

The key suspect in the murder, Boris Nevsky, had become a diplomatic pawn whom the Russians demanded be allowed to return to his native country. Even though the man had attempted to put out a contract on the life of Boston blue-blood Howling, no evidence conclusively proved that he had committed the murder or hired the murderer. His partial fingerprint was found on the presumed murder weapon, a knife owned by the gypsy Thomas Porro, and police forensic analysis had found traces of Howling's DNA on the knife. Still the evidence for murder was circumstantial. Under pressure from the Governor and the Mayor, Boris Nevsky was released from jail and spirited out of the country by the Russians. His fate was unknown.

The key accessory to the murder, Thomas Porro, whose confession to having stolen Marcello Rapello's knife and given it to Boris Nevsky for reasons that were still unclear, was released from jail the day after Nevsky was freed. Four days later his nude body was found floating in the Charles River, his throat sliced neatly in the same manner as Howling's had been. The police did not waste time investigating his death because it was presumed to have been coincidental justice for his role in Howling's murder, which was now listed as a cold case. Fulghum figured that Porro's death was likely a matter of gypsy justice, but it was not his business to investigate every murder in the Greater Boston area. The fact that Roberto Rapello was in the area at the time of Porro's murder was not linked to what was now a cold case that would never be revived.

Fulghum resolved that his role in the Howling murder was over. After all, he had agreed with Zara Rapello to help free Marcello Rapello from jail. He had done that. He had also done a favor for his friend Ken Mander of the CIA in the process, but that favor and its implications would remain forever in the shadows. The detective viewed the Rapello situation as "happily ever after" with the Rapello family now apparently resolved to break their ties to the Russians and to accept the nuptials of Marcello Rapello and May Bell Strong. That marriage assured the continuation of the bloodline with the novelty of introducing a "non-pure" Roma in the mix.

It was somewhat of a surprise to Fulghum when Ken Mander knocked on his office door to throw the whole situation back into play with a new twist.

"Hello, John. I thought you might like an update on Boris Nevsky."

"Do you think we should discuss this matter here, or while we're getting some exercise in the city?"

"You're right. Let's drive over and perambulate in Boston Square and admire the fall scenery."

"What's left of it…the rain has turned the leaves brown, and they're falling fast. Winter's coming, and the first snow can't be long. I'll bring an umbrella in case it rains—or sleets or snows. Can you believe they're predicting snow?"

The two friends repositioned themselves for the circumnavigation of the Square. As they walked, they talked. They did not smoke because the Boston police would doubtless disapprove.

"Nevsky made it to Moscow. Our people managed to pick him up in the Arbat while he was getting some exercise. We put him under extensive implemented interrogation to discover the Russian plan for using the long-standing gypsy network in the U.S. It turns out that Nevsky was a Soroca gypsy from Moldova. He was the link between the American and Russian gypsies. He did not kill Howling. Neither did Porro. Porro's friend Ollie Strong did the job. I've got a copy of Nevsky's signed statement to that effect for you, along with the English translation. I'm not sure you're going to be able to use our interrogation as evidence though it's all recorded and transcribed." Mander handed Fulghum the two documents, which the detective stuffed in his coat pocket.

"Is the case now closed from your point of view?"

"Definitely not, my friend. While Nevsky was playing the Boston angle for the Russians, Russian intelligence had another angle going in Virginia through Roberto Rapello. Both angles have now been scotched, thanks to you. Moscow is trying to pick up the pieces, and one nasty requirement of their gray men is to eliminate Roberto because he broke free from their control. They plan to go farther and extirpate the Rapello family as an example to the rest. All this is documented in our decrypts of intercepted orders flowing to Roberto's former control, a man named Alexander Ribcoff, an intelligence professional of the new school."

"Ordering the elimination of the Rapellos and assuring that the assassinations are accomplished are two different things."

"That's true—if someone knowing the plan was on the inside advising the Rapellos."

"Aha. Let me guess. You want me to use my status as an honorary member of the family to get inside to provide them and you with the information that will foil the Russians' plan and keep the Rapellos alive to serve the Agency in the future."

"I couldn't have put it better myself. We know that you are newly rich, so money is not a problem. We're willing to subsidize as necessary, but you can't be perceived as working with the Agency or you're going to be in the line of fire. I don't want that to happen."

"Neither do I. What is the timeline for our operation?"

"You've got to get into the thick of it as soon as you can. Your opportunity will come when you are invited to the wedding."

"The wedding? Oh, you mean Marcello and May Bell's wedding."

"That's right. It has been planned for the weekend after next, and you are supposed to be a guest of honor. Later today, you'll get your invitation. You'll accept and insist on providing security both in the Greater Boston area and in the Virginia Tidewater where the wedding will take place."

"Why don't you just infiltrate one of your agency stars to do this job?"

"Think it through. The CIA has no charter to operate within the boundaries of the continental U.S. We'd have to inform the FBI and turn over the case. They would take over the case in a heartbeat and fumble it. We'd end up with four dead Rapellos and a lot of finger pointing. The result would be game over. You, on the other hand, are in the perfect position to get inside and keep everyone safe."

"I can only do that if you provide intel and over watch."

"We intend to provide those things continuously."

"Then the key problem is the length of time that we'll have to continue security for the Rapellos."

"We've gamed that. Moscow never forgets, but its resources are stretched thin these days. We can't provide security forever, but we can lessen the likelihood that Russia will persist in this plan. Suffice to say that we'll be working European angles simultaneously to increase the odds of your success."

"Is Boris Nevsky still in play?"

"No. He had an overdose of heroin in the Arbat. It was most unfortunate. He was found with his lover, who also died of an overdose, in one of the fashionable apartments there. The Russians may suspect foul play, but they are just as happy as we are that Nevsky is no longer with us."

"What about Ollie, the known murderer?"

"He is still in play, and I'd advise taking him out as soon as possible. His name is mentioned in the encrypted traffic to Alexander Ribcoff. By the by, don't take out Ribcoff unless you absolutely must. We're set up to monitor and decrypt his communications. If he were to be replaced, it's going to be a whole new ball game. I've got to get you back to your office. It's almost show time. Marcello will be coming with Zara to invite you to the wedding."

"All right, Ken. What about our communication during this interval?"

"I'm glad you asked. Here, take this cell phone. Use it like your own unit, only push pound after you dial my number. That will encrypt our discussions. All your attachments of text, recordings and videos will be encrypted automatically. Do you have any other questions?"

"Has over watch already started?"

"We've been in a classic foursquare all the time we've walked today. The Rapellos will be covered after your meeting with the brother and the sister."

"Is Marcello briefed in?"

"No, he is not. He is not officially an agent yet, and he is too green to be capable of much on the inside. We have informed him that you will be the security in this time of transition. That's why you'll have no trouble selling your security services for the wedding. Isn't it great that we are back to the car right on time to leave?"

"You folks don't leave much to chance, my friend."

"We've got you covered for this one, John. Just keep us informed as you go, and use initiative when you need to. We're there, but don't count on our being omniscient."

The detective and the agent climbed into the car and drove back to Fulghum's office. Fulghum walked up the stairs alone and reestablished his position behind his desk. He placed the cash from his winnings in his safe before he lit up a Marlboro. He had no more sat back in his chair to wait when a knock on his door revealed Marcello and Zara Rapello.

Marcello said, "We can't stay long, but we thought you should know that I'm going to marry May Bell Strong in Virginia two weeks from today. I'd like you to attend and be my best man. I'd also like you to provide security for my family in Massachusetts and Virginia."

Zara chimed in, "Please come, Mr. Fulghum. It would mean a lot to all of us. The wedding would not be happening if it were not for you."

Fulghum stood up and extended his hand to Marcello, "Congratulations. I'd be honored to attend your wedding and serve as your best man. As to the security, I'd be delighted to do that as well, provided that we agree on what you all must do to lighten my load."

"You wouldn't be working security alone, Mr. Fulghum. We gypsies have our own resources." Marcello sounded confident. Evidently, he did not consider insider threats seriously enough.

"People like your friend Ollie Strong?" Fulghum asked with a straight face.

"Ollie, though a cousin, will not be attending the wedding. He'll be staying here in Massachusetts. Also in Virginia, certain members of the King family and the Strong family will not be attending either. We don't want to take any unnecessary risks." Marcello seemed to have thought through the problems in his extended family.

"Since you have thought through the internal threat, can you guarantee that you can handle your family conflicts?"

"Dad and I are reasonably sure we can take care of any family problems. He has arranged for twelve good men to help with security. They will be under his orders, and he will coordinate their activities with you."

"Mom noticed that Thunder Road won the race!" Zara said with a broad smile. "She said she hoped you took advantage of her insights."

"Indeed, I did. Please relay my thanks in advance. I'll thank her in person when I see her again tomorrow morning. I plan to spend a lot of time with you at your camp until you're ready to leave. I saw in the Globe that your friend Thomas came to a rather grisly end."

Marcello looked Fulghum directly in the eyes and said, "Yes, he did. He was playing dangerous games and lost. I'll not forget his role in my being arrested for murder."

"Thomas was a bad man. He lied and tried to kill my brother—and you also. We're glad he's gone now." Zara said, with fire in her eyes. "I've been talking with our people in Virginia. They'll be sure to have your old friend ready to meet you when you arrive."

"My old friend?"

"Yes, Jack Daniels."

"That will make the whole trip doubly enjoyable. Thank you. Well, I'll see you both at your camp early in the morning."

"Come as early as you like, Mr. Fulghum. We all rise at dawn when the cock crows." With that, the Rapellos exited the office and drove home. Fulghum settled behind his desk, poured a glass of Jack Daniels whiskey and cleaned his weapon. He prepared himself mentally for being a soldier again.

After all, he thought, *as in Afghanistan, I'm going into foreign territory on an 'impossible mission' where I won't know who's a friend and who's a foe.* The likelihood of friendly fire was high. His own rules of engagement were unclear. He did think that Ollie was likely to be his first target. Who his other targets would be, he just did not know at this point.

At daybreak as the cock began to crow and the dogs began to bark, the sounds carrying in the damp, cold air, John Fulghum pulled into the unpaved parking area by Rosa's shack. Her shop light was on, so Fulghum knocked on the door and went inside. As he entered, Rosa threw her arms around him and hugged him. She then held him back at arm's length, looked into his eyes and smiled. Under her old-fashioned floor length dress, her baubles, rings, bells, and bows, she was a good-looking woman.

"I'm so glad for the way things turned out. I'm grateful. Thank you." She smiled, her eyes twinkling as she observed him admiring her.

"As you know, I'm supposed to provide security for your family through the time of the wedding. I'm also supposed to be the best man. I'll need special advice to be effective. Can you tell me about Ollie Strong?" Fulghum was thumbing a Russian Federation flag that hung from a pole back of the shop door.

"Ollie is a cousin of May Bell. He inherited the willful genes of his headstrong family. Easily led, he liked to dog Thomas Porro's footsteps. No one knew what those two men did most of the time. They would sneak off for many days. They would return and snicker among themselves, as thick as thieves. Then they would be off again. I always suspected he was dealing drugs and stealing things. The police would come by to question him, but they never arrested him. That man Boris Nevsky came around to talk with him on numerous occasions, but they always talked alone. I don't know what their business was, but I did not like the looks of them together."

"Does Ollie own a gun?"

"I don't think so. All he has by way of weapons is his knife. He sharpens that knife all the time. He practices using it daily. I've watched him throw it at targets. He's very fast and accurate at over twenty feet. Of course, he's not as fast as Thomas was. Thomas had the quickest hands I've ever seen. I'm still amazed that you managed to disarm Thomas easily. Anyway, if we want a goat killed for a feast, Ollie's the man for the job. He knows just how to hold the animal so he can slice right through the neck."

"How is Ollie taking the fact that he will be excluded from the wedding?" Fulghum was now admiring a dress in progress on a clotheshorse. Rosa began tidying up for her day's work. She moved around the shop as she talked.

"Ollie is disgruntled and sulking. Roberto told him that someone had to be left in charge of the Boston camp while we were all at the wedding in Virginia. Ollie wants to feel like a big man in his family. He doesn't much care about our family except that with Marcello's marriage, we'll all be one big family after all. How the tide turns!"

"The Kings and the Strongs had a falling out in Virginia. Can you tell me anything about that?"

"Roberto said it was about an insult and revenge. I thought the two families were looking for any excuse to fight against each other. It's a blood feud that goes back to Europe. I spoke with Ollie about it. He has a very narrow view. He cares nothing for history. He just wants to kill all the Kings and be done with it."

"So how will the Kings and the Strongs play at the wedding?"

"They are at war. The Kings won't be invited. They'll feel disgraced and want to make things difficult for everyone. The Strongs are now out of jail for a while so they will be looking for the Kings to make a move against the wedding. Then they can retaliate. Roberto knows this. He has twelve men from other families coming to Virginia to help with security."

"We'll be going into a war zone then with the Kings and the Strongs likely to scuffle and the marriage as a likely flash point. How does May Bell Strong factor into the situation?"

"She's largely innocent. She's beautiful, spirited and intelligent. I like her. One of the reasons that Roberto was against Marcello's marrying May Bell was gypsy politics.

Roberto managed to make the peace among the families by being pure gypsy. The marriage changes all that."

"Because Marcello's family will no longer be pure, as you call it?"

"You see, we are caught in a conundrum. On the one hand, when gypsies band together, we are easily marginalized and persecuted. On the other hand, when we disperse and blend in with the population, we lose our identity as gypsies and have a hard time adjusting to societal norms."

"Have the Kings and the Strongs dispersed themselves?"

"Yes, they have done that. Their men have mainly married outsiders but they've been dissatisfied with their wives' inability to understand them. Their women have had a hard time connecting with their gypsy roots because the pure gypsies know that, given the chance with the right match, the mixed breeds break off and go on their own."

"What about the allegation that gypsies are criminals?"

"Pure nonsense! That's what the Nazis maintained before and during World War II. Do you know that until 1974 the Germans refused to pay gypsies reparations for the war because they claimed that sending criminals to prison camps was not the same as sending ethnic populations there? Nazis saw pure gypsies as belonging to a different class than mixed breeds. It's all in the documents that were produced at the Nuremberg trials. That's another reason that Roberto felt this marriage should not go forward."

"America is not Nazi Germany."

"Neither was Germany before the Nazis. Yet even after the war, we were shunned and feared as being criminals. Not all gypsies are murderers and thieves, Mr. Fulghum."

"Can you tell me anything about the Sorocans?"

"Those are Moldovan gypsies. The Strongs have close ties to them."

"And to the Russians?"

"I'm more concerned about the Russians who are working as agitators in this country than those working against the Sorocans."

"Do the Russians have anything to do with the animosity between the Kings and the Strongs?"

"That's highly conjectural." She looked at her séance desk as if she were trying to find a better answer there.

"All I have to go on is guesses at this point. What do you think?"

"I think my husband was almost killed three times while he tried to make peace among the Kings and the Strongs. Both sides had reasons to stop the peacemaker, but the Russians have their own game going. They might have been involved in all three attempts. Here comes Zara."

Zara came into the office with rosy cheeks in her green dress with the orange scarf over her hair. She wore an ankle-length, black winter coat that appeared to be of Polish manufacture. It would withstand the harshest winter weather.

"Good morning, Mr. Fulghum. If you'll drive me back to the camp, you can join us for breakfast. We're making coffee, and there's fresh bread and goat's milk. I hope I'm not interrupting anything, Mother."

"Not at all, Zara. Mr. Fulghum and I were just talking shop. It's time he had breakfast. Run along, you two, while I prepare for my first customer. He's a young lawyer anxious for a positive verdict. I'm afraid I have bad news for him, though. Mr. Fulghum, please stop by around close of business. We can talk before you return to your place for the evening." She extended her hand and he shook it. Then he drove Zara back to the gypsy camp.

When they got out of the car, their breaths were white in the cold air. Fulghum heard distant crows and dogs. He heard the sounds of an ax chopping wood. He saw Ollie in the distance throwing his knife at a target nailed to a maple tree. In the center of a huddle of trailers was a fire where a coffee pot steamed. Boys and girls in colorful clothing were toasting bread on sticks over the fire. Roberto and Marcello rose from where they were sitting to shake Fulghum's hand. Zara fetched glasses of fresh goat's milk and a round loaf of brown bread. She then poured several cups of black coffee, one for herself. They all sat around the fire and ate while they talked.

"I've just heard from the last of our twelve helpers for the wedding. The arrangements have been settled. We don't have to worry about calling for reinforcements at the last minute." Roberto seemed relieved and a little surprised.

"Seeing as we'll be going into the middle of two warring families, that's just as well," said Fulghum.

"I'm more worried about the Kings than the Strongs at this stage. That's because the Strongs attacked them in the last round before the appointed time. The Kings will want revenge."

"Besides the feuding families, do you have any other security concerns for this wedding?"

"The resentment against the Rapellos goes deep across the gypsies in this country. Who doesn't love to hate us? I'm supposed to be the peacemaker, but no good deed goes unpunished." Roberto shook his head in amazement. He drank his coffee and eyed Fulghum, who was looking towards Ollie and his knife practice.

"Ollie can throw his knife like that for hours at a time," said Marcello. "Pay no attention to him. If he comes over, act like nothing bothers you. He's mad because he won't be at the wedding, or perhaps he's angry about not being able to join in the fighting at the wedding. He's also been upset ever since they found Thomas Porro's body in the Charles River. Everyone knew they were close, but Ollie seems to be in mourning for the loss of his friend."

"I'm new at being the best man at a gypsy wedding. Can you tell me what you expect me to do?"

"The best man at a gypsy wedding brings a ton of gold and twelve white stallions. He provides the wedding feast for one hundred people. Then he broaches a large cask of wine so the whole village can carouse. Just kidding. All you really need to do is witness the wedding vows then toast the bride and groom after the ceremony. We will provide the wine for the toast."

"And I will provide the Jack Daniels so that we can continue toasting through the night until dawn while the bride and groom practice creating my descendants." Roberto was clearly looking forward to the wedding festivities.

"Zara, the goat's milk was delicious. Did you make this black bread?"

"Yes, with Mother's help, I did. And I churned the butter as well."

"Zara will make some gypsy a fine bride, won't you, Zara?" asked her father.

"Papa, it's too early for me to be married. I've got so much more to learn." Zara was animated but respectful. Fulghum felt as if he was in the middle of a continuing conversation about Zara's future.

"Here comes Ollie looking for breakfast," said Marcello. "Come on over, Ollie, and have some goat's milk and bread." Ollie smirked and approached the fire while Zara fetched him food and drink.

"When are you going to slaughter the goat for our evening meal?" Roberto asked him.

"It's already done, Roberto. The carcass is hanging behind the oak tree. I collected the blood in a zinc bucket, as always. Do you want the hide prepared for tanning?" Ollie asked as he drank his goat's milk and spread some butter on his black bread.

"Yes, we'll use everything as always," Roberto said. "I'm depending on you to keep things together here in the camp while we're in Virginia. Will you do that?"

"Yes, I will. I wish I were going with you, but, as you said, someone has to be here minding the farm." Ollie said this perfunctorily with a scowl at Fulghum. The detective held the man's gaze. "I was getting a little rusty with my knife, but slaughtering the goat and practicing to throw honed my skills just fine. I'm now ready for anything." The young man's eyes narrowed menacingly. His words held a hidden meaning for Fulghum.

"Ollie, how is Brenda, your girlfriend?" asked Zara innocently.

"I wouldn't know, Zara. We broke up a week ago. I probably won't be seeing her again." Ollie did not seem very upset with this new development, but Zara was distracted.

"I'm sorry to hear that. I know Brenda will be unhappy," Zara said.

"She's the one who ended our relationship," Ollie responded.

"I see. I still think she'll be unhappy."

A few flakes of snow fell from the low gray clouds and thunder sounded far off. Fulghum and the others exchanged glances.

"We're going to get that snow storm they've been predicting," Roberto said. "Twelve to eighteen inches are in the forecast. We'd better make sure we have what we need to last through a week of snow, at least. The generator should keep us powered up in case the electricity shuts down. The livestock should be fine as long as the generator power remains on."

"So what's the schedule for your departure?" Ollie asked.

"We'll be leaving tomorrow around noon, weather permitting. We'll be gone for two weeks and return right after the wedding itself." Roberto took a long look at Ollie. "Will you be all right while we're gone?"

"I'll manage. Do you want roast lamb tonight? If Zara will wrap some potatoes in foil, we can roast them." Ollie was already acting as if he had taken charge of the gypsy camp.

"That will be fine, Ollie," Roberto responded. "After all, this will be our last evening meal here before we leave for the wedding. It might as well be a feast."

"Roberto, if you don't mind, I'd like to have a few words in private with Ollie."

"Don't ask me—ask him!"

"Ollie, can we walk around and talk. I'd like a cigarette. Perhaps you'll join me?"

"Sure, fine, Mr. Fulghum. Lead on." Fulghum rose and proceeded in the direction of the place where Ollie had been throwing his knife. Ollie followed him. They had not gone far before Fulghum gave Ollie a cigarette and lit it for him. The two men smoked as they walked.

"Ollie, I know the score. I'm prepared to remain silent about what I know, but I need your cooperation."

"What are you saying, detective? Look, I saw what you did to Thomas. I don't want the same thing to happen to me."

"Ollie, I know you killed Standish Howling. Don't try to deny it. I have in my possession a copy of the sworn statement from Boris Nevsky detailing everything. Here is the English translation of Nevsky's statement. Take it. It's all legal—and it's definitive. Things could be very bad for you if that statement should fall into the wrong hands." Ollie took the sheet from Fulghum and read it carefully. Then he read it again and handed it back.

"So what happens next?"

"I'm not the only person who knows about Nevsky's statement, but I'm the only one in a position to keep it quiet. I'll keep it under wraps unless you make any move against the Rapello family or against your cousin. If I even suspect you caused harm to befall those people, I will assure that you are indicted for first-degree murder. Do you understand me? This is not a bluff." Ollie's eyes showed terror. He seemed paralyzed for a moment and he stopped walking forward. He stood for a moment and gazed at the low, gray sky. Then he made some sort of decision and continued walking.

"Show me the Russian version with Boris's signature." Ollie seemed to transform from a frightened young man into an older man with uncommon sense. Fulghum handed him the copy of the Russian original. Ollie read this slowly as if he knew Russian. He nodded and handed the paper back to Fulghum.

"So, detective, it is true. I am in checkmate. You don't seem surprised that I know Russian. Maybe I'm not as dumb as I look."

"You were smart enough to pull the wool over the eyes of the authorities about Howling's murder. You were smart enough—and ruthless enough—to implicate your friend Marcello. You're smart enough to make the Rapello family think that you were the follower and Thomas Porro was the leader. That, of course, was pure drama. You were the leader of the pack, weren't you? Don't try anything with your knife. You know what I can do."

"I wasn't reaching for my knife. My hands are cold. I was just putting them where they could get warm."

"Just so we understand each other, I have a knife and a gun. If you try anything at all, I will shoot you dead and use the statement to prove I shot you in a good cause."

"Why don't you just shoot me?" Ollie turned towards Fulghum and opened his arms as if to open himself for the killing shot.

"You are too useful for me alive for me to want to shoot you. But don't get any ideas because I'll shoot you anyway if I need to."

"What do you need from me?"

"First, who killed Thomas Porro? Was it you?"

"I killed Thomas on orders."

"By the same people who ordered you to kill Standish Howling?"

"Yes."

"And would the name of the man who gave you the orders be Alexander Ribcoff?"

"How do you know these things?"

"Was it Ribcoff?"

"Yes, damn him, it was."

"Would you be willing to write and sign a statement that Alexander Ribcoff ordered you to kill Howling and Porro? This would not be a confession that you committed the two murders. It would only be evidence against Ribcoff. It might get him deported so that he could not come after you."

"Why would I want him deported? He is my meal ticket."

"Explain, please."

"Alexander Ribcoff arranged for me to come from Moldova to be reunited with my cousins in America."

"So you've been a Russian agent in the U.S. since you arrived here. Is that so?"

"Yes, it's true. I had no life in Moldova. I sat on a hilltop, watching people below get rich when I had nothing. America is the land of opportunity. When Alexander recruited me, my whole life changed."

"Everything except for what you really did for a living. You were an assassin in Moldova, and the only difference between there and here is that you get paid better for your assassinations here."

"Yes. What if I won't sign a statement like the one you're asking for?"

"What if I told Alexander Ribcoff that we had this conversation and you did sign a statement? Would he believe you or me?"

"Where do I sign the statement?"

"Let's continue our walk and discuss other things. We'll wander over to Rosa's shack. She'll give you the paper and pen to write the statement. Then we'll talk some more."

As the snow came down, Fulghum and Ollie Strong walked the long way to Rosa's shack. In the course of this walk, Strong fell into a familiar pattern. For the moment, Fulghum had taken the place of the man's control. Fulghum recognized the man's need to report to his superior. He also knew when to remain silent. Likewise, he knew that his cell phone was recording every word they spoke. So, while Ollie reviewed his assassinations in all their particulars, Fulghum sternly listened and nodded as if approvingly. Twenty killings were Fulghum's tally when in the snowy field they encountered two deer that raised their heads before they bolted. The first shot sounded as if it came from a hunter's weapon except Ollie's head was suddenly a bloody mass with the brains and blood scattered all over the ground to one side. The second shot rang out but Fulghum lay flat on the ground trying to appear dead. His cell phone rang. Slowly, the detective reached into his pocket and pulled out his phone. He stopped the recorder and answered.

"John, this is Ken. Are you all right?"

"I'm fine. Ollie Strong has been killed."

"We know. Our man shot his assassin. Crawl over and check for the man's cell phone. Don't say another word until you find it."

Fulghum crawled slowly to Ollie Strong's body. He felt in the man's coat pocket and found the cell phone with its recorder still working. He silenced the recorder.

"Ken, I found the cell phone and silenced the recorder."

"Good. It seems you and Ollie were playing the same game. Both of you were feeding the voice message straight to someone else. Yours came to me. Ollie's went to Alexander Ribcoff."

"Ribcoff knew that his work was done if he did not silence Strong before he wrote and signed his statement."

"Yes, and he must have pre-positioned his shooter just in case."

"Can you use the recording I sent you against Ribcoff?"

"We can't use it in a court of law, but we can get him sent home through clandestine means. Believe me, pal, that angle is being explored as we speak. As for the shooting, this is hunting season in New England. Accidents do happen. You'd better dial 911 ASAP so the police can clean up that mess. Pocket the cell phone and hold it until I can pick it up at your office tonight. If you're up to it, continue on your mission for the Rapellos. There's no telling what else you'll turn up in the process. Goodbye."

Fulghum terminated his call and dialed 911. Within half an hour, the police arrived to discover the body of Ollie Strong in a field between the copse of trees with the gypsy camp and the roadside shack of a fortuneteller named Rosa. Fulghum told the first responders exactly what he saw—two deer that bolted and his companion's dead body lying in the snowy field. The responders cursed that they were witness to another senseless hunting accident during deer season. Probably, they opined, the hunter never knew he or she had hit a person. Such things happened too often in New England. They drove off with the corpse, but Fulghum had possession of Strong's cell phone. He knew that phone was priceless to the Agency because of the forensic evidence it contained.

The gypsies gathered around the fire later that day to feast on the goat that Ollie Strong had killed. While it roasted on a spit, Zara wrapped potatoes and vegetables in aluminum foil and laid them on a grate over the fire. The resultant feast was fit for a wake of a dead gypsy.

"Brenda was lucky to have made her break before today. She would have been heartbroken over Ollie's death, I'm sure, if he hadn't tried to rape her. That's what she told me was the reason for their split-up. She is a virgin and wanted to be married before they consummated their relationship. He did not want them to be married. So they had reached an impasse." Zara looked grimly into the fire, a glass of red wine in her hand. The snow continued unabated, and everyone's breath was white as they ate.

"Ollie was good with a knife," Roberto said, "but he wasn't lucky. Besides, he was a follower. When Thomas died, he was living on borrowed time."

"Ollie once told me that he longed for the days when he lived in Moldova with his original family. He said they were poor, but they owned their lives. Freedom, he thought, was more important than riches." Marcello shook his head and asked for another pouch of vegetables. Rosa pulled an aluminum pouch out of the embers and opened it for him. Zara poured another round of wine.

"Fulghum, you were lucky today. That hunter might as easily have shot you as Ollie Strong. It was pure chance that you survived. I thought I heard two shots. I wonder whether the other bullet hit one of the two deer you saw." Rosa said this without looking Fulghum in the eyes. She seemed to be trying to read something in the flames. Not seeing what she was looking for, she placed another two logs on the fire and waited for them to catch.

It was evening and by the fire's glow, the Rapellos ate while they reflected on the day's events. Marcello wondered what would happen to Ollie's knife. Zara called Brenda to tell her what had happened, but Brenda did not seem to be upset. Rosa said that she had not received a large tip from the lawyer because he said he only paid well for good news. Roberto said that tomorrow they would continue on their plan. His team would meet them at the Norfolk airport and escort them to the gypsy camp in Portsmouth. It may be snowing in New England, but in Virginia, it was cool and humid with no chance of precipitation.

Returning to his office that evening, Fulghum found Ken Mander waiting outside his door. He handed Mander the cell phone he had pulled from Ollie Strong's coat pocket. He invited Mander to drop in for a nightcap with Jack Daniels.

"I'm in a rush on account of the Ribcoff business, but how can I refuse JD?"

Over two glasses of the velvety brown nectar, the detective, and the spook reviewed the information both had heard from Ollie Strong that day. The recording was a mine of information about many past international cases and a few American cases that had no solutions formerly.

"I only wish we'd had the time to turn Ollie Strong and work him back against the Russians. We're going to try that trick with Ribcoff, but we don't think it will work. He's an old school agent not likely to crack or turn. I propose a toast to the 'Great Game' wherever we find it and to winning it."

"I'll drink to that, Ken. Something that was said around that gypsy campfire struck my fancy. There we were in the field—two deer, two men and, in the distance, two 11overwatch shooters. Events could have taken us in many directions. Why do you suppose the Russian shooter was ordered to kill Ollie Strong and not me?"

"John, I'll let you know if we find out for sure. I'd hazard a guess, though, that the sniper's second bullet would have been for you if he had been given the chance to use it. We got lucky. We knew where he had holed up. We cut him off before he had the time to shift targets."

"I'm off to Virginia tomorrow. Do you suppose Alexander Ribcoff will be a problem for me there?"

"Ribcoff is not going to be a problem for anyone. Rumor has it he has already packed and prepared to depart for Moscow. Maybe we'll be able to do the same service for him as we did for Boris Nevsky. Time will tell. Speaking of which, I must be going now. Thanks for the drink. Have a great time in the Commonwealth of Virginia. We'll be watching your performance there. That young gypsy Zara is one looker, don't you think?"

"I do, Ken, but something tells me that she'll not choose a mixed breed as her brother did. She'll want to remain pure gypsy. Some traveler is going to have the perfect bride."

"Let's hope he won't be a fellow traveler."

"You can say that again. Goodnight."

Fulghum was exhausted from his daycare duties with the gypsies. He smoked another Marlboro after Mander departed. He also had another two fingers of Jack Daniels. He was about to lock up and go to his apartment for a few hours' sleep when his cell phone rang. The caller was Rosa Rapello.

"Hello, Mr. Fulghum. Everything is fine here, thanks to you. We'll see you at the airport tomorrow, but I wanted to call tonight because I saw something and thought you should know it. I saw two deer in a snowstorm. A hunter killed one, and the other got away. The other was shot by another hunter. The image was very clear."

"Thank you, Rosa. I believe I understand what you saw."

"Be careful, Mr. Fulghum. We need you. Stay alive."

"I'll do my best. Keep envisaging, Rosa, and let me know what you see."

The next morning John Fulghum, PI, met the Rapellos at the airport and flew with them to Norfolk, Virginia. They were escorted from the airport to the gypsy camp in Portsmouth where all preparations were being made for the wedding. Gypsies were arriving in their trailers from all over the southeast United States. Roberto took charge of the area with his twelve watchmen standing guard in four-hour shifts. As the arrivals came, they were given locations on the farm to park their vehicles. The entire area had the look and feel of a county fair. The gypsy families turned out in colorful clothes, and in the evenings, their separate fireplaces sported foods with spices of all kinds. Fulghum remained by Marcello's side, and he made sure that he checked on Rosa and Zara often during the daylight hours. At night, he lodged in the same trailer as Roberto, and the two spent long hours discussing every detail of their evolving security measures.

May Bell Strong was sequestered by the Strong family women because she was not to be seen by the bridegroom until the wedding. The wedding dress was likewise a matter of secrecy because it was considered bad luck to show it before the appointed time. The gypsy children all had roles to play in the ceremony, and the families had positions to occupy too. Musicians played and practiced every day, and gypsies who worked for the circuses entertained the families with their juggling, acrobatics, animals, and knives. One wandering violinist became the spirit of the occasion, and his repertoire included Hungarian mazurkas as well as Czech etudes. Goats roamed among the people, and a few dogs nipped at their heels.

The increasing throng meant a greater threat to security, so Roberto Rapello and John Fulghum decided to cordon off and protect the Rapello compound especially. Fulghum insisted that the same precautions be taken with the trailers surrounding May Bell Strong.

"Roberto, can we arrange a meeting with the leaders of the Strong family to discuss the state of play?"

"Fulghum, consider it done. We'll meet tonight over Jack Daniels. I have bought a whole case for the occasion. We'll have music with Alfredo the violinist and Zara will sing. She is such a beautiful singer—you'll see."

That night a great many portable tables were jammed together and folding chairs were arranged so that fourteen people could be seated for the talks. When all the invitees were seated, and Roberto's twelve guards were stationed around the area, Roberto welcomed them.

"We are here to celebrate a wedding, not to feud. In case trouble comes, though, we are ready to deal with it." He gestured to his twelve guards. "Eat and drink Jack Daniels. If you have any information about possible troublemakers, Mr. Fulghum and I would like to know about it right away. Alfredo, play! Zara, sing! Everyone, be happy! Here's to a marvelous evening." Roberto then quaffed his drink and sat down to pour himself some more Jack Daniels whiskey. Alfredo played the opening for a serenade, and Zara appeared dressed in a fine dress and sang.

"Roberto, you think of everything. This is a fine feast. I am happy to have my granddaughter be the bride of your son."

"Ranolfo, thank you. I'm sorry about the recent loss of your grandnephew Ollie Strong. That accidental shooting was unfortunate and ill-timed."

"Yes, it was—if it was accidental. He was a distant relation on the European side, but a Strong just the same. He was involved in dangerous things for powerful people. Anyway, he lived as he wished and died like a man."

The ancient patriarch nodded and drank. His long beard and hair gave him an aureole in the torchlight. He hummed along with Zara's singing.

"Your daughter is very beautiful. She sings like a songbird. Do you have a match for her yet?"

"No. She wants education before she gets married."

"Good for her and good for her future husband. I'll keep an eye open for possible suitors for her. As for trouble, you know that the Kings are planning a few surprises for us in the next few days."

"What do you know about that?"

"They intend to strike when the wedding ceremony is occurring. They will come with knives, machetes, and guns. They will be gathering at a nearby farm the night before where they will drink courage. Then they'll be coming through the back acreage and through the trees. They'll break into two groups, one coming from the pig pens and the other coming from the barn."

"This is very good intelligence, Ranolfo. What do you suggest that we do?"

"I suggest that you attack the Kings when they have gathered for their courage. Cut them off before they even begin."

"And if the information you have is a trap?"

"If it is a trap, we'd better find out what they really intend to do and cut that off at the root."

"Were you the one who advised a preemptive attack on the Kings after the insult?" Fulghum interposed.

"If I had not done that, we would have suffered a lot of damage. As it was, two of the Kings died and all of ours remained alive to fight another day."

Fulghum nodded. "Let's suppose the information that you obtained was planted so that we preempted just as you did before. What do you think the Kings would do?"

"If this were the Strongs attacking, I'd have them go straight for the bride and groom the night before the wedding. I'd do it at the time when the security was diverted to the place where our people were supposed to be massing. That way the victims would be defenseless. They would be slaughtered, two victims to serve as revenge for two men lost."

"Fulghum, what are you thinking?" asked Roberto.

"I like what Ranolfo has said. Let's plan to send a false force to the farm where the Kings are supposed to be gathering. That way, they'll feel confident that the way is clear to attack this camp. We'll remove the bride and groom from their current lodgings and put them in another place. We'll then dispose our defenses around the cordoned areas where the nuptial pair are supposed to be staying. You and I will guard the couple as a terminal defense. Can you give orders to make these things happen?"

"I can and I will do that. I'll also arrange for some nasty surprises for the Kings if they actually follow through with the plan that they have put forward. Foot spikes in ditches by the pens and stable should do the trick, but we'll have to warn our people not to go walking there."

The plans having been hatched, the revelers caroused until late in the evening. When the Strongs had gone to their trailers, Roberto called a meeting of his security staff and told them the plan.

"We have one day to accomplish what we plan. The key element is the credibility of the force that we will send against the farm where the Kings are scheduled to meet. If we don't have enough men to do the job, we'll have to dress women as if they were men to fill out the ranks. Make your choices and have the decoy force come to see me at first light tomorrow."

The next morning twelve teenage boys and girls assembled for their instructions. They were excited about playing a part in the action, but Roberto warned them about the seriousness of their role.

"The Kings are murderers. They will have blood. If they are actually at the farm where they plan to meet, you will find trouble waiting for you. In that case, you will not engage them but retreat. If you retreat, do not come back anywhere near the pens or the barn. We'll prepare some nasty surprises there that will cripple them literally. Any questions? Assemble again here at ten o'clock tonight for launch."

Roberto and the detective supervised the placement of the foot spikes and the straw that hid them from view. That evening, they covered the bride and groom with dark fabric and escorted them to the interior of the barn where they were ensconced in two empty stables. Fulghum stood guard at the barn door while Roberto's team took their assigned positions. At ten o'clock, Fulghum met Roberto and the decoy team to give them their final briefing and launch them. Into the night went the teenagers while Roberto and Fulghum resorted to the barn door.

The Kings attacked at midnight. They came in two groups, one to attack the bride and the other to attack the groom exactly as the patriarch said he would do in their shoes. The battle was fierce, and the two groups of attackers fell back to the area beside the pens and the area alongside the barn where the foot spikes had been placed. The retreating attackers were taken totally by surprise. Roberto and Fulghum took positions alongside their security forces to drive the wounded and limping Kings off the farm. Sure that they had routed the Kings, Roberto and Fulghum escorted the bride and groom back to their separate places to continue to prepare for the wedding. Meanwhile, the decoy force returned to report that no one had appeared at the supposed rendezvous. Roberto told them what had happened in their absence and praised them for having provided such a credible force that the Kings followed through with their real plan.

During the evening, not a single member of the King family was killed, but nearly all were injured, many in the feet by the foot spikes. Several members of the Strong family had suffered slight injuries. Those were treated effectively and the bandages worn like badges of honor. After all, they had routed the hated enemy forces even though they had to overcome deceit and fraud more devious than the Kings had ever devised. The police did not come to the gypsy camp to investigate after the fracas because no one reported any trouble to them. Local physicians wanted to report the odd injuries that the Kings had suffered, but the Kings dissuaded them from making the reports.

"Roberto, consider how embarrassed the Kings must have felt to be outmaneuvered and routed in such a shameful fashion."

"Fulghum, I am in complete agreement with you. Still, we must remain vigilant until the wedding is done and everyone has gone home."

The Kings did not mount another attack. The wedding went on as planned. Fulghum served as the best man and, after the vows when all the glasses had been filled, toasted the bride and groom.

"Ladies and gentlemen, I propose a toast to Marcello Rapello and May Bell Rapello, the happy groom and bride. May they live long and happy lives together. May they enjoy the fruit of their wedding with many healthy, intelligent children. May all their dreams come true." He lifted his glass and drank. Everyone applauded.

After that, the feasting, the music, the dancing, the drinking and the kissing began. Young men and women danced with knives in one hand and scarves in the other hand. Tumblers did exotic leaps and bounds. One very young girl stood on a bareback horse while she juggled hoops in the air. A bear tamer led an enormous bear through the crowd and fed it an ice cream cone as a reward. Alfredo played his violin. Another man played the accordion. The scent of roasted meat filled the air.

In the evening, Rosa set up a table to tell the fortunes of her guests for free. Zara stood on a dais and sang a capella accompanied by ten gypsy girls. The bride and groom, wholly engrossed with each other acknowledged gifts that filled a large table. They received envelopes of cash. They danced and drank. Finally, they departed the area in the dented Saab, the back seat filled with their gifts.

Gradually the gypsies began to pack their things and depart. They did not wait until morning. As they became ready, they drove their trailers away into the night. All this time, the remaining Rapellos sat at a table where Jack Daniels was also present.

"Mr. Fulghum, you have done us honorable service. I lift my glass to you." Roberto toasted. Rosa also raised her glass. Zara was not drinking alcohol, but she raised her glass of goat's milk just the same.

"Roberto, you have a fine family and a great future ahead. I wish you all the best of everything. I'll be leaving in the morning early, but before I retire, I'd like to know how much you knew about what Ollie Strong was doing."

"Some things, my friend, are better left in the darkness and not dragged into the light. For example, the recipe for this Jack Daniels elixir is better not known. Don't you agree?"

That reminded Jack Fulghum that he had to make a phone call. He excused himself and walked into the barn to place his call.

"Hello, Ken. It appears we are in the clear."

"So it appears from my end, John. Ribcoff is no longer with us though we had a long conversation before he departed. I can't tell you the details because you don't have the need to know. I can tell you that the gypsy play in America is now the subject of a major review by Moscow Center. Congratulations to all of us for that. The Deputy

Director is beaming. By the way, she extends you a hearty, though deniable, WELL DONE! I'll keep you under watch until you're safely back in your office. Don't let that be an incentive for you to drop your guard."

"Hahaha. I believe you missed one opportunity to join Jack Daniels and me for a celebration. Consider that an invitation to drop by and imbibe. In the meantime and in any case, watch your Six. And thanks for the opportunity. I would not have missed it."

Jack Fulghum terminated his call and turned to exit the barn but bumped into Zara, who had been behind him all the time he was talking.

"Mr. Fulghum, I wanted to give you a special thanks for all you have done for my family." She then kissed him full on the lips, warmly and lingeringly. She moved right in to hug him tight, as he took her in his arms and kissed her. He gently released her and offered her his arm. She took it like the young lady that she was. The two proceeded out into the torchlight. Roberto and Rosa held the torches. No matter what they thought, they were all smiles. Zara was blushing but she held her head high. A troupe of small gypsy children with a herd of goats passed through them. Fulghum heard the goats bleating and the Rapellos laughing. All he thought was, "Mission accomplished!" Then he sought out his old friend Jack Daniels for a final round before he slept the sleep of angels.

Hacker I

Jonathan Smart, a later acquaintance of the Boston CIA prodigy Joseph Pounce, hated school but loved computers and taught himself how to write software. His history as an autodidact provided the advantages of anonymity. His happiness as a loner gave him a wide range of accomplice-free play. Jonathan surfed the web to discover the most vulnerable software systems on the planet and decided to hack them one by one, solely to wreak havoc on a world that did not understand him. A world that did not tolerate what he viewed as his extraordinary skills—stealth, surprise, malice, and ingenuity.

Jonathan had learned the power of automated systems when he was a toddler just discovering the magic of garage door openers. At five, he experimented with his parents' door opener until he knew the range and conditions of its operation. At seven, he learned on the Net how to program a garage door opener and by ten, he had built, out of parts from Radio Shack, a garage door opener code detection unit by which he learned every code in his neighborhood. Then he built another unit that could accept any number of codes.

At age eleven, when he was driven to school, as his family's car passed garages he would clandestinely press buttons to open all of them. No one ever learned that Jonathan was responsible for midnight attacks on the systems in his neighborhood. He never took advantage of his skill to steal property, but he made garages vulnerable to others who did so. People were perplexed and concerned that their garage door opener codes had been broken. When people discussed the mystery in range of his hearing, Jonathan affected not to be interested, but he was secretly excited. His mischief was working but the boy was invisible and inscrutable.

Jonathan in his teens graduated from simple hacks and became interested in hacking complex control systems of all kinds. No software was more vulnerable to hacking than control system software, and none was less likely to develop countermeasures because automated control systems were far too widely used for easy fixes. Expensive defenses or code rewrites to do the fixes would make the systems unprofitable. Jonathan saw in this an enormous unexploited opportunity, so he plunged right in and voraciously learned everything he could about programming control systems.

Because it was no fun just to program in the void, Jonathan did practical experiments to disconnect or activate commercial alarm systems remotely. As a result of his experimentation, fire and theft alarms went off unaccountably all over the city, with firemen and policemen constantly being vectored to answer false alarms. Op-ed pieces and news articles decried the rising false positives in alarm systems generally. These technical articles appearing on the Net showed Jonathan that his malice was causing a stir, but the public remained unaware of the real threat.

When he was fourteen, Jonathan decided to upscale his attacks, and he began to explore how to infect or destroy the software of control systems. He brought down the city's traffic light system in such a way that the city had to buy a new replacement system, which Jonathan also infected and destroyed on its first day of operation. Special software forensics people began looking into possible sabotage and the

IT company that developed and installed the control system code was sued by the city. However, the suit failed because nothing in the fine print of the acquisition contract mentioned vulnerability assessment.

Jonathan figured that the second replacement system to control traffic signals would have additional safeguards that would require a lot of time for him to master, so he moved on to bank-vault security systems and might have made a fortune if he were a thief.

Instead, he took grim satisfaction in breaking into the software security systems for all the banks in town and causing the local police and FBI a lot of trouble as they tried frantically to find how the systems were being compromised. As a matter of public policy, no one wanted to admit that banks had a problem with security, so many of the attacks were only discussed in classified circles and the open media's coverage of Jonathan's attacks was scant.

Jonathan reversed that trend by alarming buildings during business hours, so the banks' robbery-in-progress programs locked all exterior doors, alerted SWAT personnel and sealed open vaults. At that point, the FBI began an intensive investigation into the possibility of a terrorist attack on all banks, but no terrorist group claimed the attack and no demands were made. The law enforcement community was stymied. Could they continue to blame Russian and Chinese hackers indefinitely? Who could say?

One intelligent investigative reporter suggested the possibility that a lone-wolf terrorist had committed the bank alarm attacks, but that eventuality seemed most unlikely and anyway no one had a way to detect a lone wolf. Jonathan was intrigued that as a lone wolf, he might create perfect, but untraceable mayhem and he gravitated towards sabotaging the US national gas pipeline system as his next gig.

What particularly interested him about pipeline systems was a feature called Emergency Shutdown, or ESD, whereby in an emergency an entire pipeline system could be shut down with the push of a button—or with a software command executing the same sequence of physical operations. Pipeline systems control software network was usually kept separate from the computer network that handled general administrative tasks like data entry, storage, and communication.

Now at fifteen, Jonathan believed that at some IP address, within the administrative side, was an access to the control side that would allow him to activate the ESD. At the time, Jonathan was getting D's and F's in school, but his genius allowed him to bring down the so-called 'impenetrable' north sector of the North-South XL Pipeline.

FEMA got on the XL Pipeline case, and the report of its extensive forensics team's analysis concluded that the cause of the shutdown was definitely a terrorist attack by a nation state sophisticated enough to penetrate the control system from the administrative systems side. The unclassified version of the FEMA report, which Jonathan found online, also concluded that the attack had to be abetted by insiders on the pipeline company's administrative team.

Background checks were re-initiated on all company employees, but the likelihood of identifying the criminal was deemed low. Jonathan knew that the likelihood was zero, but just to be extra safe he decided not to tempt his fate by penetrating pipelines anymore. He shifted his interest next to airline control systems.

Jonathan was malicious, but he was not a murderer. His criminal mischief with air control systems included invading automated baggage handling systems and ground traffic pattern controls during the holiday season. Reading reportage of the confusion and delays caused by his hacking gave Jonathan a malicious sense of accomplishment. His Aunt Mildred had been delayed at Chicago's O'Hare Airport for seven hours, and even a week after arriving in Washington, DC, her airline had not located her baggage. Congress demanded that the national air control systems be given a thorough and immediate vulnerability assessment. Jonathan laughed because it was all bluff and bluster. No government had the money to do a real vulnerability assessment and besides they were only playing politics. When all the fuss and bother were over, the vulnerable systems would remain vulnerable. For Jonathan no system was invulnerable—hacking was going to be successful and success was only a function of time.

Meanwhile, at seventeen Jonathan was looking forward to the third attempt to pass tenth grade. Instead, he read online that at an open symposium of Black Hat hackers, the Deputy Assistant Secretary of Defense had put out the call for black-hat hackers to join the DoD in the fight against cyber-terrorism. More interesting to Jonathan was the reference to the Black Hat symposium itself. That became his next target of opportunity.

Jonathan saved money he made at home from manufacturing garage door opening systems, and went to the next Black Hat event under the pseudonym Arnold Schwartzhut, newbie hacker. He kept his distance from the crowd but noticed that a few others were also keeping on the sidelines. Some, he reasoned, must be Federals looking to put hackers on their lists of hacker suspects. Others, he thought, might be lone wolves like him. One tall, lanky dweeb with pimples edged up to him and suggested his attending an off-symposium meeting at midnight at a hotel suite. He said mysteriously that only a few hackers would attend, and no names would be required or given. You could even wear a mask to the event.

The clandestine, off-symposium meeting was attended by a dozen hackers. Eleven hackers were males and one was female. The objective of the evening's discussion was to analyze mysterious hacking cases that the Feds had not been able to crack, including Jonathan's signature bank and air systems hacks.

The female hacker who seemed to be the leader of the group told them that she wanted the group to solve the cases and so prove their worth to the authorities who would otherwise put them all in jail on suspicion. One of the males in the group, a short, bespectacled fellow with three cowlicks in his tousled hair, bragged that he had pulled off Jonathan's hacking masterworks.

Jonathan never liked to brag, so he was delighted to have a 'beard' falsely claim to have hacked those systems. When Arnold Schwartzhut was asked whether he would like to help out, he shyly demurred saying that he was only a novice and a newbie. He said that, surely, the others had the required expertise, particularly the person who had claimed to do the hacks on banks and air systems. Jonathan thus eluded the trap that snared the braggart whose statements about his exploits had been secretly taped as his confession. Immediate headlines proclaimed that the mysterious lone wolf had been apprehended in a joint effort of FEMA and DoD.

Jonathan now laughed out loud at the imbecility of the imposter's braggadocio. He also figured that his picture and remarks had been made part of the government's Black Hat operation records. The authorities would have little trouble penetrating his pseudonym to identify him, and they would be looking at his life with a laser-like detection in a team that probably was led by the female geek who led the clandestine meeting. He wondered why he had been identified at the Black Hat, and invited to the meeting. He also wondered what in blazes he had been thinking to attend since his going there violated everything he believed about his priceless anonymity.

After Black Hat, Jonathan for a long while avoided hacking of any kind. He assumed that his entire on-line presence was under a microscope, and he hoped that the authorities could not do back-bearings to discover the searches he had conducted. As a precaution, Jonathan slicked and then melted his hard drives, changed out all his email addresses and discontinued his garage door system business after delivering all the orders for which he had committed himself. He decided to go straight and devote himself entirely to school.

So, he racked up all A's for five consecutive semesters and two summer sessions, including three semesters at his local community college and the equivalent of two additional college semesters of credit online. His performances in mathematics and computer science were deemed so outstanding that he received awards and a full-paid scholarship to the prestigious Harvey Mudd College.

Jonathan Smart, aka Arnold Schwartzhut, became a summa cum laude graduate of Harvey Mudd and was selected among four out of a field of four-thousand applicants to be awarded a 'full-boat' National Science Foundation scholarship at Caltech for a Ph.D. in computer science.

At his graduate student orientation at Caltech, Jonathan was surprised to find the woman who had led the clandestine sting operation at Black Hat. She boldly introduced herself as Cynthia Skylark and asked Jonathan to accompany her to the Starbucks for a chat. He did not want to create a scene by being rude and she was prettier than he remembered her being, so he followed her.

At a table in the back over lattes, which the woman had paid for, Cynthia looked Jonathan in the eye and told him that she had kept an eye on him for many years. She said that everything had gone exactly to plan and that Jonathan was now ready to hear what she had to offer him. She reviewed the bidding about Jonathan Smart's performance as Arnold Schwartzhut, which she gave an A+. She evaluated his garage door opening escapades in alarming detail, which she was awarded an A-. She enumerated his exploits against banks and ATC control systems and gave each an A. She then gave a summary analysis of his personality profile and his academic performance from the time of his transformation after Black Hat.

Jonathan's face was red, and he wondered when the guys with the guns were going to break into the Starbucks to arrest him. As if reading his mind, Cynthia told the boy to relax. She said she had enough hard evidence to put Jonathan behind bars for life, but it could never be used in a court of law because, it had all been gathered illegally by her employer, the NSA.

Cynthia explained that he now faced a dilemma, which she defined as a choice between two bad alternatives. On the one hand, Jonathan could come with her to sign employment papers for work at the NSA and spend the rest of his life in the catacombs of Fort Meade—as good as a life sentence in maximum security prison. On the other hand, however, Jonathan could just walk out of this Starbucks and at some time soon be assassinated by one of Cynthia's colleagues as a potentially lethal threat to US national security. Cynthia finished her latte and pointed out the window towards a familiar large tree on campus. She told Jonathan to think things through and then to meet her at the tree with his decision in five minutes. Then Cynthia stood up, turned and walked out of the Starbucks and wandered out to stand under the tree. Jonathan looked at the gawky, geeky NSA agent standing under the tree for two minutes. Then he shook his head, stood up and walked out coolly to give the woman his answer.

Jonathan Smart chose wisely. Within three years, he had a Ph.D. from Caltech and a job with the NSA working at Fort Meade. He lived in Laurel, Maryland, well within the 'magic circle' where most of NSA's key analysts lived. He did not make a lot of money, but making money was never his objective in life. Every day he went to work to think about the most outrageously malicious acts that could be perpetrated against the US national infrastructure.

In other words, he continued doing what he had always done from his earliest years—invented ways to hack embedded systems. Now instead of hacking from the outside secretly, he was hacking from the inside secretly. His work was so secret that he had to sign papers that he would never divulge what he knew for the rest of his life. The HR folks at NSA made it clear that any infraction of the rules would be handled extra-judicially, which meant he would be quietly assassinated.

Cynthia was Jonathan's boss at the agency, and Jonathan found the brown-eyed girl was as much a workaholic as he was. She was a fine technician but her forte was management. He figured that she would be head of a Directorate some day or perhaps even the Director. Over the years, Jonathan had become a handsome single man, and Cynthia had become a beautiful single woman. They were very much aware of each other as more than colleagues. In fact, they were known to be an item and dated often. At work, they met over coffee daily in a secure room to discuss their work, and on weekends when they were not working for the agency, they found significant time to spend time together. They cut a deal with each other that no agency work was permitted to be part of their private life together.

One weekend they sailed on the Chesapeake Bay. Another weekend they would drive out to the Shenandoah Valley and hike the Appalachian Trail. Jonathan twice took her to the US Marine Corps shooting range where they both practiced their marksmanship. Cynthia many times steered him to visit the big Washington art galleries and to attend openings at small galleries that featured chilled Chablis and fine cheeses.

The NSA protocols required that employees report their significant others regularly, and Cynthia and Jonathan reported each other as such from the time Jonathan began working at the agency. When Jonathan began doing fieldwork with long absences from the Fort, he returned each time to sign a debriefing form detailing any contacts he had encountered while on assignment. As a matter of NSA policy, agents traveled in pairs abroad for safety and security. Jonathan went abroad with another agent Mildred Stewart because they had complementary skills as analysts and because Cynthia did not feel that her relationship with Jonathan was threatened by Mildred since the green-eyed blonde was not technical. Cynthia knew that Jonathan hated non-technical people of all genders, and she was the one exception to his rule of exclusion.

Mildred was the kind of agent who viewed her current mission as her life. When she was on a quest, nothing else mattered to her. People became ciphers. Mildred viewed her work in terms of time-and-distance efficiencies and results.

What Cynthia did not see was how the operational setting made Mildred's approach entirely consistent with Jonathan's.

Where Jonathan got down to the minute technical details, Mildred kept the two-person team in balance by taking care of the 'BS and bureaucracy.' Jonathan hated to lose and so did Mildred. Both viewed Cynthia as their common 'enemy' when they were overseas on an assignment because of her demanding manner for compliance and allowing no slack for independent initiatives among her people.

Cynthia's desire to control an operation was manic. She was a perfectionist. Operations were never perfect; people were never perfect; technology was never perfect. Cynthia was bound to be frustrated no matter what Jonathan and Mildred were doing, and they were bound to be rebellious and non-communicative in return for Cynthia's implied distrust. Since trust was the one great hallmark of NSA operations, this situation spelled trouble, but none of the parties saw the difficulty until it was too late to do anything constructive about it.

The straw that broke the proverbial camel's back came when Jonathan and Mildred went on assignment together in Eastern Ukraine. Cynthia, as always, watched over her field operatives' six-hourly reports like a hawk to be sure her "Gold Dust Twins" were performing at peak. Each field operations team, technically a crypto support team, had a home team working around the clock for them so that those outside Fort Meade always received instantaneous backup from those inside it. This close cooperation gave the NSA its critical edge in global operations. Cynthia caught something in a midnight report from Mildred that she thought implied an unduly personal concern of Mildred for Jonathan's welfare. Cynthia began to consider the woman's relationship to her man with envy and jealousy, but she could do nothing about what was happening between her agents in the field. She seethed about what she imagined was happening but decided she would wait until they returned to the Fort before she delved deeply into the matter.

When Jonathan and Mildred returned, they were debriefed on their operation and each declared that no reportable contacts had been made. Cynthia went over each of their debriefings with them, and she could find no lever to pry into what had happened out in Luhansk. She looked forward to going camping with Jonathan in West Virginia the next weekend more for her opportunity to probe his personal interest in Mildred than to endure another soggy adventure in the wild with her boyfriend.

The rain that fell that weekend was torrential, but Jonathan did not seem to mind. He picked up Cynthia in his Land Rover, and they drove just across the West Virginia border and camped in the woods for two days. Jonathan seemed glad to be back, and the rain kept them inside the tent almost the entire time, providing plenty of opportunities to become reacquainted intimately. Jonathan was an inspired lover, and Cynthia's responses were attuned to drive any lingering thoughts he might have of Mildred entirely out of his mind. They had no trouble restoring their physical relationship in no uncertain terms.

The rain stopped on Sunday at noon, and the two decamped and drove back to Fort Meade in the sunshine with the clouds receding to the East. Cynthia saw this as a symbol of her receding doubts about Jonathan's loyalty to her.

The next week Cynthia saw Jonathan and Mildred together often, but they were working on the same missions so that seemed natural. Not natural from Cynthia's point of view were Mildred's eyes lingering on Jonathan and the way she handed Jonathan a pen or a cup of coffee. She saw the signs of a woman smitten and looking for an opening to seize a man's heart. Cynthia decided it was time for Mildred to have another work partner, so she arranged for Mildred to be re-positioned with Susan Bridgewell and for Susan's partner Harry Black to work with Jonathan. She knew from their files that both Bridgewell and Black were transgender employees, so she felt that Jonathan and she would not be threatened. Anyway, she figured that Mildred was not going to see much more of Jonathan, or so Cynthia thought.

The first day on the job with her new partner Susan, the woman made advances on Mildred, which Mildred rebuffed. Mildred went to HR to complain but was told that she needed a course in transgender sensitivities and, if that did not work, psychological counseling. In any case, HR said, a letter would be placed in her file about the complaint. The fact that Susan had made the overture was not considered an infraction.

That night Mildred called Jonathan and asked to see him at once on an important personal matter. Jonathan was alarmed but thought Mildred only needed to talk things through, so he told her to come right over. They shared a bottle of red wine while Mildred poured out her soul. She told Jonathan what Susan had done and explained her revulsion. She wept when she told Jonathan about her interview with HR. Now, she thought, she would have a black mark on her own record, and she had no recourse whatsoever in the agency. Jonathan calmed the woman down by assuring her that they would together find a way to deal with Susan Bridgewell.

Meanwhile, Jonathan said, he was having trouble fending off the advances of his new partner Harry Black. He had been considering reporting Black's advances to HR, but now he would hold back since he would have no more success than Mildred. By the end of the evening, Jonathan and Mildred were laughing together and scheming. Mildred was happy because she knew Jonathan cared. He had even touched her on the arm and for a moment took her hand. That was a sign of something, was it not?

Jonathan brooded late into the night about what to do, and by the time he arrived at work the next morning, he had a plan. It was the kind of plan that he used to dream up as a teen, but then he was only interested abstractly in the effects of his mischief. Now he needed to focus his mischief with clear intent to achieve his objective. His objective was to probe the lives of Bridgewell and Black by clandestine means and to determine whether either person was a threat to national security on account of their transgender status.

Outside the Fort, Jonathan set up an informal command center at a local hotel's business center. He monitored Bridgewell's and Black's personal computers and discovered that each had multiple Net identities along with volumes of images downloaded from hard pornography sites, some by subscription.

Jonathan knew that an agent not reporting all identities used was an infraction that could cause the suspension or loss of one's security clearance. That violation would terminate employment with the NSA or any other US government agency immediately. Jonathan was not a neophyte, so he did not report anything to security just yet.

Instead, he continued to sift through the two agents' documents and began looking at their historical email traffic. One of the most effective means of concealment was to communicate via email but to delete that traffic immediately after sending or receiving. Jonathan reasoned that if those agents' emails were incriminating, he would have to monitor them as they occurred or to siphon off the traffic on both sides via a splitter. He decided on the splitter because then he did not have to watch their browsers continuously. After all, he still had his work at the Fort to do. Daily on his way home, he stopped by the business center to examine the emails he had harvested.

Within a week, Jonathan had amassed a solid case against both Bridgewell and Black. They were not only promiscuous, but they were indiscriminate. Jonathan had a record of IP addresses that both operatives had communicated with frequently via strongly encrypted emails sent through intermediary IPs via the Dark Net to prevent tracking. When he checked the two agents' home computers, he discovered that all these suspicious emails had been deleted almost immediately after they had been read. Jonathan told nothing to Mildred or to Cynthia. He wanted to check on whether Bridgewell or Black, or both, were being sheltered by someone higher up the NSA chain. This was a difficult matter that would require thought.

Jonathan asked for a meeting with Cynthia in a special room that was regularly swept for listening devices. He asked that the meeting be scheduled for a time just after a regular sweeping operation. When they met, Jonathan asked Cynthia what might happen if he had found two agents acting peculiarly, having unreported online relationships and communicating with suspicious IPs from their home terminals followed by erasing all such emails.

Cynthia assessed what she was being told coolly, and she said that he was making very serious accusations. Jonathan told her that he had the evidence, but he needed to know who within NSA should receive it. Cynthia said that the information should be given to counterintelligence, and she gave the point of contact for that.

She continued that if possible infractions were committed by anyone in the Diversity communities, HR would be the right place for a report, but the situation would be very complex. Jonathan and Cynthia talked this over for half an hour, and Cynthia gave him the names and NSA Net addresses of the right people. She did not ask him who his suspects were or how he had gleaned his information. She was always punctilious about NSA protocols. She thought that Jonathan should deliver his information only through the proper channels to keep matters straight and to avoid spreading personal information that should be protected as if it were classified.

Jonathan now had three new targets for his surveillance, and he did the research he needed to do. Three days after his meeting with Cynthia, he had placed splitters on the home email accounts of the three personnel from HR. Their traffic was now being harvested in the business center.

Jonathan's analysis of the harvested email traffic showed the same patterns among the three HR people as were occurring in the cases of Bridgewell and Black. Jonathan had uncovered a cabal that included, at least, five personnel. He had physical evidence of what they were doing. He wondered how far up the NSA chain this cabal reached. He was glad he had asked for a swept office for his discussions with Cynthia, and now he decided to warn her against saying anything to anyone about his suspects or the discussions he had had with her. To do so, he invited Cynthia to go sailing on the Chesapeake Bay that weekend on a rented yacht.

The weather was perfect for sailing, with a gentle breeze, blue skies, and puffy white clouds. Cynthia wore a cerulean bathing suit that brought out her curves as well as the color of her eyes. Jonathan was a good pilot, as she knew from prior adventures, so she felt confident that they could sail out and return without having problems. When they were well out in the bay, Jonathan luffed sail and let the bay water carry them along while he told Cynthia not to talk about his suspects or the other things they had discussed during their private meeting with anyone, not even the Director himself. Cynthia was alarmed and asked whether Jonathan could tell her anything more, but he stated that things were getting complex and possibly dangerous. He said the situation involved personal information and a possible pattern. He would not be drawn out to talk about any details. Cynthia's natural curiosity caused her to try to break through Jonathan's reticence, but he refused to be compromised.

Cynthia asked Jonathan to go below-decks with her giving him the look that invites a man to intimacy. They made love in the berth below as the yacht rocked gently for hours, but in spite of all Cynthia's charms and attentions Jonathan remained mum about his suspects. After many delightful exertions and risings to the occasion, he finally pulled on his swimsuit and T-shirt and went back up to raise sails for striking home.

Cynthia emerged while he was doing this work, and she admired him proudly because he was a fine looking male specimen and her exclusive lover. When he took the wheel for the sail home, she stood just behind him, touched him gently on the arm and laid her head on his shoulder. They arrived at the dock at twilight, and she was no more enlightened about the mystery that he harbored than she had been when they had set out early in the morning. Still Jonathan's physical communication made her feel as if they were collaborating without saying so. She thought he would tell her everything when the time was right.

The next Monday Mildred wanted to talk with Jonathan in the special room where he had met Cynthia. He agreed to meet, and at the meeting, Mildred burst into tears. She said that Susan was now putting significant pressure on her to date her and to "come out" as a lesbian. She shuddered when she told Jonathan where the woman had caressed her with her hands. She asked whether Jonathan had made any progress with his plan. The way Mildred said this alerted Jonathan to the possibility that Mildred was asking on behalf of someone else, not herself. So, he lied and said that he had not made any progress at all, but he was still trying to find a way.

Immediately Mildred calmed down. After thanking him and drying her eyes, she went back to her workplace. Jonathan thought for a while and decided to include Mildred in his research, so that evening he began to harvest her emails at the business center. To his surprise, her pattern fit the others. Now he had six personnel in the cabal, ironically including the person who caused him to investigate it in the first place.

Jonathan began to research the IPs with which the six suspects were communicating, particularly those requiring special encryption. He decided to run a check through the NSA active archives, using the rationale that he was checking on some legacy issues involving his Ukraine trip.

Within four hours, he had a highly classified report detailing the IPs, their owners, their locations, their communication patterns and their threat levels. Three of the IPs were located in the Russian Federation and three were located in the Peoples Republic of China. All six of the IPs required encrypted traffic.

Jonathan then requested decryption of selected traffic for those IPs. He was sent the decrypts and was informed that their encryption keys were close-hold by "A" Branch and "B" Branch, respectively. The substance of the decrypts was explosive from a security point of view since it involved details of crypto key card changing patterns throughout the world. As the implications began to sink in, Jonathan received a message from the head of "A" Branch asking him for an immediate conference in his private office.

"I asked to be informed whenever requests came in regarding these specific IPs. All six IPs you asked about are on our threat watch list. Your file requests indicated that you needed the information to follow up on what you discovered while you were in Ukraine. Fair enough. Now I'm ordering you to desist in pursuing any leads that connect to these six IPs. Am I clear? Good. That's all. Please close the door on your way out."

Jonathan was now conflicted. He had just been told to stand down. He was very glad that the Director had not probed his reason for requesting the information, but now he knew he would lose his job and his security clearance if he persisted with his investigation. He, therefore, did what he always did when confronted with authoritarian mandates—he decided to destroy all six of the IPs whose product he could no longer harvest.

That evening he stopped by the business center and used his information operations techniques to shut them down for good. He continued to harvest the emails from the six persons who had communicated with them. This gave Jonathan the chatter about the six IPs that had been terminated.

When the Russians and the Chinese established new IPs for the same purpose as the lost ones, they relayed the information to the six agents. Jonathan was back in business because only the IPs that he had killed were off limits to him. He marveled at how predictable NSA managers could be.

Jonathan no longer felt responsible for helping Mildred, and she did not seem to require help anymore. According to her emails with Susan, their relationship was progressing rather well. Mildred was going out with Susan regularly, and Susan was introducing Mildred to her friends in the local community. Mildred was having doubts about coming out, but Susan was persistent. Once Mildred came out, she could be explicitly part of the Diversity group too. That would give her protection and power. She could also progress to another level of communication with international participants in the LGBT movement. Was that not an appealing idea for her? Of course, it was appealing.

Jonathan felt that he was fortunate having to deal with Black because when he had asserted his heterosexuality, Black had backed off. They had a professional relationship now with no vantage for a sexual relationship. If Jonathan had complained about Black's advances, he would have suffered the same fate as Mildred. The difference was that Mildred was not only sympathetic to the transgender cause—she was a closet lesbian! From Jonathan's perspective, the problem with the cabal was not the sexual politics of it but the covert espionage that the overt sexuality covered. Jonathan continued to collect and arrange evidence on the six NSA employees.

Jonathan had waited for two months before he saw an opportunity he had not anticipated—an old-fashioned agency witch-hunt. He thought that no secret organization could do without periodic reorganizations and witch-hunts. The first shuffles people around, as if that mattered for security, while the second allows people to settle scores. Jonathan realized that the hotline and website that had been set up by the counterintelligence team conducting the witch- hunt would be perfect for his submitting anonymous tips. He carefully erased all connections of his evidence to himself and posted it to the website inbox. He waited for the bombs to burst in the air, but absolutely nothing happened. He reasoned that the so-called witch-hunt was merely a scare tactic, not a genuine effort to unearth spies. He was wrong in this because several people who used the hotline and gave their names were themselves investigated by HR and their management for being malcontents and disgruntled workers, possibly spies.

Jonathan and Cynthia continued to develop their relationship even though Cynthia received a promotion. She had not yet reached the level where it would have been inappropriate for her to have a full-fledged sexual relationship with a mere technician like him, so Jonathan threw a private party for Cynthia celebrating her advancement.

There was champagne. There was steak with a red Bordeaux wine. There was a carrot cake with cream cheese icing that Jonathan made especially for her. There were chocolates, coffee, and cream. Jonathan gave Cynthia a silver brooch in the form of a crescent moon because her name was associated with the moon. He kissed her gently when he placed the little box with the brooch in her hand, and her eyes suggested that they take things to another level. They went to the bedroom and leisurely undressed each other. Then they did—more than once—what made the evening memorable. Cynthia wept because she felt so beautiful in his presence. He gazed deeply into her matchless eyes and wondered how much longer their long affair would be permitted to last by the authorities.

The witch-hunt went into high gear because someone presented information and accusations anonymously. Data that had personal information and plenty of innuendoes to grab the attention of the Director himself. Personal computers were being checked en masse. Human Resources was busy sending out refresher notices about the importance of protecting personal information. Managers were canvassing each of their underlings, particularly the technicians, about their knowledge of baseless insinuations being leveled at Diversity employees.

Jonathan was asked about what he knew, and he said, "Precious little. I have no time for anything but my own work. I don't even know how to define 'diversity' beyond the information that HR sends around. Do you want me to repeat that verbatim because I can?" Jonathan was ignored. No one wanted to believe he was anything but the drone he seemed to be. Cynthia was the one exception, but she did not make the connection between Jonathan's secret and the agency's quest for a scapegoat.

Poor Mildred became the scapegoat because of the report she had long ago filed about Susan's advances having importuned her. HR forgot the fact that Mildred was now Susan's lover and an outed lesbian. Her decision to become part of the Diversity Group was read as her way of deflecting criticism from herself. Her accusations against Bridgewell and Black in her "anonymous" submittal were discounted because they were only "the spiteful and vengeful expressions of a disgruntled employee." Mildred lost her security clearance and her job at NSA. She put her house up for sale and moved in with Susan. Jonathan continued to monitor their computers, and he was not surprised to discover that Mildred and Susan shared everything including company gossip though Mildred was no longer an agency employee.

Black never mentioned Mildred or Susan so Jonathan would not have known about the two women's living arrangements without his clandestine eavesdropping computer at the business center. As for Black, he remained incommunicado about most things, including Black's having become an avid spy for China. Jonathan kept the evidence for this in his special repository. He did not know when he would get the chance to use it, but he was careful to look for any intelligence passing between his co-worker and the Chinese that might do the US irreparable damage.

Cynthia was doing very well in her new job, and the Director himself asked her to the top floor to discuss her career plans. He encouraged her to prepare herself for becoming a Branch Head at some time in the next two years. He told her he would be her mentor in the many processes that would be required for her success. He warned that one thing she should be very careful of was fraternizing personally with her fellow NSA employees at any level. He spoke like a father to his daughter when he advised to cleanse herself of any such relationships as soon as possible because the checks might begin any day. The fewer skeletons in the closet the vetting found, the better her chances to survive the process.

Cynthia nearly broke down and cried in the Director's office, but she managed to keep a stiff upper lip. That afternoon she called Jonathan and gave their secret formula for meeting at his place in the evening—"See you later!"

Cynthia arrived at Jonathan's home in an extremely sorry state. She burst into tears upon arrival, and it took Jonathan two hours to calm her down. He reminded her that they both knew this day would come. He congratulated her on her prospect of promotion and on her having the Director himself behind her in the process. He told her that word would get out about this, then the rank and file would clear the way for her advancement.

Cynthia shook her head and told him that the Director had summoned all sixteen of the candidates to his office, and he had told each the same story. She was not unique, and the

Director would delegate his mentorship to others because he had no time to do it himself when there were sixteen employees to mentor. It was going to be a chariot race where the closest to the inside track would win. She said she was on the outside track, so her chances were slim. Then too, the Director was rumored to be leaving the NSA and going to lead the CIA in a top-level executive shuffle. What would happen to her chances then?

Jonathan let Cynthia ring the changes on what was going through her mind. One moment she was exultant with the possibilities, and the next she was despairing for having to abandon her relationship with Jonathan.

He sat impassively as she fought the terrible battles within herself. She talked about wanting a family. She talked about one day becoming the Director. She said it was unfair for the agency to make her choose. She said it was unfair that she was a woman. She said she was hungry and thirsty. Jonathan poured them each a glass of wine and placed the bottle within easy reach to replenish their glasses.

So Cynthia became, in turns, Dido on the funeral pyre, then Cassandra with the flames of Troy at her back, then Cordelia trying to support her Director, and finally Cynthia, the goddess of the moon going through her many changes in quick succession.

Jonathan listened, computing silently. When she had finished, he rose and gathered the woman up into his arms. She breathed a sigh and placed her head on his chest. She grabbed his arms as if they were a life preserver in a tempestuous sea. He led her to his bed and held her close. They undressed each other carefully, placing their clothes on two separate chairs. They admired what they had revealed and came together. The night was one sleepless cycle of making love and taking showers. Cynthia was, at first, the vulnerable lass then the shy violet and finally the warrior princess. What Jonathan gave, she offered back with cries and moans of ecstasy. They were the perfect meld—every time he became spent, she spun him up for another venture and braced herself as he took her far beyond her expectations.

When the light broke in the morning like a cock crowing in a crowded stable, Jonathan lay with his arm around her head, and Cynthia laid her hand on his chest. They breathed deeply, and then they both laughed deep and rich laughter. They rose for one last shower, and then they dried themselves off and dressed. There was work to be done, but first breakfast.

"So what have we decided?"

"That we can still give each other extreme pleasure in spite of the pain that life inflicts on us?"

"And about your future, Cynthia?"

"Last night is my future, and all the rest is hokum. You make me feel alive."

"Hold that thought. Let's see whether we can shake you of your habit."

"My habit?"

"Me."

"Hahaha. That's a habit for life, I think. What do propose to do about that?

"Propose. Cynthia, dearest, will you marry me?"

"Someday, perhaps, Jonathan. We shall see."

"That is precisely why we should make a pact."

"Go on."

"We should meet each night right here and do what we did last night until you are thoroughly tired of me and I am tired of you. Then we'll have had enough of each other, and we can go our separate ways."

"You don't mean it! Jonathan, don't shake your head for yes! How cruel!"

"We should face facts as they are. If I could tire you in, say, two weeks, that would tell us both something. I'll guarantee I'll never tire of making love to you all night. Let's see if the same's true for you."

"Being practical, we are deciding to finesse the agency rule about relationships."

"Who needs to know?"

"Do you think we could keep us a secret from the most powerful eavesdropping agency the world has ever known?"

"Zeus kept his liaisons secret from Hera in mythology."

"So you think when we are married, you will have secrets from me?"

"I believe in secrets so much, dearest Cynthia, I think everyone should have some of his or her own. I have secrets you don't know now, and you have secrets I don't know too. Yes? Well, then. Did I just hear the words, 'when we are married'?"

"A premature slip of the tongue. Where were we? Oh yes, your immodest proposal. A duel really about sexual mastery. Who will say 'uncle' first, you or I?"

"You're on. So after work today, you'll come back here after twelve hours' rest to begin our cavorting, rollicking, heavy petting and sex? Please say you will. That will be the first of fourteen days of struggle."

"Some struggle when all I want is you, all day and night."

"And if we are irremediably addicted to each other, what then?"

"I suppose I'll have to say, 'I do.'"

"We can spare ourselves the trouble by your saying, 'I do' right now."

"Then we wouldn't have our game, which sounds like fun to me."

"Plato said that women should use gymnastics, not cosmetics for heightening their color. You look simply ravishing."

"I'm quite sure I look ravishing because you ravished me."

"I'd do it all again starting right now."

"Tempting, really, but I've a nine o'clock and so have you. Pour me another coffee. Then we've got to be going. This was fun. Thank you for being here for me. I'm not going to like it the least bit if I lose this match we've decided upon."

"You'll lose for certain."

"What bravado, sir! Beware hubris. Pride will have its fall."

"Tonight we'll play to see what rises and what falls."

Jonathan and Cynthia drove to the Fort in separate cars. Neither had slept the night before, but both looked ruddy and refreshed anyway. The spring in her step showed she had been fulfilled in some unspecified but very physical way. The manner he took in diminishing himself indicated to Black that his co-worker had definitely had a sprightly night with someone.

So all that day the work went like clockwork until the clock struck five and the mausoleum of the dead that some call the Fort became a tangle of bodies, arms, and legs necking down to the parking lots and from there to the suburbs of Maryland.

Jonathan arrived at his house before Cynthia, and he quickly changed and prepared dinner for two. He expected Cynthia at any moment, but the dinner had cooked before he received her call. She was so very sorry, but the Director had called her to his office. They had discussed some things that she had to do for him right away. It appeared that she would have to work most of the night. She did not know when she would be able to eat. She did not know whether she would be able to make the tryst that they had planned. Jonathan said he was disappointed but tomorrow was another day. He told her he did not want to win by default, but he knew, in his heart, that was exactly what had happened. She did not come that night.

The next day Jonathan and Cynthia were both embroiled in the daily grind, and Jonathan drove home, fixed a meal for two and then left it cooling while he drove to the business center to check his harvest. There he found evidence of a kind of treachery he could not abide. The Chinese were planning an enormous cyber-attack for that Friday, and the five remaining cabal members had provided the means by which the attack would be a success unless Jonathan thought fast and acted faster.

He received a call on his cell from Cynthia, who had reached his house and now sat at his dining room table. She was heating up their dinner. Jonathan, this time, had to tell her he was working late on a special project of his own. When she told him to stop kidding her, he said he was deadly serious. She did not need to know what he knew or what he was going to do about it, he said. She was furious and ordered him to say what he was doing. He flatly refused to do so and hung up.

Jonathan turned back to the evidence and began to see what he must do to stop the attack. His fingers flew over the keyboard, and he managed to send emails that contradicted and countermanded the emails that had caused the trouble. Then he initiated protocols that would bring down all the IPs that were active—the five spies' IPs and their six corresponding IPs in Russia and China. Jonathan knew that the emails that he sent would be read just before the IPs went down hard, so there would not be enough time for the Russians and Chinese to reconstitute their attacks by Friday. He grimaced when he realized that a business center had become the main line of defense against a crucial cyber-attack from America's most cyber-adept enemies. Jonathan was exhausted when he reached his home, and he discovered his dinner was on the table cold and Cynthia was in his bed hot under the covers. He chose Cynthia over his cold dinner, and she thought that was the right choice.

She told her man that she intended to make up for their missing last night's contest by doubling up on tonight's activities. She was insatiable, and that was fine with Jonathan although he wondered at odd moments whether they would each get the general recall notice ordering them to return to the Fort to protect the cyber grids of the world against the final threat.

Cynthia's liveliness through the night proved that she was capable of far more than she had demonstrated thus far and more than he had ever imagined. When daylight broke, she was fully awake with a light in her eye that he had never seen before that moment. She asked Jonathan whether he thought he could do what he had just done again right now. He reminded her that they had only a little time before they had to depart. She countered that they would skip breakfast and grab something when they arrived at work. Both eager in the new day to make something of each other, Jonathan reached for Cynthia. Her cries of ecstasy rose with his touch until at last she smiled, stroked his broad back, and softly moaned, "Yes." They had to hurry through a shower and then they were off through the traffic to the Fort. Strangely, neither felt the least bit tired from their exertions.

Jonathan found in his morning classified email traffic that during the night a major cyber-attack had been miraculously halted. No one knew why that had happened, but everyone at NSA was urged to be vigilant because another attack was deemed imminent. One wag said that the whole story was a "fund-raiser," by which he meant that unscrupulous contractors often staged events to raise awareness in Congress so that votes for increased funding could be passed when without an emergency they might fail. Jonathan shook his head when Black repeated the fund-raiser story.

Jonathan told him, "What nonsense some people will invent when they are clueless!" Black did not know what to say to that.

The Fort was in an uproar trying to discover what the cyber-attack was supposed to do and what had been done to stop it. The Director himself sent out an All Hands email asking for any information about what stopped the cyber-attack. His major source of information about the attack was an article in the Bangkok Post reporting the attack as a fait accompli. That meant that the story about the attack was planted in advance. The scope of the reported attack was so vast that it was very lucky something or someone had deterred it.

Around noon, Cynthia called Jonathan and asked him to meet her in their secure room, which had just been swept for bugs. He broke off from the menial tasks he was performing to meet her. When he arrived at the room, he discovered two people there, Cynthia and the Director, who motioned that he should close the door without comment.

"Jonathan, I just want to shake your hand. Thank you. I don't want to know how or why you did what you did, but this agency owes you and I owe you. Keep up the great work.

Cynthia, you recruited this national asset, and I'm very proud of you for keeping him fit and in his prime. Keep up the good work on your part. If you do that, you'll become not only a Branch Head but much more than that. I've got other obligations, and this is a busy day, but the worst is behind us, thanks to you. Goodbye."

When the Director had departed and the door was closed again, Cynthia burst out laughing. Jonathan did not know why she was unable to control herself, but he joined in.

"Don't ever accuse me of not thinking on my feet!"

"I never have done so and never will."

"The Director came into my office and asked who stopped the cyber-attack. He wanted a name—one name. I was so flustered, I blurted out your name, and he wanted to meet you right away. That's why I called you. Thank you for coming and playing the straight man for me. I was so worried you'd blurt out something that would indicate you knew nothing about it. So, whew! Now let's get back to work. It's going to be a long day. And at the end of the day, we've got new heights to hit and I want to be ready. Are you okay?"

"I'm fine."

"Well, you look surprised. I'll see you tonight unless we get that cyber-attack they've been talking about. Maybe it is a funding exercise after all. See you later! Don't be late."

Jonathan was stunned by the whole episode. Now, what could he say? He had stumbled into the best deception and cover possible—Cynthia's need for advancement. What did it matter whether he did or did not do the hack of a lifetime last night? His girl had hit the heights, and tonight they would be looking past the early morning triumph to vast stretches of Himalayas as far as the imagination can project. He would win this contest, he thought, easily. She was made for it, that was for certain, and he was game.

When Cynthia disappeared, Jonathan was beside himself with worry for two weeks. She had not appeared at their last appointed meeting at the apartment though he waited for her all night. He could not reach her at any of her ordinary numbers or email addresses. For reasons of secrecy, the Agency did not announce her disappearance even within the Fort. Since agents often went on deep assignments for months, this was not unusual. Nevertheless, two weeks after her disappearance, the NSA reported her absence to the police and circulated an internal memo asking employees for information about her whereabouts.

The NSA cooperated with the police in their investigation of her disappearance, but rumors abounded that she may have defected. Then her bloated body was discovered, floating in an inlet of the Chesapeake Bay. The police were clueless. When Jonathan realized that Cynthia's murder was going to become a cold case, he wracked his brain about how he could discover the truth about who killed her. During an interagency operation, he happened to be paired with an acquaintance, a very young man at the CIA named Joseph Pounce. Pounce seemed receptive, so Jonathan explained his concerns.

"I was very close to a fellow operative, Joseph, but she turned up dead. Now the police are about to give up and label it as a cold case. I don't know who to turn to. I can't let this go. The whole thing is driving me out of my mind."

Pounce countered, "Jonathan if anyone in the world can get to the bottom of Cynthia's death, it will be John Fulghum. Don't call him—you don't want to be visible in this matter. Instead, go see him in his lair. I'll give you his address and I'll call him to let him know someone is coming to see him about solving a murder. Don't worry about security.

Fulghum is trustworthy. He has worked on Agency cases before. One thing, though—don't bullshit this man. If you have to talk about classified matters, think out of the box."

The next day the NSA agent used his vacation days and took the first available flight to Logan International Airport. He had no trouble finding Joe's Malt Shop and Fulghum's second-story office above it. The detective was in and ready to talk.

Hacker II

Jonathan Smart found himself sitting in a captain's chair looking across an old wooden desk at John Fulghum, who was enshrouded like an enigma in cigarette smoke. An overflowing ashtray lay on the desk in front of the detective while he chain lit a Marlboro. A dim light shot through a grimy window raised high above the littered desk. The smoke rose in swirls to the ceiling where it mingled with earlier smoke. Smart saw that on the floor against the wall were stacks of racing forms.

"Let me get this straight. A successful NSA agent named Cynthia Skylark, formally a missing person, was fished up dead, out of the Chesapeake Bay. Police forensics determined she had been tortured, raped and murdered, in no particular order. Law enforcement spent four weeks trying to piece together evidence but finally had no joy. Now they want to label her murder a cold case. From what you suggest, your agency is doing the same. The NSA, you said, was just happy the woman did not turn up a defector."

"That's a succinct version of what I just told you, yes."

"Joseph Pounce told me that you had a job for me. What is it?"

"Mr. Fulghum, help me find Cynthia's killer. I don't have a lot of money, but I don't have a lot of student loans either. I am willing to pay what it takes. Will you help me?"

"Your involvement with Cynthia—was it personal?"

"Very. Against all the rules, we were lovers."

"Did you kill her?"

"No, I did not. Would I be here now if I did? If I killed her, I'd be very happy to see the case go cold. I'll bet the killer feels that way."

"That's fair enough. You imply that you're continuing to investigate the case on your own."

"I'm doing what I can. I can't do the kinds of things that you can do as a private detective. I don't want my investigations to be visible within the agency. The murderer might be one of my colleagues."

"I can understand that. Do you have any ideas about why Cynthia was murdered?"

"I have a few dozen. She was very good at what she did. People were jealous of her. Then there was her caseload as an agent. She was playing with several live wires."

"I'm not sure how much I can be allowed to know about her work for the agency."

"I'll sanitize what I tell you without getting either of us involved in a compromise."

"All right, I'll take the case. I'll require a five-thousand-dollar retainer. My fees and expenses will come out of that. When I need more money, I'll ask."

Jonathan brought out his checkbook, wrote a check for five thousand dollars and signed it. He slid the check across Fulghum's desk. The detective picked it up and looked it over carefully. Then he folded the check and placed it in his shirt pocket.

"You are now my client. So tell me what you think really happened."

"Can you fly down to Laurel and check into a motel there? I'll need to go over a few things I've gathered through the local library computer."

Fulghum accompanied Smart on his return flight to Maryland. He booked a room in a motel in Laurel for a week. That night Jonathan showed the detective what he had discovered about espionage among his agency colleagues. The detective sat back and whistled when he reviewed the evidence.

"Does your security head know about what you've found?"

"Mr. Fulghum, Human Resources would skin me alive about the personal information I had to invade to get this evidence. That's why I used a third-party machine off the grounds of the Fort. I know how to cover my tracks or I would not have had a chance. Anyway, the evidence is compelling but cannot be used either in the NSA or in a criminal court."

"Did Cynthia know what you've found?"

"No. I did not want her caught in the crossfire."

"Of course, someone might have thought she knew."

"I don't think anyone knew what I've found out, particularly about Harry Black."

"Is he your chief suspect?"

"Near enough, yes, but I've got others who come close."

"Like who?"

"Susan Bridgewell and Mildred Stewart, for two. They both blamed Cynthia for getting Mildred fired."

"What was the official version for the firing?"

"Mildred was outed as a lesbian. That made her a target. She moved in with Susan after she was dismissed from the agency. Susan is still with the agency but she is invulnerable because she is lesbian."

"I take it Cynthia was heterosexual?"

"She definitely was that."

"And Harry Black is gay?"

"As a jaybird, yes. He made a move on me but I rebuffed him. Now we're just colleagues who share an office. Look, I've got to go to my apartment to get some rest tonight. Tomorrow I'm back at the grind. I'm working with Joseph Pounce."

"Say hello to Joseph for me, but please don't mention I'm down here in Maryland. Let's not get him caught in the crossfire, shall we?"

"No. I mean, yes. You know what I mean."

"I do understand. Do you know where Black hangs out when he's not at home?"

"He likes the Silver Diner because it's a good pick up location. It's odd he frequents the place because the NSA brass also goes there."

"Give me three days to do some wool gathering. Then we'll meet here again. Don't call me unless you have an emergency need to do so."

"That's fine. Mr. Fulghum, I'm glad you could come. I hope you'll call me if you find out anything interesting."

"I'll do that. Now let me get to work. The clock is ticking."

Fulghum went straight to the Silver Diner and sat in a booth drinking coffee nonstop while he waited for Black to arrive. He did not have long to wait. The man matching Harry Black's picture showed up within a half hour of Fulghum's arrival looking for a match up. Fulghum ignored the man while observing him in action. He was smooth and scored within twenty minutes. Fulghum took the two men's photos with his cell phone camera. When Black and his match left the diner, Fulghum followed them to a motel where they booked a room under the names Smith and Jones. They clearly intended to spend the night.

On a hunch, Fulghum sent the pictures he had taken to his friend Officer Pounce of Boston Homicide. His covering email asked Pounce to run the photos through his facial recognition databases. He knew that Pounce would need time to run the pictures against the algorithms and the archives, so he made the same request of Agent Ken Mander of the CIA. Then he went to his motel to grab some rest before he returned to the lovebirds' motel in the morning to follow Black.

At three o'clock, he received an urgent email from Mander asking for a crash meeting about the pictures. Fulghum texted that he was not in the Boston area at present, so Mander phoned him to talk.

"John, this is Ken, you've got a hot one. That Chinese man is on our hot list of agents of a foreign power—in this case, the PRC. The other man is a known operative of the NSA. Why in the hell did you take the pictures?"

"Ken, I'll have to invoke client privilege on that question."

"You are in a red sector, pal. Is there any chance you could follow the Chinese for me? I'll have you relieved on station with one of mine. Just tell me where to catch you."

"I'm in Laurel, Maryland. The photos were taken in the Silver Diner there. I expect your man can pick us up there if he hurries."

"He'll be there by seven. His work name is Maxwell."

"If he has the picture of the target, Maxwell and I will not have to meet."

"That would be best. Thanks. Later."

Mander terminated their call. Fulghum wondered what he had gotten himself into this time. Instead of waiting until four o'clock, he went immediately to stake out the motel where Black and the Chinese man had taken a room. It was fortuitous that he did as the Chinese man was furtively leaving when Fulghum arrived there. He climbed into an Uber car and the detective followed him to the I-195 to the airport. Enroute Fulghum called Mander to update him on the situation, but the agent's voicemail answered. Fulghum left a brief message and decided he would have to act on his own. When the Uber car dropped the man off at the departure gates, Fulghum jumped out of his car, called to the man and waved. The man turned to see what the commotion was, and the detective was able to close the distance between them. Fulghum did not hesitate but executed a flying tackle, bringing the man to the pavement. He then scurried to stand up and held out his hand apologizing.

"Take my hand. Stand up, quickly. We haven't much time."

The Chinese man warily took Fulghum's hand and pulled himself up. Fulghum noticed that the man's cell phone had fallen on the walk. He picked it up and pocketed it. Then he flashed his concealed weapon and said they should walk to his waiting vehicle. The Chinese man looked around and then shrugged. He went quietly with Fulghum to the car and got into the passenger's seat. Fulghum got behind the wheel and pulled out. He drove to the airport exit while he spoke.

"Listen to me carefully. You've been caught in a difficult situation."

"My country will be outraged. In fact, when I tell the police about what you are doing, you will be in grave trouble."

"I think not. I observed you at the motel you just left. I know what you are. The authorities have photographic evidence of your liaison. I don't think you'll want to inform on me when I can blow your game sky high."

"Why are we driving around for no good reason? Take me back to the airport so I can catch my flight."

"You can change your flight. I'm taking you for breakfast. Relax. I didn't catch your name."

"Hahaha. All those intimate details and no name. My name is Fu Wan Shin."

"Fu, I'm not pleased to meet you. I'm John Fulghum, private investigator. I have a few questions for you while we drive to the Silver Diner."

"What do you want to know, Mr. Fulghum?"

"How often do you meet Mr. Black to receive the materials he brings you?"

"This is preposterous. Tonight is the first night we ever met."

"You had a one-night fling, and having been refreshed, suddenly you're flying home? I don't buy it."

"You're fishing for information, gumshoe. Why should I pay any attention to you?"

"Perhaps you're right, Fu. I think you're owed what I'm going to give you. Just sit back and be quiet while I drive."

Fu Wan Shin did just that. When they arrived at the Silver Diner, he got out of the car and walked to the door with determination. Fulghum thought he might be heading straight for the nearest phone. As he entered the restaurant, however, he was spun around by a tall, athletic looking man who took him by the arm and led him out again. As the two passed him, Fulghum handed the athletic man the cell phone of Fu Wan Shin. Now that the Agency had its prey and its prey's cell phone, Fulghum decided it was time for breakfast. As he ordered coffee, Mander called his phone.

"Great timing, John! We're going to put our friend through a little QA session. If we find out anything interesting, we'll let you know. What can we do for you in return?"

"I may have a couple more pictures for your analysis later this morning. If you can expedite the analysis, I'd be happy."

"Roger that. Later."

Mander terminated the call. Fulghum settled down to a lumberjack's breakfast. The detective wondered how he was going to execute the next phase of his plan. In essence, he had to take pictures of two lesbians in a way that aroused the least suspicion. He decided on the direct approach—he would proceed to Susan Bridgewell's apartment and knock on the door.

"Hello, Ms. Bridgewell, my name is John Fulghum. Harry Black said you might be the person to see about a bit of trouble I've run into in my job. You see, it's about the prejudices we all face these days."

"Say no more, Mr. Fulghum. Come right in for a cup of coffee."

"May I smoke? I'm dying for a cigarette."

"Sure, light up. While you're at it, light one for me and one for my friend. Hey, Mildred, come out wherever you are. Mr. Fulghum has offered us cigarettes and wholesome conversation."

Fulghum lit one cigarette and chain lit two others, which he handed to the ladies. They migrated to the kitchen table and sat down.

"It's a bummer what we LGBTs face these days, isn't that right, Mildred?" Susan asked with affected concern.

"I was fired after I came out. Thank goodness, Susan let me stay here." Mildred took a long draft of her cigarette. Fulghum laid his Marlboro box on the table as a peace offering.

"So what's your story, Mr. Fulghum?"

"Please excuse me while I check my phone. It buzzed a moment ago." Fulghum used this opportunity clandestinely to take photographs of the women and turn on the cell phone's voice recorder.

"Harry Black told me that he's afraid to turn around with all the persecutions going on," Fulghum lied.

"You know, Harry and I used to be a team. Imagine a bull dyke like me and gay old Harry sharing a tiny office at the Agency."

"He told me about that. Do you know why they split you up?"

"HR is always shuffling the deck. Probably it was a security matter."

"Was it that? Or was it someone in the know?"

Mildred interjected, "I think I know who it was. I don't have proof, but I think it was Cynthia Skylark." When she said this, she fingered a silver moon-faced brooch that was pinned to her sweater.

"Oh, Mildred, no one knows whether that's true."

"Anyway, she's dead and gone," added Fulghum to steer the conversation in the direction he wanted.

"We heard the news. It's awful. Think of her floating in the Bay with all the blue crabs pinching at her flesh. It makes me shudder to think about it."

"She wasn't one of us, though," Fulghum stated, shaking his head as if he regretted that fact.

"No, she wasn't," Susan agreed as she selected another cigarette and chain lit it from her first.

"Why are you here?" Mildred asked Fulghum.

"I'm a bit outraged, actually. I followed Harry to the Silver Diner last night but got scooped by a Chinese man named Fu Wan Shin or something like that. I had expected to have a long night of fun, and I got left out in the cold."

"Don't be jealous, John. He does that all the time."

"I was hoping you weren't going to say that. Do you mean he's that promiscuous?"

"Not precisely," Susan said, "He's got a special thing going with Fu. He meets him once a week. It's usually Fridays, as I recall. The man's a regular. Seeing that yesterday was Wednesday, they must have met off schedule."

"Not my luck," Fulghum said with a sigh. He reached for another cigarette. "Is Fu in B Group?"

"Fat chance of that," said Mildred. "He's not even American much less agency."

"It's best for us not to go down that road, Mildred," Susan warned.

"Why not?" Fulghum asked them trying to look clueless.

"Harry hasn't reported his meetings with Fu or several other people he sees regularly. They're all in our LGBT community. Security would not understand our special needs." Susan stopped to take a long drag on her cigarette. Then she chain lit one and handed it to Mildred.

"John, since you're here, why don't we step back into the bedroom? I'm feeling especially randy this morning for some reason."

"I'm hard over gay, girls. I hope you'll understand. What do you do, if you don't mind my asking?"

"No problem. Mildred here is lesbian morphing from hetero on her way to bisexual. I am fully bisexual and love group sex of all kinds. I especially like the ménage a trois." Susan looked Fulghum over with an eye that stripped him naked.

"I thought I'd keep things simple with Harry, but I guess I shouldn't have figured he'd not want to play the field."

"Things are never that simple, John. Are they, Mildred?"

"I'll say. Anyway, what Harry does with those men of his is anyone's guess. I'd lay odds he doesn't do much sex with them at all."

"What do you mean by that, Mildred?" Fulghum asked her.

"Harry has things to do related to his job. Those require him to be promiscuous in a good cause." When Mildred said this, Susan shook her head in agreement.

"So, is Harry still doing his counter-intelligence work?" Fulghum took a blind stab.

"That's all he ever did if you ask me," Susan said.

"Harry would even go with women for the job," Mildred said. "We all make whatever sacrifices we need to make." She got a faraway look in her eyes. Susan looked at her and nodded.

"If only others knew what we do for national security," Susan declared.

"That's a far cry from what Cynthia thought," Mildred said.

"Are you glad she's gone now?" Fulghum asked.

"Damn straight we are. We couldn't wait until she met a bad end. Not that she had to end that way. But she deserved it."

"Because of the way she persecuted us?" Fulghum said as he pulled out a second box of Marlboros and placed it on the table.

"Listen, John, don't get the wrong idea about us. We're glad she's gone. But others in the agency are just as bad, and some are a far sight worse than she was."

"Does it go right to the top?" Fulghum asked.

"Who knows? We LGBT's are few, and the others are many."

"But HR stands beside us, doesn't it?" Fulghum opined.

"We have to keep them on the straight and narrow," Susan said.

"How do you do that?" Fulghum asked.

"We have friends on the inside, the same as us, really," Susan averred.

"That must run right to the top of the HR organization." Fulghum helped the discussion along.

"Nearly so, yes."

"And I suppose a little blackmail helps!" Fulghum suggested.

"Whatever it takes," Susan said. "If you're not here to have fun, why are you here?" She was getting impatient and bothered. "I'm getting the hots for you, John. I can't help myself. If I don't get back to that bedroom in five, I'll be jumping you right here in the kitchen on the floor."

"We can't have that, Susan. I'm going to leave my Marlboros right on the table for you two to use. I've got another appointment now, so I'll run along. You two have fun. Keep the flag flying. I've only one last question for you, though. If anyone in the Fort had the hots for Cynthia Skylark, who would that have been?"

"The scuttlebutt was Jonathan was screwing her silly."

"We never had proof of that, did we, Mildred?"

"No, we didn't. The Director was another candidate, but that would have been difficult. The man may be a machine, but not a sex machine. Hahaha. The very thought of that makes me laugh."

"Thank you, ladies, for your time. Ta ta. I'm off. Please don't let Harry know I feel as I do. I like to play hard to get, don't you know?"

"Goodbye, John. Drop around any time you like. In the meantime, you should think seriously about going both ways. From your looks, you have what it takes. Anyway, I'd take you for a ride solo. I really would." Susan leaned forward to show her cleavage, and she licked her lips. Mildred grabbed her by the arm and pulled her towards the bedroom. In the confusion, Fulghum made his way out the front door. He was glad to be in the open air again. He walked towards his car when he heard behind him Susan's voice.

"Hey, John, if you're in B Group, think about having Fu yourself. Harry says he's great! Ta ta!" Then the door slammed again. Fulghum shook his head as he climbed into his car and started it. He stopped his cell phone recorder and drove for a while. Then he pulled off the highway to forward his pictures and recording to Ken Mander. Satisfied that he had done everything he could under the circumstances, he went to his motel, showered and sacked out. He felt filthy and exhausted from his encounter with the two sirens. Glad to be alone again, he thought about Susan's final shot about B Group. That group, he knew, was the anti-Chinese cryptological group within the NSA. Susan had explicitly connected Fu, who was Chinese, to that group, which considered the Chinese to be the enemy.

He chuckled when he thought, "I tackled Fu just today. Perhaps, though, that was not what Susan had in mind. Mander will figure that out—I hope." He fell soundly asleep and slept until his cell phone rang importunately.

"John, it's Ken. Why are you always sending me dirty pictures?"

"Not again!"

"This time, your ladies are very indiscreet. We have to talk ASAP. Can you bring your agency friend to a meeting?"

"It'll be a walk in the park."

"Exactly. Laurel Park. Three o'clock give or take. Later."

Fulghum looked at his cell phone as Mander terminated his call. He then called Jonathan and invited his voicemail to the meeting. Likely as not, Jonathan was in some SCIF where cell phones are not permitted. Fulghum thought the NSA agent would check his phone—or not—and that would determine whether he would be at the planned meeting.

Laurel Park was almost deserted when Fulghum and Mander made their rendezvous. Jonathan was not present for the first few minutes of their conversation.

Mander said, "That's just as well, pal. I've got a few details that he has no need to know. First, we got everything Fu had in his memory banks by implemented interrogation. He's been getting a weekly feed of NSA goodies from Harry Black, and he is the paymaster giving Black a boatload of US dollars in a numbered account whose contents are now Agency property. Second, Fu set up Cynthia Skylark for a Chinese intelligence hit on US shores. She went out on a boat named Sea Spray where she was beaten, tortured and interrogated before they killed her and threw her overboard. Whatever she knew, they now know. Third, Susan Bridgewell was in league with Fu. We can place her pier side when Cynthia boarded Sea Spray. We think she participated in the murder."

"Anything else?"

"Yes, the treachery of Black is beyond belief. He was playing the Chinese off against the Russians. Everything went to the highest bidder. Fu stated that Black was a shrewd bargainer who always brought top value product. Key lists, codes, lists of broken cipher traffic. Whatever Fu's masters wanted, he obtained one way or another."

"Was anyone else working with Black?"

"Wittingly or unwittingly, the entire LGBT community was involved. Susan was the ringleader for the community."

"Here comes Jonathan. Hello, Jonathan, this is Ken."

"Do you have something for me?"

"Yes, but I'm not sure how much of what I have can be conveyed to you. It has to do with need to know and classification security. Ken, what can we tell Jonathan?"

"The man you are looking for is Fu Wan Shin. He was the mastermind and primary agent who orchestrated the death of Cynthia Skylark. Don't get excited because we have him in custody and he is not likely to live much longer. He's been under a lot of strain."

"I hope he doesn't live much longer. Is that the whole of it?" Jonathan asked Fulghum.

"Jonathan, you mentioned to me in my office that you gave Cynthia a silver brooch in the shape of a moon. Please describe it for me."

"It was finely wrought. It looked exactly like the moon with all its features. Why do you ask?"

"I saw that brooch this morning on the sweater of Mildred Stewart when I saw her in Susan Bridgewell's place."

"What are you saying?"

"Somehow the brooch made its way to Mildred. I'm just guessing, but I think Susan gave it to her as a gift of affection."

"How did Susan obtain the brooch?" Jonathan asked excitedly.

"I believe she got it directly from Cynthia just before or just after she died."

"That's all we have for Jonathan, Fulghum."

"Does that satisfy our contract, Jonathan?"

"It does. If I can know that Fu is dead, I'll be satisfied. Now I can tell you a couple of things that I've discovered in the interim since I last saw you. I located the numbered accounts that Harry Black was using to park his illicit money. They've all been cleaned out."

"What do you mean?"

"All the traitor's accounts have been zeroized. It happened in the last five hours."

"So you knew about Black's traffic with the enemy?"

"Yes, but I didn't know how to inform security about it because I got the information by hacking via the backdoor outside the NSA grounds."

"Can you provide me what you've found out?" asked Mander with an edge in his voice.

"If you'll take care of business, I'd be happy to do that. We can go to the library where everything is stored in an encrypted file, and I'll give you the file plus the decryption key."

"What else do you have on this man Harry Black?" Mander pressed.

"You're probably interested in the Russian side of the equation."

"Yes, very."

"I've got a file on that and another on the Chinese side. I've got nearly everything you'd need to take action. None of it could be taken to a court of law, though."

"I don't intend to take anything to a criminal court. The Agency takes care of business all by itself. If you tell anyone what I just said, I'll deny it."

"Ok, Ken, let's go to the library to get your files. John, that's all I need from you. Please send me an accounting once you get back to Boston. Anything remaining of your retainer, you keep as a bonus for outstanding work."

"Well, I'm outta here. If you're ever in Boston, just drop by for a chat. My friend JD will be there with me. Goodbye." Fulghum extended his hand and both men shook it. He then went back to his motel, packed and left for the airport.

He flew back to Logan, arriving late, and drove to his office. The room was the same as he left it. He did not hesitate to light a Marlboro. He sat in the captain's chair behind his desk and pulled open the second drawer on the right to reveal his old friend Jack Daniels Number 7 and three glasses. As the smoke rose, he lifted the bottle and unscrewed the top. He raised one glass, dusted it with his handkerchief and slowly poured two fingers of the brown elixir. He raised the glass and examined the liquid with a refined eye. He took a sip and let it swill in his mouth before he swallowed. It burned slightly all the way down and made him feel right at home.

As if on cue, his cell phone rang. It was Mander with a brief message.

"Tell JD that Fu did not survive. Black is bleating and may not survive the night. Susan and Mildred have become locked in their last embrace. I never called to interrupt you, and you never stopped smoking and drinking. Later, John, and thanks."

Ken Mander terminated his call. Fulghum did not have to say a single word in response. As he contemplated the reach of justice in a world gone mad, Fulghum wondered how much corruption could be managed at the fringes and how much remained when justice had been served.

"Here's to you, Ken Mander, master of the black arts!" Fulghum toasted out loud. "What would we do without you?"

The next day the NSA called a news conference about the rash of strange deaths that had occurred recently, particularly of women and of those whose diversity was openly apparent. The Director lamented the tenor of the times but made no mention of any security breaches. He turned the conference over to the HR team, who promised to provide additional diversity sensitivity training and to help the police bring the perpetrators of the dastardly murders to justice.

In a side note, the Chinese Embassy protested the disappearance of a registered foreign agent Fu Wan Shin. They suggested foul play but could bring forward no evidence of any wrongdoing. The US State Department promised the PRC Government that a full investigation of the disappearance would be conducted. American law enforcement, the spokesman said with gravitas, would form a task force for that purpose.

Jonathan Smart did not directly communicate with John Fulghum, not even to acknowledge the accounting that Fulghum sent via email to him. Nothing in the detective's accounting spelled out what Fulghum did as his 'investigative services.' That was all right with both the detective and his client.

A brief note from Joseph Pounce, CIA agent, arrived in the mail late in the week afterward expressing only,

"Thank you, John Fulghum. Your Friend, Joseph P."

Fulghum affixed the note with a pushpin to the corkboard that hung on his wall with other treasured trophies. He chain lit another Marlboro cigarette and pushed through his racing forms to the one that he needed. Running his finger down the form, he stopped when he found the nag he was looking for—Cynthia the Moon. He thought that might be a good bet at the track. He mused on that idea for a good two minutes before he was convinced and wrote down the odds.

"What a man has to do to discover a winner these days!" he said aloud. Then he swung back behind his desk to his captain's chair. He was expecting a guest, and he had to get ready. The solid knock on the door and the quick entrance of the man in the police uniform confirmed that Officer Nigel Pounce of Boston Homicide was right on time.

Bloody End of the Line

It was hard work in the hot sun, and the worst part of it was the combined stench of sticky, drying blood, human excrement and the unmistakable sweat of fear. The candidates were arranged in four lines corresponding to the level of infraction with the capital offenses on the left and the merely suspected on the right. All the candidates were, of course, guilty though no trial had been held and no evidence provided. Any reprieve, such as it was, lay on the raised wooden platform at the center of a viewing area surrounded by terraced ranks of seats filled with shouting spectators. A hooded man with hairy shoulders on a bare scarred back and short pants, backed a large, rusty haulage vehicle right up to the platform. The five black-hooded figures on the platform carried, dragged or swept the sundry bodies, heads, entrails hands, feet, and limbs into the haulage cavity where the refuse of the morning had been piled and now buzzed with a coat of flies, wasps and honey bees.

Blood was so plentiful that the haulage cavity seemed like a stew of humanity roiling in a mixture of ordure, blood, and miscellaneous secretions. Prominent on top of this mass was the head of a blonde female still fixed with the sneer she had given the headsman who had removed it with a single stroke of his sword. Here and there were the bodies of infants that had been cut laterally in half and now bobbed in the goo. When the platform had been cleared, the lead executioner moved to the center of the platform and announced the next event—a simultaneous execution of seven persons by a single bullet from a 30-30 rifle.

"This would," he said with a smile, "be a Guinness world record event, and the rules are complex." After the seven persons had been stripped and beaten, they would be aligned front to back in a human sandwich, and the marksman would stand five feet away from the lead victim. If the rifle bullet passed through all the bodies and killed, the marksman would be awarded the right to declare whether the corpses should be beheaded, or not. If the rifle bullet did not pass through all the bodies, then the survivors and the marksman would be decapitated. A great roar of approval arose from the audience, and some laughed at the wit of the rules.

One man laughed so hard that he drew attention to himself, so much so that the lead executioner motioned for him to climb the platform stairs and join the fun. He ordered the man caned with thirty strokes. Two of his assistants stripped and strapped the man to a bench on the platform and began caning him so that his back and buttocks became a mass of bleeding flesh. Trembling with pain, he was given back his clothing and descended to rejoin the other onlookers while the seven victims were led to the platform for their own experience of caning on the model they had just witnessed.

The seven were then tied in a single unit standing face to back, and the lead executioner raised the 30-30 rifle in the air to resounding applause.

In a booming voice, he asked who would be the marksman. A hush fell on the assemblage because no one dared to risk his own life for the attempt. The lead executioner pled for a volunteer to step forward. The alternative, he said, was for him to select the volunteer and have him caned for not stepping forward of his own volition.

A victim raised his voice and said, "I volunteer!" This instigated a roar of disapproval from the crowd and might have caused uproarious laughter too except the crowd had learned what laughing meant.

A boy of twelve stood up tall in the stands and raised his hand. The lead executioner tried to avoid seeing his nephew's hand, but inevitably, he had to acquiesce and invite the boy to the platform. The boy stood at the required distance and aimed at the throats of the bound victims. When he saw that his targets lined up perfectly, he pulled the trigger, and the bodies fell as one. The lead executioner examined each body, and he announced that the boy had, indeed, won the record. He also said that two of the victims were still alive. He drew his sword and offered it to the boy, who ordered the survivors to be taken to the beheading area on the platform where he neatly lopped off the two survivors' heads with two clean blows.

As always in these cases, the blood of the victims spurted from the necks from the force of the still-beating hearts. The boy took a blood-soaked towel and wiped the blade before returning it to his admiring uncle. He whispered a few words to his uncle, but his uncle shook his head and indicated sternly that his nephew should return to his place in the stands.

All afternoon, the work continued until all persons in the first line had been beheaded. All prisoners in the second line were scourged then hung until they were dead. All prisoners in the third line had been flogged along with their right hands removed and then returned to the holding area, and all prisoners in the fourth line had been caned and returned for reprocessing. The humdrum routine of the proceedings made the spectators uneasy with boredom. They grumbled and made up games to liven things up.

The lead executioner had foreseen this turn of events, and he had a special treat to crown a successful day. When the platform had been emptied of all refuse into the rusty haulage cavity, the lead executioner ordered a large container to be raised by pulleys onto the platform. He then opened the doorway of the container to reveal a beautiful woman, who he said was a dangerous spy. He raised his hand to quell the clamor of the indignant crowd, and while he enumerated the woman's crimes, he attached a canister with markings and a valve to a flexible pipe leading into the container. He said that the canister contained a blister agent that would burn and blister the woman's skin and finally kill her. He closed the door of the compartment and fastened it, and then he turned the valve until it would turn no more. The sounds of the struggling woman could be heard by the entire crowd, who remained hushed so they could savor every plaint and groan. When the noise stopped, the lead executioner turned off the valve and ordered that his associates remove the container from the platform with extreme care.

The lead executioner then announced that today's festivities had ended, but the same—and more—would take place the next day and every day this month because so many did not choose to follow the righteous path. He did not preach or sermonize beyond that. He and his associates policed the execution area, and then they retired to their individual homes for a good night's sleep.

After the evening prayer and a hearty meal, the lead executioner went out into the night to visit the area where the container with the female spy had been placed. Over his arm, he carried a burqa. When he reached the area, he saw that the container's door was still closed and locked as when it was on the platform. The lead executioner looked all around to be sure no one saw him, and he opened the door. There the female spy sat, very much alive. With a crooked smile, she said the oxygen in the canister had worked to keep her alive just as she said it would. Now she told her accomplice that she had to travel, and she took the covering from the man and put it on, covering her entire body, everything but her flashing, coal-black eyes. The lead executioner walked with her following at the prescribed distance through the darkness as if he were walking one of his wives. At the edge of town, the woman bade him farewell and promised to return.

The bloodshed of the next week was extensive. According to the records kept by the executioners, seven hundred men, women, and children were tortured and then executed or, if they were luckier, maimed for life. Many who lost their limbs eventually died from infections or from loss of blood. The lead executioner's nephew grew to manhood in that time with twenty-five deaths, all told, credited to him by his uncle. His reward was a black hood of his own, and he joined the executioners on the platform proudly. He did not need to boast of his exploits because he had become a legend to his friends and a wonder to his people.

On the seventh day, the woman spy returned with a burqa-clad group of two dozen women. As their spokesperson, the woman spy claimed they were fleeing from enemies who had killed everyone else in their village. The group remained uncharacteristically silent, as if mute while she made a public request to the lead executioner—let those in the required garb attend the executions so that they could see for themselves the vengeance that was to be wreaked on the unbelievers.

The lead executioner, who defined the rules as he went forward, agreed to the woman's request and showed her where in the stands the people in burqas should be seated.

The next morning before the day's proceedings began, the lead executioner announced to the crowd that special guests were among them and that they deserved a hearty welcome because they had been wronged by the enemy. Looking out over the multitude, the lead executioner noted that it was a beautiful day to die and that he had an announcement to make—that his assistant would lead today's proceedings, seconded by his nephew who had recently come of age. He made a ceremony of handing over his sword to his relief, and he salaamed the crowd in all directions before he left the platform and headed out of the execution area. He saw as he departed that the first victims from the four lines were being led to the platform, and smiled to hear his assistant capably shout his orders above the din.

When the shooting started, the lead executioner went straight to the container that had held the woman spy, entered it, turned the canister's valve to full on, pulled the door closed and locked it from the inside. The shooting continued for well over an hour, and the Special Forces team who threw off their shrouds were loaded to the teeth with weapons that served their purpose.

The first to die were those hooded figures on the platform, whose death dances, at first, pleased the fickle crowd until they realized that they were the next to die. The Special Forces soldiers did not stand down, or relent or give mercy. They head-shot as many as they could of the teeming multitude, then drew their sharp knives and ripped the remainder apart from the gut to the heart. Finally, they used their bare hands to break necks, shove noses into crania and strangle those that needed it.

The SF leader laughed and said, "Now this is the kind of women's work I like!" He then turned to grab one of the would-be spectators by the arm and showed him how it could bend in ways he never had expected. With the man's red arm bone, he stabbed another spectator and then another. His compatriots followed his example but with variations, one taking a leg apart, another reaching inside a man to rip out his rib to make a knife. The cowardly crowd was no match for these ruthless killers, who lived on blood for a living and prided themselves on their ability never to tire or slow down.

Seeing the turning of the tide, the lines of prisoners swept out to join the SF troops, and the mayhem began in earnest. Those who were slated to die this day were the slayers themselves. Those who came to watch people slaughtered were themselves slaughtered. The man who was scourged on the first day because he laughed was found by the woman spy and gutted while she laughed and looked him in the eyes as he died. Now the prisoners manned the platform, and they signaled for the truck with the haulage cavity to be backed so they could fill it with carnage. When it was full to the brim, they ordered it to be emptied and then returned for a refill. Heads were lopped off and people were hanged all around the platform and from every overhang around the town.

Covered with blood, the soldiers continued killing until they saw that the prisoners had things well in hand. Following the female spy's lead, they withdrew to the area where the container had been deposited. There she unlocked and opened the door, but immediately slammed it again when she realized that the leader of the executioners had turned the valve of a canister of blister agent that had been substituted for the canister of oxygen. In all the noise of what became known as the cleaning operation, no one heard the minor drama that was occurring in the container. The SF leader shook his head with a smile.

"Those who live by the sword shall die by it." With those words, he picked up his radio phone and called in an air strike on the town's position. He ordered up the very best munitions - daisy cutters, which would leave nothing above ground alive. Then he formed up his men and, with the woman spy in their company, proceeded to the safe area outside of the red zone of the air assault. From that vantage point, they were treated to what few witness and survive—the daisy cutter bombs at work. No human carnage can compare with that. Satisfied that the air support had completed their mission, the SF troops prepared for an immediate helo evac with no casualties and no regrets.

****

Years later on the second floor of a Greater Boston area building that housed Joe's Malt Shop, up a narrow, enclosed stairway from the street level was the office of John Fulghum, PI. The detective sat behind his dusty desk poring over his racing forms and trying to decide where to place his bets. Between the thumb and index finger of his right hand was his third Marlboro cigarette of the morning. Smoke rose in lazy swirls to the ceiling where it mixed with a dense cloud that was pierced by a shaft of light from a single grimy window high up behind the gumshoe's desk. In the man's left hand was a slip of paper with scribbles that might be names of horses. The slip of paper had been shoved under the office door before Fulghum arrived, delivered by the daughter of a gypsy fortuneteller that he knew. She had once given him a tip that made him a lot of money. He was not averse to repeating that exploit.

A loud knock interrupted Fulghum's reverie.

"Just twist and push," the detective barked.

The door opened on a tall man, rakish thin and angular with a mustache setting off a manly face with dark eyes and a military haircut. The visitor stood in the doorway watching the detective and waiting for him to take notice.

"Fulghum, is it really you in the back of all that smoke?" the man asked.

The detective recognized the voice as he tried to place the physiognomy and tone with his memories of military service in foreign lands. The detective processed what he saw and heard narrowing memories rapidly through Afghanistan, Helmand, and Special Forces to the name Landsdowne.

"Marty Landsdowne, come right in, shut the door behind you and sit down," Fulghum said to his old comrade in arms as he rose to shake the man's extended hand before he gestured to the captain's chair opposite to his own. "You haven't changed a whit. Have a cigarette." He pushed his box of Marlboros across his desk and his visitor took out a cigarette and lit it before he continued.

"You haven't changed either, but the world has changed around us. The people think we've been superannuated." The man fixed Fulghum with a stare that was severe as well as serious. It was clear to the detective that Landsdowne did not feel superannuated.

"I hadn't noticed," said Fulghum with a wry smile. "What brings you to Boston?"

"You may recall I used to work with a woman in the field. The name she went by was Alia." Landsdowne hesitated while this idea sank in.

"I would not forget Alia. She was quite a woman."

"She still is. She's here in Boston now." Landsdowne might have said, *Duck, live grenade!* with the same effect. Fulghum was clearly stunned by the information.

"What does she do these days?" the detective asked already guessing at the answer.

"She does what she has always done. She loves the kick that she gets from being close to danger. Alia is the natural double agent. She was born to spy and a natural with wet work."

"Is she spying on anyone in particular here in Boston?"

"In fact, she is. She's infiltrated the local Muslim community and provides our best HUMINT on the target."

"I suppose you're in the game as well."

"Yes. Like her, I would be bored not to be in the game, as you call it."

"CIA?"

"Something with a military flavor, actually. If anyone asks you about our meeting, it never happened."

"Should we be talking in this room?"

"Only if you are going to report what we say to the local Imam. I sincerely doubt that you would do that. Some things don't change."

"Like the nature of the threat. Like the way we have to deal with it."

"You've got it. Do you remember that operation we performed against the terrorists when we all wore burqas and brought down the air strike with the daisy cutters on those bastards?"

"It was your finest hour," Fulghum said as he chain lit another cigarette and nodded for Landsdowne to do the same if he liked. He did like, and he took his time to chain light another cigarette while he plotted his next revelation.

"We're very close to having the enemy in our sights."

"You mean here in Greater Boston?"

"Close enough."

"And you're cleared for wet ops within CONUS?"

"We're deniable, but there may be blood." Landsdowne nodded to emphasize his point.

"Why are you telling me these things?"

"Our interagency liaison told me to seek you out and give you the gist."

"What do you expect me to do with such forbidden knowledge?"

"The intelligence I've just given you is for deep background only. I expect that you will be asked by the police to look into certain crimes that will be committed in the near future. Knowing Alia and I will be involved may help you with your future investigations."

"So, let me get this right—if a daisy cutter bomb just happens to take out a boatload of Muslim tangos in Boston Square, I'll know the signature?"

"Hahaha. Not exactly. You'll know where not to look for the murderers." Again, Landsdowne hesitated so that Fulghum could absorb the implications of what he had said.

"Marty, I've got a license. I like practicing in Massachusetts. I like the relationship I have with the local police. I don't want to have to go clandestine, relocate and start all over again somewhere else."

"You won't be put in a compromising position. Trust me, John."

"Didn't we always say to trust no one? Look, don't bring my name into any of your discussions about what you are doing. Make no guarantees about what I will do or not do. I will not be part of your operation. Be very careful because if I can trace a crime to you or Alia, I will not hesitate to do so. This is not Helmand, Marty. This is home."

"The terrorists have brought Helmand to our home, John. I fail to see any distinction in the difference except that the potential for collateral damage impacts American civilians and not Afghan civilians."

"Is your interagency team in touch with Boston Special Ops?"

"I've been told she's in the loop, but that part's not my business." Landsdowne had the look of dangerous boredom now. Fulghum had seen the look on many occasions. He knew that Landsdowne was mission oriented. He would do what he had been ordered to do, efficiently and effectively. He was not subtle in execution, but you could depend on his competence and he never failed to complete a mission. Fulghum made a snap decision to clarify where he stood.

"Likewise, what you are doing is none of my business. You weren't here this morning. I don't recall anything about you or Alia or what you did in your special operations in Helmand. Be very careful not to cause too much collateral damage in Boston. I won't question your methods of target identification or your orders. To the extent that you're taking out genuine threats to national security, we are in complete agreement."

"That's all I wanted to hear from you, John. Thank you. I've got to be moving on. Maybe after everything has settled down, I can return and meet your closest associate. Then we can have a drink and talk about old times."

"Maybe so, Marty. Mr. Daniels is a powerful friend in times of need."

"I'll see you later, friend." With that, Martin Landsdowne rose, pivoted smartly, and walked to the door. He gave a mock salute as he exited. He then secured the door and Fulghum heard his footsteps as he clambered down the stairs.

For a while, Fulghum stared at his door trying to gauge what had actually happened during the last fifteen minutes. Martin Landsdowne, a fellow former Special Forces officer, had dropped by to inform him that a black wet operation was currently underway in the Greater Boston area. The operation involved a mutual acquaintance and master spy with the working name Alia. Everything that he knew of both operatives suggested that the threat they were hunting was both viable and extremely dangerous.

Landsdowne had never lied about what he was going to do. Fulghum deduced that very soon mayhem was going to break loose in New England. The detective knew from what Landsdowne had said that the interagency unit behind the hit expected that he would become involved in the aftermath of their attack. Fulghum could not guess why he had been informed about the matter in advance. *Perhaps,* he thought, *things might be moving too fast for me to be informed as the operation segued to its denouement. Perhaps the operators want me to know rather than surmise about the signature of the operation. Is Landsdowne laying down the basis for collaboration after the fact?* He resolved that he would know soon enough about that.

Fulghum shrugged and decided to go back to his important work of the morning—his horseracing bets. It warmed his heart to learn that Alia, the woman with the flashing black eyes was still alive and working against the enduring threat of the radical Islamists. In Afghanistan, she had been as beautiful as she was ruthless. She was also lethal. The detective tried to visualize what age might have done to the spy's beauty. He had no trouble visualizing her face and body, which had been etched permanently into his imagination.

He took another look at the scribbled note on his desk. There he read the name, "Aliant." Perhaps, he thought, the fortuneteller was not referring to a horse but to a person. His eyes narrowed as he factored the odds. He then called his old friend Ken Mander with his cell phone and left a message in coded language that was their way of arranging an urgent meeting. To anyone trying to decipher the message, it was gibberish. To Mander, it meant, "Urgent lunch tomorrow at Dalia's Restaurant on Route 4 in Bedford."

The next day Fulghum arrived at Dalia's fifteen minutes early and asked to be seated at the table nearest the front window looking out on the parking lot. Five minutes later Ken Mander emerged from the bathroom of the establishment since he had taken the precaution of arriving earlier still. He removed his trench coat and laid it on the back of his chair as the waitress glided over to take the two gentlemen's lunch orders. Since the weather was chilly, soup and coffee were the starters.

"It's your nickel, John. We'll have to make this a quick lunch because I'm in the middle of something that's up to my clavicles."

"Speaking of being up to your clavicles, an old friend visited recently. The friend was a colleague overseas specializing in the kind of work we'd all hoped would remain overseas. Now the work is being done right here in Greater Boston. Do you know what I mean?"

Mander's eyes squinted slightly as he answered, "I know precisely what you mean. I recently told such a man to come see you. I guess you managed to meet."

"Well, that's the funny thing, Ken. We never did meet, and I don't recall ever knowing the man anyway." Fulghum looked out his window and saw that snowflakes were beginning to fall. "It's cold outside. I expect that, ironically, it's going to get hot very soon."

"You don't know the half of it, John. Let's finish our soup and drive around a little. We'll talk and I'll drop you back here afterward."

The men finished their soup, paid the bill and proceeded to Mander's car. While Mander drove out to the interstate, he briefed Fulghum on the state of play.

"John, we've got a convergence happening at the mosque. All the big players associated with a major terrorist action are meeting there tomorrow night after prayers. We don't know what their plan is, but the bomb maker, the operators, and logistics personnel are all in play. Funding has been flowing through the usual conduits. When a meeting like we're monitoring happens, all the players go off in different directions afterward. Then the evil begins. Our plan is to take out the major players in a lightning strike."

"That sounds like a big mess with all kinds of implications for the authorities."

"When we strike, we're going to take no unusually noisy measures. In fact, you can think of the operation as a surgical removal of a nasty cancerous growth."

"That sounds promising, but the local Muslim community will seethe."

"Only a few will know about the operation, and they'll be in no position to complain. Are they going to say that five of the worst terrorists in the world were present at the mosque? I think not."

"I won't ask how you are going to do your job. Why did you want Landsdowne to come to me?"

"You're our insurance policy, John. I don't want you to become involved, but I don't want you or the Boston police to cross-thread the operation either."

"But you're surely working with Boston Special Ops?"

"Yes, but only to a point. Some things we cannot let them know." Mander took out a cigarette and lit up. Fulghum did the same.

"We have an inside person whom you know."

"Aha."

"We don't want her to get caught in the crossfire. She's much too valuable for our continuing surveillance to sacrifice her."

"What do you want me to do?"

"Stand by and wait. If we need you, I'll call you. I'm not sure what we'll need to have you do. We all have to remain flexible."

"Is there any chance that your agent has been blown already?"

"She is always under suspicion, but she's a big girl. Right now, she's playing the Imam for all he's worth. When the action comes down, she'll be pleasuring him as a diversion. Depending on how things go, she may need to have a safe house not controlled by the Agency because only a handful of people in the Agency know her status as a double."

"So she'll be taken with the others in the raid?"

"That's the current plan, but if things go wrong, we'll have to use our wits to get her clear and keep her safe."

"Does Landsdowne know about your plans for her?"

"How can he? We don't know how things will work out yet."

"When the action starts, he will have his own plans to protect her."

"Yes, but she is to be protected, at all costs. Landsdowne is expendable."

"I see. Landsdowne might be targeted by the threat and she can't become collateral damage."

"I couldn't have put it better."

"So what is my time window of engagement and where should I be situated in case you need me to support?"

"Work late in your office tomorrow night. Be there from ten until midnight. Don't meet our friend Jack so you'll be action ready. You won't have to come out—at least, I don't think you will. We'll come to you. After midnight, if nothing has happened, drive on home to your apartment."

"It all sounds too easy."

"For all the tricky pieces of this thing, it all boils down to easy actions taken one at a time. We're lucky to be taking out the major players rather than trying to stop a terrorist attack in progress."

"Let's hope by taking out the master planners, the terrorist strike will be disrupted."

"Amen to that. We don't need another bombing incident like the one we had at the Boston Marathon."

Mander completed this wishful thought just as he eased his automobile alongside Fulghum's in Dalia's parking lot. The men shook hands, and Mander drove off. Fulghum drove back to his office through the snow. The bleak winter landscape was like a reflection of Fulghum's dark thoughts about the impending operation. He could not help but play out every conceivable possibility about his role tomorrow night.

As he climbed the stairs to his office, he noticed water on the stairwell as if someone had preceded him. He unholstered his concealed pistol as he continued to mount the stairs. He saw that his office door was closed and locked, but he had the sense that someone lurked inside. Keeping his weapon at the ready, he unlocked and entered his office to discover a dark, immobile figure sitting in the captain's chair that faced his desk.

"Stand up slowly. Make no quick movements, or I'll shoot you. That's right. Now turn around slowly." The figure that stood before him was dressed in a burqa. Fulghum switched on the light so the figure could see his drawn pistol aimed at the head.

"It's true, then. John Fulghum. Do you remember me? It's Alia."

As he closed the office door behind him, Fulghum kept his pistol pointed at the figure's head.

"All right, then. Take off your burqa, slowly. It's been a long time." She did as he asked. When she was finished taking off her robe, she laid it across the back of the captain's chair and stood looking at him with a crooked smile on her face. Her eyes were flashing black. Her hair was black. She was little changed from the last time Fulghum had seen her in Afghanistan.

"See? It's me. I'll turn around so you can see that I'm not armed. Do you want to frisk me? You can put your gun away. I've not come to harm you this time. I needed to know that the others were not lying to me. I needed to know that it was really you. My life is at stake, after all." She then walked towards Fulghum, pushing his gun aside as she invaded his personal space and raised her head to kiss him on the lips. He returned her kiss and took her in his arms. They embraced and continued to kiss, long and hard. Then she pushed back to catch her breath and look him in the eyes.

"You are the same. You taste the same. Is it possible you really do remember me?"

"Alia, you are inimitable. How could I ever forget you? Why don't you have a seat and tell me what you've gotten yourself into now?" He re-holstered his weapon as he moved to his captain's chair behind the desk and gestured for Alia to be seated across the desk from him.

"Please have a cigarette."

"In my present position, I cannot smoke. You know how they are about smoking and drinking. Perhaps later, we'll do both once I've finished with my current assignment."

"You'll never be finished. I thought we discussed this in Afghanistan. Your mission, you said, would never end."

"Sometimes I can take a rest after a strenuous operation or between the phases of a particularly long one."

"Just being in this office will make your clothing reek from stale cigarette smoke."

"So take me somewhere else where we can be smoke-free for a while."

"I know just the place, but you'll have to promise me that you'll be on your best behavior." Fulghum looked at the beauty with an arch expression that told her he sincerely doubted that she could behave properly.

"I'll be good. Where are you going to take me?"

"I'm taking you to the house of a friend. When do you have to be back on the job?"

"I must return for evening prayers. That gives us four hours." She batted her eyes at him flirtatiously.

"Turn off your charm, Alia. The reason I'm going to introduce you is for your protection. If there is one place in Boston where you'll be safe, it is with the family I know."

"Let's be going. Do you want me to wear my burqa, or not?"

"We'll take it in that large bag that's sitting against the wall. Put on that hooded coat from the coat rack. Now you look like any other frumpy New England woman. Take my arm so you can look as if you're my companion. I'll have to assume that you've not been followed, but I'll take precautions on our way to be sure we're clear."

"Frumpy, am I? Considering that I've been wearing that cloak all the time since I arrived in this city, it will be nice to blend in for a change. Can you tell me about this family I'll be staying with?"

"I will tell you only after I've determined that you're not being followed. I don't want to lead your terrorist friends to the best safe house in the city." The edge in Fulghum's voice told her to take him seriously.

Fulghum and Alia went down the stairs and climbed into Fulghum's car. He at first drove making frequent switchbacks, and then he set out in the opposite direction from his destination. Finally seeing that they were probably in the clear, he drove a circuitous route to the residence of Officer Pounce of Boston Homicide. At the door, he and Alia were met by Molly Pounce, who was surprised to see Fulghum with a beautiful woman hanging on his arm.

"Molly Pounce, this is Alia. Alia, this is Molly Pounce. Molly, may we come in for a cup of coffee at your kitchen table?"

"John, please come in. I'm in the middle of a dozen projects, but I'd be happy to have coffee with you. Would you like something to eat? I just made a rhubarb and strawberry pie."

"Unless Alia is hungry, we won't have any food, Molly. But the smell of fresh pie is redolent."

"I'll just have coffee, please, Mrs. Pounce," Alia said as she followed her hostess down the hall to the kitchen where she always had a pot of coffee ready for guests. Molly poured three cups of coffee and placed them on the table along with sugar and cream, three silver spoons and cloth napkins.

"Molly, Alia may need a place to stay during the next few days. Do you still keep a guest room ready?"

"John, I just made up that room this morning. Alia, if you need to stay, just drop by at any time. You can use the room and eat with the family. Do you have any dietary restrictions?"

"Molly, I'm grateful. No, I have no dietary restrictions," she said while she looked gravely at Fulghum.

"How long have you two known each other?"

"We've known each other for over ten years. Isn't that right, John?"

"That's right. We met in Afghanistan during the long war. Imagine that Alia landed right here in Boston only very recently, and I saw her only this afternoon when she stopped by my office." Fulghum gave Molly a look that cut off inquiries yet made his hostess curious.

"Where are you staying, Alia?"

"I'm staying with a community downtown. It is a convenience."

"Well, the Pounce family is not a community, but we can lend you a room if you need it anytime. If you'd like to see the room, let's go up right now. John, you wait here and finish your coffee. Come with me, Alia. He'll be all right while we're gone."

Fulghum sat and drank coffee while the women went to see the guest room. When they returned, the detective was pouring his second cup of coffee. He could see that the women were smiling together and becoming friends. He did not know what Alia had told Molly, but the policeman's wife seemed relieved at what she had heard.

"Molly, thank you for your hospitality," Alia said. "I hope to see you again soon." The two women embraced, and the arrangement was now in place.

Fulghum, not one for chitchat, departed the Pounce residence and drove Alia back to her car. On the way there, he gave the female spy his cell phone number. He did not pry into the nature of her current operation or the details of the plan to take down the terrorist cell the next evening.

"Alia, your dangerous games are likely to get you killed one day, but I don't want you dying in Boston. Call my cell number if you need me. I'll be in my office from ten pm until midnight tomorrow."

He saw that she was looking straight ahead through the windshield as she said, "John, it has been good to see you again. It's close to show time. Wish me luck."

"You'll need it. Do you want to come up to the office to get back into your outfit?"

"I can manage right here." She took off the coat that Fulghum had loaned her and put it in the back seat. She then took out the burqa from the large bag, and with a neat sinuous motion, slipped the covering over her head and edged it down her body. "See how easy that was? Now drop me off a block before we arrive at your office. I'll get out and walk the rest of the way to my car. One thing more, our mutual friend Marty Landsdowne from the bad old days may be a problem."

"What kind of problem?"

"I think he has a crush on me."

"I can understand why he might. I certainly did once upon a time." He smiled to recall that interlude in his complex life.

"Let's not get started again, John. We sorted out our relationship years ago."

"You sorted out our relationship, Alia. I'm just glad you're still alive. As for you and Marty, don't you think his not being Jewish could be a problem?" Alia did not answer his question because they had come alongside her car.

Fulghum dropped Alia off. Then he drove forward to his usual parking space across the street from Joe's Malt Shop. He used averted vision to observe Alia walking to her car. She looked anything but normal in her burqa navigating the snowy walk. Fulghum noticed that she wore the garment as if she had been born to it. In the Middle East, she would have fit right in. She shuffled just like an Arab. The detective made a mental note of the license plate of Alia's auto before he ducked into the entrance to his stairwell. He stamped his feet and went up the stairs to his office. Just as he was about to sit in his captain's chair, he received a call on his cell phone.

"Fulghum. It's your nickel."

"Jack, it's Ken. The timetable has been advanced by twenty-four hours. Tonight is the night, my friend. Is that a problem for you?"

"Not at all."

"You may have another visitor before ten o'clock tonight, so can you remain in your office without a break till midnight?"

"I'll be here."

"Great. Later."

Fulghum took a deep breath. The mission clock was running and adrenaline was kicking in. He had the impression of involvement without knowing what to do about it. He realized that he had refrained from smoking the entire time Alia was in his company, so he lit a Marlboro and dumped the contents of his overflowing ashtray into the wastebasket under his desk. His long wait had begun, but he did not want to twiddle his thumbs. He went back to the puzzle of his racing forms and became lost in thought. The hours streamed by without his being aware of it.

At seven o'clock Marty Landsdowne knocked on his door and entered quickly.

"Hi, John."

"A little bird told me you might be dropping by. What's up?"

"I just dropped by for a cigarette. Do you mind?"

"Not at all. Take a seat. Do you want to talk?"

"I can't say a thing. You know that."

"Suit yourself."

After he lit his cigarette, Landsdowne sat down and looked at his watch. Fulghum had witnessed the man's behavior before operations on many occasions in war zones, but he never felt that the operative was personally invested in any of them. For this op, however, he was clearly nervous. He looked around Fulghum's office. His eyes fell upon the awards display with Fulghum's three bronze stars. He shook his head.

"Friend, it wasn't so long ago we were in Helmand hunting and killing tangos."

"You have that right."

"The rules of engagement then were fairly clear."

"For you, maybe. Everything for me was ambiguous."

"What do you mean, John?"

"Even the clearest orders were written so I was left making the hard decisions, not the bureaucrats or staffers sitting behind their desks. If anything went wrong, I had to be ready to take the fall for it."

"I know all about that. I guess it only becomes an issue if someone's life depends on what you do."

"Someone's life always depended on what I did. The same went for everyone in Special Forces. Marty, what are you trying to tell me that you can't tell me?"

"I've fallen for Alia."

"All right. What does she say about it?"

"She won't take me seriously."

"Perhaps she can't take you seriously on account of what she feels compelled to do for a living."

Landsdowne's cell phone rang. He stood up and walked towards the office door.

"Right. Right. Understood. I'm on my way." The operative terminated the call and pocketed his cell phone.

"It's show time, John. I'm off. Wish me luck."

Fulghum nodded as Landsdowne exited his office and sped down the stairs. The detective reflected that his supply of good wishes had just diminished for the second time that day. He had a hard time directing his attention to the racing forms. He stood up and paced his office. He straightened the stacks of papers on the floor along the wall. He decided to clean his firearm, but he did not clean it after all. He knew he might be called at any moment. He did not want to be caught short with a disassembled weapon on his desk at the time of the call.

At eight thirty, Officer Pounce of Boston Homicide called Fulghum to confirm the arrangement Molly had made that afternoon. He did not pry into the detective's reason for needing a room for his friend. After less than a minute, he had to terminate the call with Fulghum to take an urgent call about police business. Fulghum thought that might be significant to the clandestine case he was following, but he had second thoughts and laughed because Pounce was always complaining about the calls he received from the police station throughout the night. Murders were frequent events in Greater Boston. The city did not experience killing on the scale of New York or Chicago, at least not yet.

At nine-thirty pm, Mander called Fulghum and said only one word, "Incoming." The CIA agent terminated his call immediately afterward. Background noise in the call had included police and emergency sirens. Fulghum lit another cigarette. His senses were aroused by the prospect of action. He could not concentrate on his racing forms. He checked his weapon and safed it.

At ten o'clock, he heard footsteps on the stairs and then a knock. When the door opened, Alia stepped into the office without her burqa. She was fiercely alert and shivering.

"It is done. Will you please drive me to the Pounce residence now?"

"Are you sure no one followed you?"

"Anyone who could give me trouble has been rounded up. They have been taken away."

"Just the same, we'll observe a few precautions. First, pull on that jacket on the clothes tree by the door." She did as he advised. She remained standing.

"Have a seat and try to calm down for a minute. You look like you're in shock."

She nodded vigorously. He came around the desk and folded her in his arms. The consummate female spy melted in the detective's embrace. Her mouth fought to find his mouth and kissed him greedily. She then laid her cheek against his chest and snuggled there. She trembled and began to sob. Fulghum held her close while she wept uncontrollably. Her pent up fear and anxiety rushed out in a torrent of tears. She balled her hand into a fist and thumped his chest. Fulghum's right hand stroked her hair soothingly. Gradually she stopped crying and recovered her composure. She looked up into Fulghum's eyes and saw sympathy.

"I'm sorry, John. This is very unprofessional of me."

"It's just after-action shock. When you think you can sit down, please do so and just talk about anything at all. That will help." Fulghum handed her a handkerchief. She dabbed her eyes and blew her nose. She broke free from his embrace, shook a little and sat down. The detective went back to his captain's chair.

"Would you like some bottled water?"

"I'd like that very much."

Fulghum drew out a bottle of water from the package that lay against the wall to the right of his desk, unscrewed the top and handed it to the woman.

"Drink a little at a time. Shock causes thirst. Relax a little if you can. Breathe deeply. That's right."

"They're all gone, John. All the terrorist leaders who came to the mosque have been taken." She had a grim look of satisfaction on her face as she began to tell her story. Fulghum had no desire to know her secrets. He had no need to know them. She did not care. She needed to talk to someone to release the demons inside her. While she spoke, Fulghum understood that she was reliving her experience in her mind.

"The mosque has a secret room where the visitors stay. The sixth visitor arrived earlier than expected and I called Marty on my cell phone. Everything—all the plans—had to be moved up by twenty-four hours. I prepared the food for the evening meal. It contained the drug just as we had planned. Everyone in the secret room and the Imam ate the food and went into a profound sleep. I called Marty and told him everything was ready for the emergency vehicles. I was afraid they would take too long and some of the terrorists would awaken. In fact, they came with sirens and lights almost immediately."

Fulghum nodded, keeping his eyes fixed on hers and not interrupting. He thought about the sirens he had heard in the background when Mander called. Because of the timing, those must have been different sirens from the ones she was describing now.

"The first responders took out the bodies, one at a time, all but the body of the Imam. They left him in the secret room where he had slumped off his chair onto the floor. He looked like he was sleeping peacefully. Finally, all the first responders were gone. Marty was there, and he asked me to leave with him. He knew I could not do that. I had many things to do. For one, I had to clean up the dishware so that no trace of the drug would be found. For another, I had to be in the women's quarters so that I would not be suspected. Marty was importunate. He tried to drag me away, but I wouldn't go with him. He became angry and said things he didn't mean. I told him to get lost. I worked fast to clean up. Then I went to my room."

Alia took a drink of water. The main action had been clarified, but she had more to say. Fulghum waited patiently to hear her out. She shook her head as if to clear it and she continued.

"I waited in my room for the inevitable explosion of fury from the Imam. Around an hour later it came. The Imam rushed in frantic but still somewhat under the influence of the drug. He shook me and beat me with his fists. He accused me of betrayal. He said I had drugged him. He wanted to know what had happened to the others. I had never seen him so vicious. He had hatred in his eyes, and I thought he was going to kill me. For a while, he wouldn't listen to my protestations. I pleaded with him to listen. I asked him why, if I had betrayed him, I remained at the mosque rather than fleeing. I suggested perhaps that while he was asleep, the others had decided to go away on a mission. I asked why he had fallen asleep all of a sudden at the table. I stroked his beard and looked into his eyes with understanding. He was distraught and inconsolable. He finally stopped beating me and started pulling my hair. He began fuming about what to do next."

Alia took another sip of water. She braced herself for what she was about to tell me.

"Marty returned to find the Imam pulling my hair and yelling right into my face. I saw the fury in Marty's face, and I tried to wave him off. I knew he wouldn't understand how much I had to suffer to do my job. Marty wouldn't heed me. He clapped his hands over the Imam's ears hard, so the Imam collapsed on the floor in front of me. He then began to beat and kick the Imam senseless. He would have kept on beating him until he was dead. It was all I could do to stop him from doing that."

She paused and Fulghum thought she might have liked the idea of Marty's killing the Imam except that her mission required otherwise. When she began, another theme came out, loud and clear.

"Marty looked at me with such anguish and longing I knew what was in his heart. He didn't want to kill the Imam as much as he wanted to sleep with me. I told Marty I now had to revive the Imam and make up a story that would account for what had happened. Lucky for us, none of the other women would come to the room. That was because the Imam was always beating one of us. Together Marty and I laid the Imam in my bed. I placed a wet cloth on the man's brow. I was stern with Marty. I told him to leave before anyone else saw him. I was afraid that the Imam would come to and see Marty. Then our mission would have been blown, for certain. Marty took me in his arms and swore that he loved me. He said we should just leave and find a way to get free of what we did. He was crazy. He knew I couldn't step out of my life for him. I told him things could never work out the way he planned. I cut him off and turned to revive the Imam. Marty stood there for the longest time watching me. Then he got jealous. He stormed out of the room and slammed the door behind him. Where he went after that, I don't know."

"So you revived the Imam?" Fulghum interjected to bring her back to her main story line.

She nodded, "He was groggy and hurt as he recovered. He hurled abuse at me. He would have started beating me again except he had severe pain in his chest and arm where Marty had beaten and kicked him. I told him I was going to dial 911 and get him to the emergency room for a thorough examination. I said he had collapsed from a stroke or heart attack and broken some bones. I then dialed 911, and the real emergency people came. Over the Imam's protests, they tied him to a gurney and took him away. As they went about their business, the Imam fulminated that I had done something awful to him. He was still yelling about that when the ambulance doors closed and the siren began."

"Was that when you decided to take off your burqa and come here?"

"Not quite. It was cold and snowy. The ambulance activity had roused all the women from sleep. I wanted to let things quiet down before I departed. I knew that whatever I did, it would be reported to the Imam by the other women. They are insanely jealous of the Imam's attention and will use anything against me that they can. Anyway, I was in my room waiting when Marty returned. He threw open the door. He had clearly been drinking. He was enraged that I had sent him away. He threatened me. Then he threatened to shoot himself if I did not come with him right away. He drew his gun and aligned the barrel with his temple."

She stopped and shook her head at the memory.

"Did he pull the trigger?"

"No, he did not. He lowered his weapon and looked at it strangely. Then he broke down and cried. I just watched him, a grown man, weeping for love—of me. When he recovered, he looked around my room. He saw that I was adamant about staying. Then he got a wild gleam in his eye and left. I don't know where he went. I don't really care.

We've worked together for all these years since Afghanistan. We were a great team. Now that legacy may be over."

"Then after he left, you came here."

"Yes, I took off my burqa and drove here."

"Is it time for me to drive you to the Pounce residence?"

"Yes. Thank you, John, for listening. You were always such a good listener."

"Do you want to stop by the emergency room at the hospital before you call it a night?"

"No, I don't. Muslim males don't appreciate being reminded of their infirmities. They think injuries are the will of Allah. I'll return to the mosque late tomorrow morning. I'll then go through the normal, boring routine. I'll keep my eyes and ears open for any news. That's what I do." She smiled faintly and stood. Fulghum rose as well. They walked down the stairs to Fulghum's car. He drove her to the Pounces' home where she spent the night in the guest room. En route they did not speak because there was nothing more to say.

The next morning Fulghum picked up Alia and returned her to her car. She shook his hand before she took off his borrowed coat and pulled on her covering. Then she drove back to the mosque while Fulghum, with his spare coat over his arm, made his way up the stairs to his office. At the top of his stairs, a figure was waiting for him.

"Good morning, John. I said I'd be back."

"Hello, Marty. Come right in and have a smoke."

The two men settled in the captain's chairs on either side of Fulghum's desk. They took their time lighting their Marlboros and smoked while they gauged each other before either said a word. Fulghum saw that Landsdowne had the after-action bearing of a man who had completed a complex mission.

"I take it all is well after a busy night."

"All did go well. The mission went as planned without a single hitch. Imagine accomplishing a counter-terrorism mission without a single drop of blood having been shed."

"Remarkable. So what happens now?"

"I'm on to pastures new. I requested reassignment back overseas. The stateside action is too tame for me."

"Calling down air strikes with daisy cutter bombs is more your style?"

"You have that right, John."

"What about Alia?"

"She wants to fend for herself. I've decided to let her do just that." From the pained look in Landsdowne's eyes, it was clear to Fulghum that he was not over his infatuation with Alia yet. "By the way, thanks for helping out."

"I did damn little."

"Sometimes they serve who only stand and wait. John Milton wrote that line in a sonnet, and he had a point. I appreciated your just being here. This mission was about more than just the terrorists."

"Do you care to expound further on that?"

"Not now. I've got to catch a whole series of flights ending in Djibouti, of all places. Wish me luck?"

"I do indeed wish you the best of luck. I hope you finally find what you are looking for."

"I already found what I was looking for in Alia, but that will not work for either of us now. I'll have to find something else instead."

"When you find it—if you feel inclined, stop by and meet me and a few friends to celebrate. Jack Daniels will be among the celebrants."

Marty Landsdowne rose and extended his hand. Fulghum shook it firmly. Then Landsdowne turned and walked out the door and down the stairs. Fulghum mused about his friend looking for anything worthwhile in the Horn of Africa. Philosophically, the detective knew what passed for meaning could be found in any location on earth if you opened yourself to the possibilities. With that sentiment, he chain lighted a cigarette and pulled up a racing form.

Who knows? he thought. *The winning horse is surely here somewhere only I've just not found it yet. My lead is 'Aliant' but that doesn't seem to be sufficient.*

Headshots I

Enzio Pinza was a perfectionist at what he did, and his work was known throughout the enemy's ranks. They knew when he was in the field, and they knew when he was absent. They could set their watches for the death count when he began firing, and he completed firing when all his ammunition was spent. Headshots were his specialty, and for a sniper usually shooting smoke free from one to two miles out, to make only headshots was more than excellent—it was considered miraculous.

A successful headshot is a splattering, blowout event—particularly when the victim's head seems to burst in all directions in a pink and red cloud of blood and the body collapses in a heap. It is both a kill and a grisly omen. Sometimes the sound of the sniper rifle's report comes a second before the gourd's explosion and sometimes afterward. Aficionados say they know the distance of the sniper by the differential between the impact and the sound.

Simply put, if a target was hit anywhere but in the head, the enemy knew that sniper was not Enzio. So it went for a year and a half in Afghanistan before something remarkable happened that changed the pattern and the attitudes towards heroism and towards Enzio. None of the enemy could say precisely when the new pattern emerged, but it was likely in May during the year of the first American withdrawal from the country. Around then headshots became common in two tactical areas simultaneously. Either Enzio had developed the capacity of being in more than one place at precisely the same time, or somehow the inimitable hero had been cloned.

A small fortune of a bounty had been placed on the life of the headshot expert, so counter-sniper activity was always active in any battlefield of the war. The enemy disposed its counter-snipers at superior elevations where they were least likely to be seen and taken out. Though they all dreamed of firing a bullet that would pay the sniper back for all his kills at once, none had ever detected the headshot expert, much less brought his weapon to bear with a view to a kill.

The rugged hills of Afghanistan provided an amphitheater where the enemy could line the ridges as it invited the bulk of the enemy in one location. The Afghan tribal opposition forces or the Taliban forces, or both might be involved in any action. The more members of the enemy present, the greater their potential to rain fire and kill their hated prey.

A strategic trick was to telegraph the US Army troops' movements and allow the enemy to come forward to shoot American soldiers from a superior position. Against such an elevated force, the US troops appeared to have a distinct disadvantage as they would fire upwards and reveal themselves in the process. To offset this difficulty, the US forces used two countermeasures, each having merit.

One was an expert sniper who remained detached from the throng of US forces and the other was the Tactical Air Control Party. These two airmen would call down air power at precisely that moment in the fight when the enemy was most confident and advancing. The combination of these two pincers was lethal and a deterrent to further fighting. The enemy could not eliminate the snipers nor the aircraft and were forced to flee to the rugged hills, withdrawing into the landscape to wait for the next opportunity. The modus operandi of the departing enemy included providing the coup de grace to most of the severely wounded.

It was on this day that the greatest massing of enemy forces ever seen in Afghanistan took to the heights in an amphitheater in Helmand Province to await the arrival of an Army company with its JTAC and TACP. The enemy numbers were significant because their intelligence at hand—courtesy of the Russian-provided ultra-lights—presented priceless intel that the headshot sniper was active far to the north and would not support the Army troops on the ground this time. Their revised strategy was to first take out the two air force personnel before they could vector strike aircraft, then, kill all the Americans with a hail of fire.

Much to the enemy's surprise, as the US Army troops and the TACPs arrived within range, one by one the headshots came in flashes of red and echoing sniper rifle reports. As one man raised his head and tried to aim, his head exploded. The game of whack-a-mole could not have a better analog for the match because the sniper fire was predictable—as each enemy head appeared, the headshot signature appeared just afterward and a decapitated body hit the ground. The bodies—forty-odd of them—lay all over the amphitheater before the enemy realized that a change of strategy was necessary. They decided on a mass firing to take out the TACPs before they could call down an air strike.

This change of strategy was noticed by the Army company commander in the instant that over three hundred heads loomed over the amphitheater and prepared to fire. He called for air support in a shout, and the TACPs went into the action. Their message was passed by radio, the TACPs dove for cover just in time to miss the first volley of lead from above. The repositioned Army troops fired upwards at what were now clear targets, but the angle was too great and the distance was too far. Still the regular tempo of the sniper's fire rang out with headshots being scored on every third enemy combatant. By the time the air support arrived, one hundred of the three hundred enemies were dead by sniper fire.

The recipe given by the TACPs was for daisy cutters, and the strike aircraft did not disappoint. Four of the monstrous bombs detonated over the amphitheater in a blossoming torrent of fire that no human could survive. When the dust began to settle, only a few enemy combatants, lucky enough to be on the edge of the action, remained alive. They threw down their weapons and ran with the sniper still taking a toll on the living with red signature headshots until only three survivors remained. The sniper fire ceased because, according to SOP, some enemy must be left alive to report what had happened to their commanders. A mist of dust, blood and smoke remained suspended over the battlefield. The shooting was over for the day.

The day's tally told the story of the action. Zero were dead on the American side, with two wounded—the JTAC and TACP with superficial wounds from enemy fire. Two hundred ninety-seven enemy forces were dead—one hundred with headshots and the remainder killed with shrapnel from the daisy cutter bombs. The JTAC and TACP would probably be awarded Purple Hearts. For the JTAC, this would be his fifth such award, and for the TACP the second such. The memory of the engagement would remain a caution for the enemy, and American withdrawal was now assured. Blood and sacrifice were the cost of a secure withdrawal, and blood was written all over the amphitheater where the fighting had occurred. When asked his thoughts on the action, the expert sniper merely smiled and with his rapidly opening fingers, imitated the explosion caused by a headshot. One hundred targets in a single engagement was Enzio Pinza's new record to date, and he was quietly proud of his achievement. He knew why the enemy was led to believe he had been at another engagement to the north, and he knew the secret of his having had enough ammunition to make the hundred bloody headshots, but official secrets would go to the grave with him. Tomorrow another engagement was likely, with fewer enemy combatants who would be increasingly on their guard. The expert sniper's tactics would vary, but one thing would remain the same—his signature bloody headshots.

****

Seated across the table from John Fulghum, PI, at Dalia's Restaurant in Bedford was the almost inimitable Enzio Pinza, renowned sniper, now presumed to be retired. He had the misfortune to be the prime suspect of the Central Intelligence Agency in a series of long-shot assassinations. Fulghum and Pinza had known and respected each other from their Special Forces days in Afghanistan. Pinza had asked Fulghum whether he could help find the real assassin and remove the suspicions surrounding him. That was the reason for their leisurely lunch on this beautiful fall afternoon.

"So John, as background let me tell you the story about Kuala Lumpur. You know Ken Mander of the Agency, right? Well, I rode shotgun with him on one of the wildest Agency assassination escapades ever in Southeast Asia."

Fulghum knew that Pinza was as good a storyteller as he was a sniper. He could modulate his voice to imitate many different speakers, and he could put you right into the action as if you were experiencing the tale from the inside. Hearing operational details about Ken Mander's past from another perspective was also interesting to the detective. He had not yet decided whether he could help Pinza solve his mystery, and this story might provide information he needed to make his decision.

Fulghum raised his hand to get the waitress's attention. "Miss, please replenish our coffees and please keep doing so as you see we need the refills."

"Go right ahead, Enzio. Put me in the picture." Saying this, Fulghum nodded to imply he had all the time in the world to hear his friend's story.

Pinza plunged right into the middle of it, "This is how the conversation went down John:

> "Ken Mander and our five-person CIA hit team arrived at Kuala Lumpur International Airport and made our covert transition to the five-star hotel, the Mandarin Oriental, where we had been booked under our work names for seven days, the duration of our clandestine in-and-out assassination mission. The country team had tracked and lined up the target for her appearance with the notables assembled to discuss global business and policy on the seventh of July. The humidity and blistering heat of the sprawling, modern city was livable only if you had air-conditioned accommodations and travel, which we naturally did have, compliments of the Agency. The logistics team that provided the weapons and ammunition for the hit arrived one week earlier. Everything had been prepared meticulously for the hit, but 'Mr. Murphy' was always ready to upset the best-laid plans."
>
> "What are we looking at, Enzio?"
>
> "Ken, everything is on plan. Give or take three hours, this plan will work."
>
> "So give me the boundaries and probabilities."

"First, the set-up is for a downward, unobstructed shot at just under one mile to an outdoor podium. Weather prediction indicates clear skies with a slight wind. The firing position includes an established tripod. Overwatch is provided. The locals have been bribed."

"But will they stay bribed?"

"That's the sixty-four-thousand-dollar question, Ken. We just don't know."

"And the target?" Ken asked me.

"She goes where she wants when she wants. Unpredictable would be an understatement. She knows the city and the way her nation's security is supposed to work as well as anyone. She distrusts everyone around her for good reason, and on a whim, she'll switch her itinerary, canceling her most important appointments five minutes prior. Her praetorian guard follows her in an identifiable formation wherever she goes while she is in the country. The lady has very special treatment from the country's police force and intelligence agency. Abroad is another story entirely."

"So who do we have working this on the inside?"

"Indira, a female Indian ballplayer, is the target's executive assistant, and she works for us. We'll know within three minutes of any change in the target's plans as long as she has her cell phone. The trouble is that we'll have to adjust over all Southeast Asia wherever the target flies. She'll take a private plane on a whim anywhere she pleases after putting out a raft of BS to the local media pointing them in a dozen conflicting directions. The last time she dropped from view she flew the coop in Vietnam where she was visiting her lover on a weeklong fling. She put out rumors that she was heading for Wuhan, China, but she ended up fifteen hundred meters from where she had been scheduled to appear talking with Vietnam War orphans about their future."

"How trustworthy is our Indian scout?"

"Totally. I've worked with Indira before. She's loyal to our cause, and she's paid very well for what she does."

"I want to meet her tonight at the finest restaurant in KL. Make the reservation happen and provide security for the meet."

The waitress interrupted the recount and asked if we needed anything more. We did not but waited until she was out of earshot before Enzio continued.

"That night at the Mosaic Restaurant right at the Mandarin Oriental, Ken Mander met Indira, the Indian agent who would vector our team, in a ten-person private dining area where they were the only two guests. The renowned chef Kamarudin himself came to their table to take their order personally. When their order had been served, Mander told the server that he wanted absolute privacy. He took out his white-noise generator and placed it on the table. Then the sensitive talks began.

"She has stuck to this political item on her schedule for the last five months. She really wants to have the chance to talk before this brainy international group. It means headlines for her. How could she resist?"

"We're prepared for that. But what if she doesn't want to talk and changes her plan at the last minute?"

"She's done that many times in the past. She'll make the decision, and then everything will move around her. I'll be with her, of course, but I'm not sure how easy it'll be for me to communicate her movements to you while they are happening. I'm tied to her hip, and her people are everywhere. Even though I'm supposed to be her EA, I'm not entirely trusted."

"Yet we'll be able to watch your movements through your cell phones."

"True, but you won't necessarily have the information that will allow you to take the shot."

"We're prepared to take that risk. Do you have any idea where she might bolt if she decides to do go off the rails?"

"Her next scheduled appointment is two days later in Ho Chi Minh City. Despite this meeting, she's actually going to Vietnam because her current lover will be there at the time. She's done this gig before on two former occasions."

"So that liaison will be our fallback opportunity."

"Yes. The likelihood of the target and her lover being in Ho Chi Minh City is ninety-nine percent. Of course, in Vietnam, you won't have the cover story that you planned here. It makes more sense that a fanatical element with the means could take her out in Malaysia rather than in Vietnam."

"I want to be sure we don't endanger you in this operation."

"Danger comes with the territory, Mr. Mander. I accepted that when I signed on."

"They talked for about an hour, eating as they discussed the probabilities and the odds. When they had finished their dinner, Mander left the room first and took a cab into the city, switched cabs four times and then returned to the hotel where he checked his back before he returned to his hotel room. There he placed three secure cell phone calls."

We waited while the waitress ushered others past us to their table. Enzio stared at the customers for a moment while he gathered his thoughts and continued:

"Mander's first call was to the Deputy Director of Operations, the DDO, at CIA Headquarters in Langley, Virginia. "Listen, Crow, we're setting up for a contingency in Ho Chi Minh City. It's only a fallback, but we've got to be sure on this one."

"Mander, you're the lead agent in the field. Do whatever you have to do, but I want that woman down within seven days. Period."

The second secure call Mander made was to the Station Chief in Vietnam. "I'm sending a small team in to prepare for a hit on a Malaysian national. I want no problems on entry or exit. I want a cleaner team ready. I want a safe house as well as deluxe hotel accommodations. Can you do those things?"

"Yes to all. Definitely, I can do what's required. I'll be there personally to meet your team lead at the airport on his or her arrival. Our placard outside the baggage claim area will read, 'Semblance.'"

"I like that."

Mander's third secure call was to Indira.

"We're setting up for the primary here and for a new secondary at Ho Chi Minh City. Send me what you can find about the target's plans to meet her lover."

"I'll send an email with photos and her itinerary. The country team can use the information to set up your people in Vietnam. Is there any chance that I can get a transfer in the likely case that your mission is successful? After you eliminate my boss, I'll need a new job."

"We'll see about that. I think we can work something out. The Agency looks out for its own. Just keep the intel coming."

"The target's been acting strangely. Are you sure we've not got a leak on our end?"

"What do you mean by acting strangely?"

"She's not been as communicative lately as she was before. I'm only fed details ten or twelve hours before an event."

"You're the person on the ground. Trust your instincts. Let me know of any changes in the subject's attitudes towards you."

That evening Mander split his team into two parts of three agents each. One three-agent group stayed focused on the mission in KL; the other three-agent group flew the next morning to Ho Chi Minh City. Mander's KL team tracked the target continuously for the next forty-eight hours. The woman did not vary from her normal routine. Reports from Indira indicated no surprises. Mander was beginning to become suspicious at the regularity of the erratic woman's behavior. At the end of the forty-eight hours, the target dropped from view entirely, and so

> did Indira. They had evidently removed their SIM cards from their cell phones, and their whereabouts was anyone's guess.
>
> Mander didn't panic, but he didn't have great hopes for making the original shot as planned. He appeared at the location where the rifle had been positioned in case she decided to keep her appointment, but the target never showed.

Enzio paused to drink his coffee that was steadily cooling while he briefed Fulghum.

"So what happened next?" Fulghum was intrigued by Enzio's story.

> "Mander updated Crow on his progress. "No joy. The target has vanished. I'm shifting to Ho Chi Minh City ASAP. The country team in Malaysia will continue the search. Two of my team will remain on station at the Mandarin Oriental for the duration in case the target can be acquired again here."
>
> Mander made the transition to join his half team at the Lotte Hotel on Ton Duc Thang Street in Ho Chi Minh City. That was coincidentally the hotel where the target and her lover had stayed the last time they decided on a tryst in Vietnam. The Station Chief met Mander at the airport and had his driver escort him to the hotel in a limo that had been swept that morning.
>
> "We've no intelligence about your target having made a transition to Vietnam from Malaysia."
>
> "This is a long shot, but it's the best chance we've got. We'll give it two days and see if she turns up."

The next morning after Mander's arrival, Indira called him on his cell phone. "The target has flown to Tan Son Nhat International Airport. She'll be staying at the Lotte Hotel. Her lover has preceded her, and he's staying in the hotel now under an assumed name. His room number is 843."

"Any details on her flight?"

"None. She booked a private charter. I was kept entirely in the dark. Her bodyguard took all our cell phones for security. I just received my cell phone back a few minutes ago."

"Consider this call compromised. Change out your phone. Call me on another phone with any changes."

Mander then called the Agency Station Chief in Ho Chi Minh City to update him. "We know the target's lover is staged at the Lotte Hotel in Room 843. Request 24/7 surveillance of that room by all available means. Notify immediately upon arrival of the target. Disguise is probable."

"John, our team went on 24/7 alert, ready to jump on a minute's notice. Mander liked the direct approach. He was impetuous and innovative."

"Go on. I follow you."

"He asked the Station Chief to supply a native stringer who could serve as a valet for the guest in Room 843. The valet provided was connected with the target's lover and managed his wardrobe and movements. That way, Mander had both an inside man and the country team working the surveillance.

"Mander, we have movement. A transfer from the airport is being effected for two females via limo as I speak. Their ETA at your hotel will be eleven o'clock local time." This came from the Station Chief one hour prior to the limo's arrival at the Lotte Hotel.

"John, Mander shifted his location to the firing position, and he took one team member—that was me - with him as the second shooter. All the time, he continued communicating with all the players in his game," explained Enzio.

The valet called. "The guest in Room 843 has ordered two dozen fresh cut roses and a champagne brunch for two via room service for noon."

"Can you help deliver the order?"

"Yes. I'll deliver the champagne brunch."

"Excellent. I want a cell phone photo of the people who visit the guest of Room 843. Send it to me as soon as you've taken it."

At precisely eleven o'clock the valet reported, "The limo just pulled up in front of the hotel. A woman stepped out of the limo with another woman, who appears to be her assistant, in tow. The woman made her way quickly inside with her assistant taking care of the details. The assistant has checked herself into Room 222 on the second floor of the hotel and has gone there without communicating further with the other woman. I'm taking the luggage to Room 843 and will send you the picture of the woman as soon as delivery is complete." The picture was received thirty minutes later.

Indira called Mander on his cell phone at eleven forty-five. "Target has arrived at Room 843, Lotte

Hotel, Ho Chi Minh City. I'll be standing by for instructions in Room 222."

"Inform me of any changes in movements immediately." Mander then terminated the call.

The valet knocked on the door of Room 843 at noon precisely. When he was asked to enter, he rolled the meal with the champagne in an ice bucket into the room and began to uncork the bottle. He was told to desist and to depart the room. The guest tipped him well.

When he was clear of the room, he informed Mander, "Guest and target are alone in Room 843."

"Stand in the hall and watch the door to Room 843. Tell me if anyone comes out of or goes into the room."

The shot was to be executed from one mile away, and it was a clear shot through the window of Room 843 of the Lotte Hotel. Mander was the primary shooter, and I was the secondary. We were in place and fully ready. He and I would shoot almost simultaneously. My shot would break the glass and Mander's shot would hit the target. Mander planned a second shot once the first shots had broken glass, depending on the results.

The target appeared at the window with her lover, a glass of champagne in each of their right hands. As they toasted each other, Mander called for the shots to begin. I pulled the trigger and Mander fired when he heard the report of my rifle. The target fell from view. Her lover, startled and covered with glass looked down amazed at what had happened. Mander then shot the man in the head.

"Knock on the door of Room 843," Mander ordered the valet.

The valet did as he was told.

"There is no answer."

"Call the concierge and tell him you think that there's been trouble in Room 843. Stay right by the door until someone arrives to check."

"Standing by." A few minutes had passed before he communicated again.

"The concierge is here. He's opening the door. He's gone inside. He's come outside again. He's closed the door but not locked it. He's running down the stairs with his cell phone to his ear."

"Go inside the room now quickly, keep your cell phone active and report what you see."

"I'm inside now. I see two bodies, a man and a woman, on the floor. Glass and blood are everywhere. The man's head is shot off. The woman is hit in the chest, and the bullet came out her back. Her back is a mass of blood."

"Check the bodies for vital signs. Do it now."

"There is no pulse on the woman."

"You're sure?"

"Yes. There is no pulse on the man."

"Good. Now get out of the room and stand well back from the door. Report everything you see."

A ten-minute interval of silence followed. During this time, Mander and I tore down our firing stations and prepared to depart our shooting locations.

Finally, the valet reported, "The concierge and three uniformed policemen have gone into Room 843."

"A man in a suit has gone into Room 843."

"A rescue team with stretchers and body bags has gone into Room 843."

"'One body in a bag has been carried out of Room 843 on a stretcher."

"Another body in a bag has been carried out of Room 843 on a stretcher."

"A woman has come to Room 843. She is knocking on the door. The concierge is talking with the woman. The woman is making a call on her cell phone."

"Mander, this is Indira. I've been diverted to your voicemail. The target and her lover are down. I repeat - the target and her lover have been killed. Both are dead. I'm at Room 843 now. I've talked with the concierge. Three policemen and an intelligence professional are at the scene."

Mander called Indira's number and said, "There's nothing you can do now, Indira. Return to your room at the hotel. In one hour, call me again to receive your instructions." He terminated the call because he had other calls to make right away.

"Team, this is Mander. Calmly check out and depart the hotel quickly. Take a taxi to the international terminal. Flight arrangements have already been made by the Station Chief. I'll call en route to confirm details."

"Station Chief, this is Mander, mission accomplished. Team ex-filtration is now in progress. ETA at the flight line is three o'clock PM local, latest."

"Crow, this is Mander, mission accomplished. The team is returning to Kuala Lumpur and after that to home. Stringer agent Indira is a loose end. Request disposition."

"Mander, this is Crow, well done to you and extend congrats to your team. Inform me when all are safe in Kuala Lumpur. Indira's reassignment will be relayed directly to her in two hours."

"Indira, this is Mander. Expect contact from Company in two hours. Stand by. This number will no longer be available for you starting now."

"The ex-filtration proceeded without incident. Our team returned to the Mandarin Oriental Hotel and took advantage of all the amenities of that five-star luxury hotel and the hot, humid, teeming city. We ate the famous street food. We took the time to see some of the local sights while we were there, for example, the Kuala Lumpur Bird Park, the Islamic Museum and the National Mosque of Malaysia. But, we only were able to stay in the city for forty-eight hours after our arrival. At the end of our first day back in KL, Mander received a scrambled call from his boss, the red-haired DDO, about another urgent assassination assignment for our team in Caracas, Venezuela. Only after that mission could we return home to Langley Headquarters. This is how it always went for Mander's special team—so many lives, so little time. He informed us that we would have to make the best of our last twenty-four hours in paradise. We did our best to make our stay worthwhile and ignored our voucher limits for that time. After all, we might not be back that way again for a long while.

"That's the whole story, John. The point is that I was the backup shooter, not the primary. The primary in a CIA operation is always the team leader, in this case, Mander. Why are you chuckling?"

"The operation you described seems to have been very efficient. It was classically planned and executed. Bravo. Ken Mander and you are two of America's finest snipers. Unless you have an unsung, close competitor, you must be guilty as hell as the Agency suspects. Who could possibly compare with you two?"

"I have another story to tell you. This one is from a different angle, but you'll get the gist. You may not recall but I set the record for kills in a single engagement in Helmand. We managed to mass the enemy tangos by making them think that I was in another province at the time. That was only convincing to the enemy because the shooter we planted for the deception could make long-shot assassinations as well as I could. That man was actually a female Air Force sharpshooter named Adrienne Poirot."

"Are you saying that the Poirot woman is the shooter the CIA should be seeking?"

"I am. All the shots they said I made had her signature, not mine."

"What defined her signature and ruled you out?"

"First, she positioned herself at the farthest possible vantage from her targets. That means she never wanted to be at the optimal site from the shooter's point of view. Rather she wanted to be at the farthest possible distance that was still within the kill radius. Her aim was to get clear after the shot."

"It makes good sense that the shooter would want to escape."

"I agree, but when you weigh accomplishing the mission against escaping with surety, I always favor the former."

"Okay, what else defines her style?"

"Second, she never takes a night shot. All her recorded kills have been accomplished in daylight. In fact, sunshine seems to be a requirement for her."

"Anything else?"

"Third, she always uses overloads."

"You'll have to explain that."

"We all load our own shells, and we're careful to use a normative number of grains of powder. Her shots indicate that she uses more grain than other shooters. There's good reason for that as she takes, on average, a longer shot."

"Put this information together for me."

"The shooter is at a disadvantage because she cannot shoot at dusk or at night. She compensates by shooting long and using powder to assure the kill at range."

"Doesn't she also have to use a spotter scope at the extended range?"

"Yes, she does. And she would prefer no wind, a normative temperature, pressure and humidity. In brief, she shoots like a dilettante or a prima donna."

"In contrast to your macho style?"

"Call it what you will. I've shot around the clock in all weathers from a wide variety of ranges. I keep close records. I pride myself on being within a quarter's distance of any target I spot."

"So even if the sniper in question has unrecorded shots, they should fit within the pattern you've established."

"If I were hunting her down, I'd have to bank on her data."

"You said that you had another story that might clarify these ideas."

"Indeed, I do. If you have the time to listen, I'll tell it now. If not, perhaps another time."

"I've got an important meeting at my office late today, but I can put that off. I need to have something I can sink my teeth into though. I'm not yet sure I can help you with your problem."

"I'll put myself in her place and see what it gets you. It's something we in the sniper business call the Shooters' Society." Enzio continued with her background as he knew it.

"The best research and development man in Iran had just been assassinated in the center of Teheran with a long-range shot that hit him squarely between the eyes at a distance estimated at two miles. The news headlines told Adrienne Poirot that she would get the business of assassinating the man or woman who had accomplished the hit if she decided to bid for it. It was only a matter of time, so she took the risk and began planning her mission. She recorded her hours worked as if she had a contract running and could actually bill the hours. This way she managed her time because, as all professionals know, time is interchangeable with money. Freelancers like her have to answer international tenders just like ordinary contractors. When the mission is deemed impossible, then only members of the Shooters' Society will prequalify to bid. Bids are entered secretly by the few who have been prequalified.

"That substantially narrows the number of bidders for two reasons. First, no one knows the entire membership of the Shooters' Society—you have to be invited to join, but the contract is always awarded blind. Second, eligibility for a contract that involves taking out a world class assassin includes, at minimum, three verified kills and no incriminating brushes with law enforcement or intelligence agencies. She could guess how many shooters belong to the society, but she will never know how many shooters like her exist. She will never know any of the shooters' names. The number of shooters necessarily varies. She is only worried about getting the optimal contract and delivering the required service on time and within budget—and, of course, staying alive.

"Her work may seem lucrative to an outsider. Since she left the Agency to open her clandestine consultancy, she had never made less than the equivalent of $14 million plus expenses for a single hit. Her highest negotiated contract netted her $25 million. Do not think she got rich on that amount. She lives frugally for many reasons. She ploughs most of her earnings back into her business for weapons, computers, planning, intel, identity services and security.

"Security is the essential expenditure for her. She is her own back office staff. She has no one working for her. She is not a sociopath. She is extremely careful. This is just as well since she can trust no one to share the secrets that she has to keep. Put simply, operational security for assassinations cannot be outsourced. The fewer who know about an operation, the better. The best case for security is for her customer and her to be the only parties with the need to know."

"It is running a small business with very few people knowing what you do and how you do it," Fulghum suggested.

"Very much so and it is best that way," Enzio replied, pausing a moment to recall the details surrounding Adrienne.

"The hit person who executed the Teheran assassination operation was someone just like her, a private contractor. No official military or intelligence asset could have made that shot. That was good for her because she does not want to have governments after her for killing one of their prime assets. We contractors, on the other hand, are expendable. Our deaths do not really matter to anyone.

When she manages to kill this contractor-assassin, no one will come after her unless she is careless or unless she is somehow part of the security equation. She makes it her business to perform flawlessly. That is why she can command the top prices. She watches her own back. She has been part of the security equation on roughly half of her missions. She has had to kill to avoid becoming part of clean-up operations. That is why she remains flexible. She always has to be ready to make a new start.

"Within four hours of studying the problem in open sources on the Net, she deduced that the assassin was most probably a man named Juan Carlos, a crack Venezuelan sniper-for-hire. She could not help but admire his work. He was reputed to have made seven hits without being apprehended. Juan Carlos made sense to her as the contractor for the Teheran job because his travel could have been arranged through the regular government-chartered flights that connect Caracas and Teheran. Those flights are supposed to be open for anyone to use. In actuality, they are conduits for clandestine Iranian and Venezuelan equipment and personnel.

"She did not care to analyze why the Venezuelan had done the hit against a key person for Venezuela's ally Iran. Geopolitics is not her area of expertise. She did plan informally to check out Juan Carlos' security at his villa, on the Isla de Margarita in the Caribbean, but that quick trip was not going to be a vacation for her. She hates Venezuela for many reasons, not least for the omnipresence of agents of Cuban intelligence in the country. She wanted to know just how closely this asset was guarded and to discover a vantage whereby she could accomplish her future mission efficiently and effectively.

"She landed on the island within two days of her decision to go there. She used one of her alternate identities for the trip. She had no trouble finding Juan Carlos' villa and scoping out the man's security, which was full of holes. She even got a glimpse of the sniper himself on the second story balcony with his comely consort. They looked as if they did not have a care in the world except each other. She took a few snaps of Juan Carlos and his security arrangements for further study. She learned to blend right in, so she had no trouble learning everything she needed to know quickly without attracting attention to herself.

"Incidentally, she noticed two other persons on the island who may have been doing surveillance on Juan Carlos. For completeness, she took photos of the gentleman and the lady. She suspected that they each returned the compliment by taking her photo, but she did not care. Only one of the Shooters' Society would get the contract. Not getting the award, the others would most likely stand aside until the work was completed. If they tried to interdict or kill the shooter, they might bring trouble to their own doorstep."

"Enzio, you make it sound as if you're a bona fide member of this secret society."

"John, draw your own conclusion. I'll continue my story if you like."

"Sorry for the interruption, Enzio. Please do continue."

"Shooters like to live in the deep shadows. They do not trespass on their kind because they might lose their own cover in the process. They are acutely aware that another shooter is a formidable threat.

"Adrienne saw right away that a rifle shot would not be necessary to take out Juan Carlos. She could enter the target's villa and use a silenced handgun for the assassination. She visualized the ingress, the room for the shot, and the egress. She pre-positioned all the equipment that she would need to do the job.

"She was in and out of the island in forty-eight hours. In addition to obtaining the intelligence she needed on Juan Carlos, she established her cover story. She was a computer software sales exec who would be making multiple trips to the island during the next few months. No waves would be created by returning suddenly after brief absences.

"Having completed her surveillance of the target, she returned to her home base and waited. She spent some time at the shooting range to hone her handgun skills. Four days later, she received an encrypted email with a tender asking for a firm fixed price quotation for the work of assassinating Juan Carlos, the Venezuelan sniper, within the next seven days. Bingo! Her quote was due within six hours.

"To prepare for this moment, she had created a fully ready proposal with all the details of her plan and justification for her expenses, and she adjusted the plan for the time window. The price she quoted was $25 million, a firm fixed price. The requester then immediately asked for her best and final offer. This was not unusual when multiple quotations had been received. She responded that her original quotation could be adjusted for time to completion. The full $25 million would cover a two-day period of performance. For a reduction to $20 million, she would perform the same service for a seven-day completion period. She gambled that time was a major factor, and it apparently was. Her offer for a two-day period of performance was accepted. She had won the contract.

"Adrienne flew back to the Isla de Margarita on the next available flight. She executed her planned assassination of the shooter Juan Carlos flawlessly. The way she did this was straightforward. She made a night incursion onto the grounds of Juan Carlos' villa precisely where the cameras offered a visible gap in coverage. She climbed to the second-story balcony where she had seen Juan Carlos with his consort. She slipped through the French doors and into the bedroom where the assassin slept. There she killed the assassin and his consort with two silenced shots to the head. She then retraced her steps, buried her weapon, mask, and black pull-ons. She returned to her hotel through the front entrance as if returning from a late night stroll.

"The next day she flew back to her home base. When she arrived, she sent her customer an encrypted email stating she had accomplished her mission successfully within the required time and included her invoice as an encrypted attachment. She stated that payment should be made as per her original proposal's instructions. The customer acknowledged her request and stated that payment in full had been ordered. When she checked the balance of her offshore account, she saw that it had been incremented by $25 million. This was as good as it gets—a clean transaction with no loose ends. All was apparently well, but fortunately, she did not drop any guard—especially as there never was a media report of the assassination of Juan Carlos or his consort. In official terms, his assassination had never happened. Clearly, Venezuela had an interest in keeping the killing out of the press. Adrienne was not naïve, but she wondered whether she had been used to tidy up a Venezuelan operation that was too hot for the Venezuelans to handle.

"As I mentioned before, she was careful to watch her own back. It was a good thing in this case since the woman assassin whom she had seen on the Isla de Margarita now had her under surveillance for a kill. Adrienne decided to terminate this intruder on her privacy as a personal security precaution. She, therefore, awaited her opportunity and reversed their roles. The huntress was now hunted by her. She had no time to waste because her opponent's contract likely had a near-term date. This woman was, at least, a double threat. She knew who her target was. She knew what her mission had been. She likely had been given a contract to kill Adrienne so that the loose end that she represented could be eliminated.

"Adrienne circled above her target's prone position on a low hill overlooking her home base. Her target was so intent on watching through her sniper sight that she did not see or hear her target approach from her rear. In broad daylight at a distance of thirty yards, Adrienne put a bullet from her silenced handgun through her opponent's skull. She took her picture. She left her and her weapon where they lay as a message to the person who sent her to kill. She decided that her customer was the likely link between this woman and her mission. She was now determined to hunt down her customer and finish the business, her way.

"She sent an encrypted message to her customer's email address requesting an immediate meeting in person for discussions. She included as an attachment her picture of the dead female assassin. Her customer agreed and returned the time and place for their meeting.

"She knew precisely what would have occurred if she had followed his or her instructions to the letter. She would have been a sitting duck for an assassination. What the woman assassin had not accomplished against her, others would accomplish. Instead of doing what was expected, Adrienne assumed a clandestine over watch of the meeting location twelve hours in advance. She witnessed from that high position how two shooters were stationed to cover all the fields of fire to take her out when she arrived for the meeting. She thought that over, and then she decided to shift position while leaving a decoy target where she was now situated. When she had shifted, she saw a third shooter taking position to cover the eventuality that she might take precisely the same over watch position that she had done. The third shooter set up to take out what was now a decoy.

"Her problem had become a little more complex than before. She now had to take four shots, not three as she had originally planned. As the countdown to the time for their meeting progressed, she lay with two scoped sniper rifles ready side by side. She decided to take out the overwatch shooter first, then the two shooters who were covering the field, and finally her customer. Ten minutes prior to their meeting time, a woman in no-nonsense Agency business dress appeared near the table where their meeting was to occur. At precisely three minutes prior to the meeting time, the woman moved towards the table. She saw the field shooters take aim. She saw the overwatch shooter aim where her decoy lay. Adrienne simultaneously took aim at the overwatch shooter and squeezed the trigger. Then rapidly she shot the two field shooters—first left, then right. Finally, she took aim at the woman at the table. She did not hesitate. She shot her through the left temple.

"Adrienne waited and watched in case other parties had been involved in her customer's lethal plan. She looked around a full 360 degrees. She saw no activity indicating that other shooters were present. Confident now, she pulled off her sweatshirt, her latex gloves, and her cap. She abandoned her weapons where they lay. Looking like a woman out for a run, she jogged down the nearest jogging path and ran down the hill to jog along the river.

"When she reached the main road, she began looking for a taxi. She kept jogging while she scanned the traffic to hail a cab. The cabbie picked her up and took her to the airport. There she fetched from an airport locker a full change of clothes along with the passport and identity papers that she had used to get to the Isla de Margarita twice before. She bought a ticket for the next flight out.

"In the waiting area for her flight, she mused on the fact that she had now abandoned her home base forever. She flew back to the Isla de Margarita savoring the irony that she was essentially, taking the place of Juan Carlos as the island's resident for-contract assassin. She also considered that during the Juan Carlos operation and its aftermath, she had taken out four expert shooters. Perhaps her odds of getting another shooter's contract had improved slightly because the field had been decremented. Who could say for sure?

"Anyway, she rationalized that her security in Venezuela could not be much worse than it had been in the US. She knew the location of a nice villa from which she could operate. Its owner had met with unfortunate circumstances. Of course, the security arrangements would need improvement. She resolved to watch her back while she looked for another contract worthy of her skills."

Enzio sat back in his chair and watched Fulghum's reaction to his tale. The detective ruminated on what he had just heard. He had allowed his friend to tell his tale almost without interruption so as not to break the flow of the narrative. The detective's coffee cup was filled by the smiling waitress. He took a sip. Then he began questioning his lunch companion.

"All right, Enzio, let's assume that there is such a thing as the Shooters' Society even if it doesn't really have that name or any name. Let's also assume we are talking about a female assassin and you haven't changed the sex of the sharpshooter to protect the guilty. Wait a moment; please let me finish. Let's also assume that a long-shot sniper has other assassination skills that you've described. My impression is that you have a vivid imagination or inside knowledge. If the latter, you are very close to the sniper you are describing. The relationship may be in the bloodline, or it may be the mentor-protégé relationship, which sometimes can be even closer than a blood relation. I don't doubt that your double in the Afghan theater would have segued to the CIA after long experience. Where else would the opportunities for exercising such skills be more abundant? It is also possible that a world class shooter might just escape the boundaries of propriety and go private. How am I doing so far, old friend?"

Enzio was smiling and nodding when he said, "They said you were good, John. What else do you deduce?"

"Enzio, I've had a lot of experience dealing with the Agency. Usually, they know a lot more than they let on. They indulge in the myth that they are like the Keystone Cops bumbling through a labyrinth they made but has come to ensnare them. I know better, but not from any special intelligence. I know how things have to work. So I'm going to assume that you are still with the Agency. You don't have to confirm or deny this. I'm also going to assume that your target is also with the Agency though the story goes that he or she is a rogue agent acting without sanction."

Pinza's face was reddening but his eyes remained fixed on the detective's. When the waitress approached to refill his coffee cup, he nodded without looking at her. He drank from the cup and after a moment responded.

"Again, John, I ask, what have you deduced from the stories I have told you? Let's grant that your assumptions could be true. Who could or who would verify them if he knew?"

"Before I answer, please tell me whether you had a protégé in Afghanistan and whether that protégé is the CIA's real target in their investigation or you are." Fulghum put down his coffee cup and gave Pinza a look that implied they had reached a critical point in their discussions. He waited while Pinza did the calculations. The man could end the lunch and leave without the detective's help, or he could answer truthfully and take whatever came from that.

"John, I have never lied to you. You have found me out. The Agency has me in the crosshairs, but I am not the assassin they are looking for. I know who the real assassin is, but she is my protégé as well as my lover. I would rather die from an assassin's bullet than be untrue to her."

"Why, then, are we having lunch today, old friend? You've already made your decision about how to deal with the situation. What can I possibly do to help you or your protégé?"

"When a man is confronted by an insurmountable obstacle that will stop any attempt he makes to go beyond it, he resorts to extreme measures. I am the best sniper in the world. That is a documented fact. You, in my estimation, are the best investigator in the world. That is a matter of shared opinion. Ken Mander thinks the world of you. He told me that if anyone could help me, you could and I believed him."

"So, assuming we are not bullshitting each other, what would you have me do? Ken Mander has the ear of the Deputy Director of Operations. She would have to sanction a hit on you or your protégé. A Presidential Finding would normally have to be sought. What is missing from this picture? Enzio, I've all the time in the world. Tell me what I'm missing. There must be something else that you've not told me. What is it?"

"John, someone is trying to remove the best two snipers in the arsenal for a reason. I don't know who is doing this, but the best minds in the Agency can't figure out the motive.

Crow and Mander are stumped. The Director hasn't a clue. The threats around the world would revel in the fact that the two best assassins in America were suddenly terminated with extreme prejudice. Consider the implications for a minute."

Fulghum brooded on this new perspective. He thought back through the stories that Pinza had told him. The story about Ken Mander indicated how a complex Agency assassination was carried out in detail. His story about Adrienne Poirot indicated how a rogue private contractor operated against the Agency personnel who were programmed to remove her after a mission that needed deniability as well as absolute security.

"How much time do we have, Enzio?"

"The clock is ticking, John. If the Agency persists, a great many people are going to die unnecessarily. They will be directed to attack us. We will be constrained to counterattack. Our services will no longer be available. Very soon, I will have to go clandestine as my protégé has done. I won't beg you for your help. I don't want to get you caught in something that might cost your life. I only ask that you think about what could be done. Here's my card. If you have any thoughts, please let me know."

Enzio Pinza handed Fulghum his business card. The company name was, "The Shooters' Society." A cell phone number and email address were provided on the obverse. On the reverse in white letters on a black field was the Latin motto, "Quis custodiet ipsos custodies?" Translated it meant, "Who will guard the guards?" It was an ancient motto suggesting that even the most sacred security institutions required constant watching. Fulghum called for their check, but Pinza picked it up and paid. He added a generous tip because they had spent the entire afternoon at the table talking. Pinza left the restaurant while Fulghum visited the john. When the detective emerged from Dalia's, the police had already arrived. A man had been shot in the head by a long-range sniper bullet. The body was being handled by first responders and the whole parking lot was surrounded by the yellow tape that read, "Crime Scene – Do Not Trespass." Fulghum went to his car, which was parked outside the police cordon. He drove onto Route 4 and proceeded to his office above Joe's Malt Shop. Once there he brooded for a long while before making his inevitable call to Ken Mander, who, according to his recorded message, was not available to take it.

Fulghum left a voice-mail message: "Good man down, another to follow. Request meeting ASAP. John."

Headshots II

Enzio Pinza's death by sniper fire to the head in the parking lot of Dalia's Restaurant in Bedford, Massachusetts was ironical. Pinza held the record for scoring the most kills in a single battle in Helmand Province of Afghanistan. His prowess as a sniper was thought to be unparalleled. Just before the fatal assassination, Pinza had finished a long lunch with John Fulghum, PI. During that lunch, the sniper had asked the detective to help him prove his innocence in a series of long-shot assassinations around the world. The real perpetrator of those kills, he maintained, was the female sniper Adrienne Poirot, Pinza's protégé.

At his office desk on the second story of the building that housed Joe's Malt Shop, Fulghum sat recalling the two tales that Pinza had told him while they were at lunch. The first was about his work with Ken Mander on an assassination in Southeast Asia. The second was about the modus operandi of his female protégé, who killed one of the world's foremost shooters in Venezuela. In his left hand, the detective fingered the business card that Pinza had given him moments before his assassination. The card contained his company's name, The Shooters' Society, with a web address on the obverse and a Latin motto on the reverse. Fulghum was waiting for the return of his call to Ken Mander's voicemail. He needed information and intelligence fast because the next to die was likely going to be Adrienne Poirot. The detective did not have a client relationship with Poirot any more than he did with

Pinza. His soldier's sense of honor dictated that he unscramble the mess that the slain Pinza had left in his wake. Enzio Pinza had paid for the detective's lunch, after all. Besides, something about his cryptic tales was compelling Fulghum to investigate the reason for the veteran's death further.

Fulghum chain lit another Marlboro cigarette with his right hand. Still thumbing the business card with his left hand, he strained his memory to dredge up the details about the sniper whom Adrienne Poirot had killed. That man, according to Pinza, had made a long-shot in the streets of Teheran at an incredible distance. The man and his mistress were slain at his estate on the Isla de Margarita in Venezuela. Poirot was supposed to have settled there after she killed her own customer and three others with long shots and subsequently fled the country.

Fulghum's cell phone rang interrupting the detective's reverie.

"Hi, John. Your call had to be about Enzio Pinza."

"Hi, Ken. Good guess. We had just finished lunch. I came out of the john afterward and discovered the police and emergency folks picking up the pieces. It was a clean headshot. The man was assassinated. Can we discuss this somewhere quietly?"

"Did you have a client relationship with Pinza?"

"Not really, but I feel obligated to investigate the man's death anyway."

"You mentioned another possible assassination in your voicemail."

"Yes. That's the crux of the meeting."

"You know Margarita's on the 225 near the Interstate?"

"Yes."

"Three-fifteen, give or take. Sit right opposite facing the entry passage."

"Roger." Fulghum terminated the call and looked at the time. He had four hours. That gave him time to snoop around the Internet for data on a couple of related matters. He did not want to use his own personal computer for a variety of reasons. Instead, he went to the nearest Barnes and Noble bookstore and logged on as a guest. Within two hours, he had the information he needed to get what he wanted from the Agency. He went to the website for The Shooters' Society and clicked the contact button. In the response form, Fulghum entered the query, "Do you know who killed Enzio Pinza?" He signed with his cell phone number. He then entered the Orbitz website and booked a one-way refundable flight from Boston Logan to the International Airport of Caracas, Venezuela, departing the next day. Satisfied that he had done what he could without further data, he drove out to Sentinel Park where he smoked and thought as he walked through the colorful autumn landscape.

At three-fifteen Fulghum was sitting in Margarita's Restaurant facing the entry. He had just finished asking the waitress to bring water, chips and salsa when Ken Mander darted into the entry and gestured for Fulghum to follow him out into the parking lot. Fulghum dropped a five-dollar bill on the table, and followed Mander to the agent's car and climbed in.

"Thanks for coming on short notice."

"No problem. Coincidentally, we have the same interest—finding what happened to Enzio Pinza. Do you mind if we drive while we talk?" Mander pulled out without waiting for an answer. Both men lighted cigarettes.

"I'm on the trail of Pinza's protégé, Adrienne Poirot, who may be on the Isla de Margarita in Venezuela. Convince me why I should not get on a plane tomorrow and fly there."

"Following up with Adrienne is predictable. If I weren't otherwise deployed, I'd go with you."

"I'm also on the trail of The Shooters' Society. Here's the business card Enzio gave me minutes before he was assassinated."

"I've heard of The Shooters' Society. In fact, they tried to recruit me once upon a time. I've never seen the business card. Here, you hold onto it. Have you got anything else?"

"Pablo Enterez, the sniper whom Adrienne Poirot supposedly killed along with his mistress at his estate on the Isla de Margarita, is listed as presumed dead with no details about how or where he died."

"All right, I'll fill in a few gaps, but no one has all the pieces to this puzzle. We have a five-person team working the details 24/7."

"Were they on the case when Pinza was killed?"

"Yes. Why do you ask?"

"Pinza thought you had a hit team focused on him. Did you?"

"The Agency has many factions. One faction favored the simple way out—kill Pinza plus Poirot and be done with all issues. Another faction wanted to ignore all the evidence against one or both of the snipers. The third—mine—wanted to know the truth before any drastic action was taken. If the Agency made the hit, the first faction I mentioned was behind it."

"So you don't know whether the hit was done by the Agency?"

"No, I don't. The Deputy Director is upset. She went ballistic when she was informed of the killing. She wants answers yesterday and heads on platters by tomorrow. She has put out a cease and desist order against anyone going after Poirot. I sincerely don't think that Ms. Crow ordered the hit or knew anything concrete about it beforehand."

"Fair enough. What do you know about Poirot?"

"She's a fiction."

"What?"

"Her name comes from the female poet and the French detective. It's a pseudonym. Did Pinza tell you anything about her besides her being his protégé?"

"He said she was his lover."

"Hahaha. That's rich. If she was his lover, then it was incest. The woman is Enzio's daughter, Hyacinth. She was the first female sniper in the Afghan War. She was the model for a whole cadre of female snipers who came afterward."

"She must have been very young over there."

"Very. He lied about her age to get her in. Once she began to do her sniping, her shooting record made the case all by itself. The Agency spotted her early and picked her up for advanced training in a whole boatload of tradecraft. She became an ace female assassin. She then went rogue and set up on her own as a private contractor."

"Pinza seemed conflicted about his own daughter."

"Tell me more."

"He was trying to tell me that she was responsible for a series of long-shot killings that had been attributed to him. Imagine a man turning on his daughter like that."

"I don't think he was throwing her under the bus."

"What other motive would he have had?"

"He wanted you to be on her trail, gumshoe. Maybe that way if he took a bullet from the bozos in the faction that wanted him dead, she might have a protector. Congratulations to both of you for his being right."

"Tell me about the mysterious series of hits."

"Five years ago the DDO noticed a series of unsanctioned hits with the long-shot signature. The word "unsanctioned" means that no Presidential Finding authorizing the assassinations had been signed. For one reason or another, all the targets were known enemies of the USA but someone in power wanted them kept alive."

"So some person or entity was liquidating our enemies without sanction. So what?"

"Labyrinthine politics, John, combined with a penchant for control. Those who play assassination games don't want anyone to make the life or death decisions outside narrow confines. A known enemy spy may be useful even though he or she is costing US lives by trafficking intelligence. A known assassin may have been turned to go rogue against his or her fellow assassins. A bent politician might be blackmailed for small favors in some godforsaken shithole country. At one level, all the knowledge and the favors come together. The DDO goes for Findings all the time. One vote against on the FIAB, or on the Security Council, and the request is denied."

"Someone was taking care of business, and that someone was the subject of a Finding?"

"Close, but no cigar, pal. Whoever killed Pinza had no Presidential Finding."

"So one rogue takes out another?"

"Perhaps, but from another perspective, we may be dealing with the threat."

"Can you be more specific?"

"Let's say you were sitting in the wet ops section of a known threat nation. Further, let's say you know that the Agency is concerned about unsanctioned hits. What would you do to wreak havoc?"

"I'd orchestrate hits designed to turn the Agency inside out looking for rogues."

"Bingo. So I'm looking for the winners in this game. They are the most likely rotten apples. Every day I ask, 'Who has the most to gain from a certain rogue action?'"

"What patterns have emerged from that approach?"

"Just a second while I light my cigarette, that's better. I've a pattern that must have been apparent to Pinza as well. The key assassinations have been against difficult targets and could only have been accomplished by an exclusive group of shooters in the world."

"Enzio saw it that way also. He sounded like a conspiracy theorist."

"At the level we're considering, conspiracies really do exist."

"He told me that the pattern of the rogue, long-shot assassinations eliminated him and included Poirot absolutely."

"So the perpetrator used the general pattern to take out Pinza while ignoring the specific pattern that pointed to Poirot. Did he happen to mention whether Poirot had any equals or rivals?"

"He did not. In fact, he was so focused on her that I thought there was no one else in her league. Of course, he considered you were in his league, but she did things that even you would not have done."

"Such as?"

"Such as taking all her shots long. Such as overload her charges every time. Such as ..."

"I get it. By the same logic, an enemy sniper would want to keep his or her distance so as to be sure to escape after the shot. I wouldn't exclude a female shooter."

"Let's not get locked down into a single answer just yet. We don't know enough to do that."

"John, I know you like evidence. You like to connect everything so that no doubts remain before you pull the trigger. In Agency work we usually have to go with a lot less evidence and a lot more gut."

"That lays you wide open to subterfuge."

"And gives us more latitude for taking decisive actions."

"And more possibilities for being dead wrong."

"We are in complete agreement."

"Yes, Ken, about the boundaries, but not where we stand within them. We'll have to agree to disagree and still be friends. How does that sound?"

Mander smiled broadly and nodded. "John, when you get to Venezuela, watch your back. We have no idea whether Hyacinth is still alive. Her identity may have been assumed by someone else. If she is alive, she will suspect anyone approaching her to be in league with those who killed her father and mentor."

"Are we sure that she was not the shooter who eliminated her father?"

"No. Anything is possible."

"Do you have a list of Agency shooters who could have made the long shots you've been analyzing?"

"Pinza, Poirot and I were on that list. Crow would have made the list if she kept her quals up to date."

"And the opposition sharpshooters?"

"We have a list of five, three females and two males. I can email the names."

"What about others in outling states and stateless private contractors?"

"Two only. One is Brazilian, the other Moldovan. Both are females."

"Please email me details on them also if you can."

"If you run into trouble, just call me. I will try to help. Don't wait until you are in extremis. Again, use your gut and make the call even if you don't have all the data."

"Understood. Can you drop me back at Margaritas so I can drive home and get packed?"

"No problem. I must say that this Massachusetts landscape is brilliant this time of year."

"We were lucky not to have an early rain. Everything you see would have been brown and at the first cold snap, all the leaves would have fallen."

"One more thing I'll send you is a picture of Hyacinth. I warn you—she is a bombshell. She must take after her mother for looks. You'll be smitten if you find her."

"I'll find her."

"I hope you do, for both your sakes."

"Meaning what?"

"Meaning she needs your help for one. Meaning you need to find her before she puts you in her sights. She's lethal, and not only with the long shots."

"Her father's story bears that out."

"I won't bore you with her dossier because it's classified. She's as good as we get."

"Better than you?"

"Myself excluded, but she reminds me to keep in shape. It's a jungle out there, pal. Eat too much or drop your exercise routine for twenty-four hours, and you may find yourself dying."

"Hold on a minute. I've got a call from an unknown number. Hello, this is John Fulghum." The detective listened for a minute while the caller spoke.

"If you are who you say you are, you'll be able to tell me your first name. Thank you. I'll be flying tomorrow. Call me at four pm local time and we'll arrange to meet." Fulghum then terminated the call.

"That was Hyacinth. She wants to tell me who killed her father. The game's afoot."

"Yes, and we have complications already because you spoke over an uncovered, public channel."

"You said earlier that we had to go with our gut. Here we are. At least, I'll have dinner with a bombshell in vibrant Venezuela."

"Don't change your money. The Bolivar dollar won't buy its weight in toilet paper. By the way, take plenty of that along. Take a separate suitcase of it. You may find it's worth the effort."

As Mander drove, the spy and the detective had a lot of fun at the expense of the hopelessly socialist regime of Maduro and his Chavista cronies in Venezuela. Mander dropped Fulghum in the parking lot of Margarita's and then sped off on his other Agency business. Fulghum went shopping for toilet paper and visited his ATM for cash. His was not going to be a luxury tour, to say the least. Just before midnight, he received a call from Hyacinth Pinza informing him that she would meet him at the airport in Caracas. He would know her by the sign she sported just outside the baggage area.

Fulghum was used to international travel. His only objection was the no smoking rule. His flight was not unpleasant, but the airport was a madhouse of activity. Fulghum took the precaution of carrying his wallet in his front pants pocket to make pick-pocketing difficult. He snatched up his bag and looked around at the throng outside the baggage area. Near the back was a sign that rose above the rest with the word, "H'ya." The detective thrust his way through the press to the sign, which was held by a slender woman in a black pants suit, a black beret, and tinted aviator glasses. She said nothing but turned as he approached and walked towards the exit. He followed behind her across the causeway and into the parking garage. She climbed into the driver's side of a black Mercedes. He stowed his bag in the back seat and climbed into the passenger side.

"Hello, Mr. Fulghum, I'm Hyacinth Pinza, aka Adrienne Poirot." She took off her glasses and extended her manicured hand. She was a stunning beauty with sparkling blue eyes in a face that would launch a thousand ships. Her auburn hair was stylishly long. Around her neck was a green scarf over a solid gold necklace. Fulghum shook her hand.

"Please accept my deepest condolences on the death of your father."

"Thank you. Did you know him well?"

"We were acquainted in central Asia. He was in touch with me about clearing his name. We had lunch together just before he walked out of the restaurant into the bullet that killed him."

"We have a lot to discuss and little time. I'll show you the traffic jams of Caracas while we talk. If you want to smoke, go right ahead. If you smoke Marlboro reds, I'll join you."

Fulghum gave her a Marlboro and lit it. He then lit one for himself.

"I expect my father told you something about me or you wouldn't have known my name."

"Hyacinth, your father did not give away your real name. I don't think he would have done that, and you know it. He used the name Adrienne Poirot as if it were your real name and not a pseudonym. I learned your real name from a friend who works for the CIA. Don't worry. I'm not Agency. I'm not sure, though, about your status."

She took a long drag on her cigarette and exhaled before she nodded. "I was an agent once but decided to make my living on the outside as a private contractor."

"Your father gave me a business card, The Shooters' Society. That's how I found your website. You remember the question that I asked via the website?"

"Yes, and that is why you are here—to learn the answer. I don't know for certain who killed my father, but I have a few ideas. First, though, I need to know the business relationship between my father and you." She glanced at Fulghum with a raised eyebrow.

"None, I had not agreed to a client relationship before your father died. I was still trying to decide whether I could do anything to help."

"Would you accept me as your client?"

"I might. It would depend on whether I thought I could do anything constructive for you. What would you want me to do?" Fulghum was looking directly ahead at the colorful stream of automobiles and people as the Mercedes nosed through the crowds.

"I want you to answer the question that you asked me definitively. I want you to discover who killed my father. I'm offering to pay triple your normal hourly rate—whatever that is—plus expenses and a performance bonus."

"All in Bolivar dollars?"

"Hahaha. No. US dollars or Euros-your choice. If you give me the numbers for your account, I will deposit a retainer of ten thousand dollars there this evening."

"Tell me enough to give me a warm fuzzy feeling that I'll be able to deliver what you need."

"That will take time."

"I'll give as much time as it will take."

"I don't want to bore you by repeating what you already know. I assume my father told you about my work in Afghanistan."

"I know enough about that work. I was in that theater as well. What happened after that to connect you and your father to the Agency?"

"The CIA is jealous of anyone with world class skills, particularly with assassinations. After Dad's famous operation in Helmand, he was a celebrity. The Agency knew my secret role in that, so it approached us with a package deal, all or nothing. We were supposed to become agents with a limited purpose for the period of ten years with the option for another ten years after that. We were offered training and incentives. My father's training was refresher marksmanship only he became the teacher of the Agency's teachers instead. My training was more expansive. I was trained as an assassin. Does it surprise you that I would do that?"

"No, Hyacinth, it does not. You have all the advantages of being a woman in that role—if you don't mind the bloodshed. I deduce that you didn't mind that then. Since you are still in the game, I would guess that you don't mind it now."

The assassin nodded, a dark look coming over her eyes as she did so.

"I worked through my ten Agency years. Then I had the chance for another ten years or something on the outside. I talked the situation over with Dad. He suggested that the only viable alternative was going private. That's when he invented The Shooters' Society as a business to do contract killings. The Agency was not happy about that, but what could it do? Dad and I figured that the CIA would be our best customer. That was a good estimation—until I killed the man who made the Teheran long-shot. Do you know about that?"

"Your father told me his story about that, yes. I was curious about some of the details, but your having been CIA trained answers most of those. I'm more interested in what happened after you killed the sniper-assassin and his mistress on the Isla de Margarita. I have your father's version but I need to know how the events flowed from your perspective."

"Mr. Fulghum, my profession requires eternal vigilance. Customers can become enemies overnight. I don't get contracts for easy kills. Most of my contracts come with hidden strings attached, sometimes political strings. My work on the island had the disadvantage that people who ordered the hit wanted me dead. Instead of cooperating, I killed everyone who was sent after me including my former customer. The fact that they were Agency crossed my mind, but my motive was survival. I did what I had to do, and I survived."

"Brava. Did that solve your problems, or did it open new problems?" Fulghum chain lit two cigarettes and handed one to her. He patiently waited for her to respond.

"From the start of our private company, our relationship with the Agency was ambivalent. We were considered useful rogues, but we were also expendable. They could terminate one or both of us with extreme prejudice at any time. We knew that."

"Why would your father tell me that he was the CIA's prime suspect in a string of assassinations done all over the world?"

"One reason is that any assassination not ordered by the Agency has to be attributed to someone. He was a convenient patsy."

"Then your father told me that you, not he, had done those assassinations. Why would he have done that?"

"I really don't know, Mr. Fulghum. My father never worked against me. I'm not sure I believe that he said what you claim." She seemed a little nervous and edgy when she said this. Her eyes narrowed somewhat as if she mistrusted Fulghum now.

"My thought was that your father knew he was being targeted. He wanted to protect you so he did two things to bring us together. He gave me your company's business card. He told me things that made me curious about you. Maybe he thought I could help protect you from the forces that were trying to destroy you both."

"Well, you're here—and you came paying your own way. Did you come expecting me to hire you? Did you come to see the curiosity that my father described? Why did you come here, Mr. Fulghum?" Hyacinth laid things right on the line, as she looked right at Fulghum accusatorily.

"It's an old-fashioned notion, but your father and I both did covert work in a war zone. He was killed in a new secret war, and I was left with some of his mysteries, including you. I did not make a decision about helping him when he was alive, but his death made my decision for me. I called a friend for clarifications, and that's how I found out who you really were. I did some research in open sources. My query through your website was intuitive. Your response brought me here, but I already had purchased the one-way ticket. I suppose, if you had not responded, I might have canceled my ticket. So why did you respond at all?"

"You are a detective, Mr. Fulghum. I fear you have the curiosity disease. I know the symptoms because I have that disease as well. Your question made me curious about you. I thought for a while about your query. I responded because we were asking the same question. I thought our having a talk would clarify whether we could work together on an answer."

"Give me your analysis of why your father was killed."

"Dad received warnings about a contract on the lives of a whole slate of national assets. The names and addresses of older heroes had been posted on the Internet. His name was among them. Dad's Agency friends told him that once a name was made public, it could be targeted by anyone. So the clock was ticking, and eventually, someone would take the fatal shot."

"Tell me about the slate of national assets on the web."

"That's old news now, but it was posted by ISIS as an open threat. It was like a fatwa, a religious order to the so-called faithful. Once it had been posted, though, all the names were at risk from almost every conceivable direction. Old scores that needed settling, that sort of thing. Dad said that all his old enemies would have a field day. He called it a turkey shoot. I disagreed because, at a turkey shoot, you win the turkey for shooting at some other target. My observation doesn't seem very clever right now."

"It may be cleverer than you think. What if your father was killed as a message to someone?"

"Mr. Fulghum, you aren't thinking like an ordinary detective."

"That's not the first time I've been told that. Listen. Did your father tell you who his mortal enemies were?"

"We talked about that. Yes. Dad said those closest to him were most suspect. You know the motto on the back of our business card. That's what he meant. He said the Agency would protect him. They seem to have failed to do that."

"I've been told an Agency team was working on his protection. Yes, they failed."

"But did they kill him?"

"The Agency has many faces. One faction evidently wanted both you and your father dead. My contact told me that the Agency had no sanction to kill your father."

"Hahaha. No sanction. Well, that means nothing to me, because my father and I rarely had sanction for our assassinations. Of course, a hit on either of us would not need to be sanctioned."

"Did your father mention anyone in the Agency by name as an enemy?"

"His worst enemy was an old agent whose work name was Brutus Higard. He hated my father from way back. I don't know the root of their enmity. Higard was deeply involved in black ops. He was an operator, not a desk man. He loved the shadows."

"You talk as if the man was dead."

"He disappeared and is presumed dead. I just don't know. Aside from him, we have the usual suspects."

"What do you mean by that?"

"Wannabes and shoulda coulda woulda's. Everyone who was jealous. Those who could not compete on the same level."

"They will always be with us, but they don't usually kill their betters."

"So the long list would include Islamists who would want revenge for Dad's kill record, one possibly dead Agency man with a grudge, and everyone wanting to kill a US national asset on a posted list. That leaves out the wild cards."

"Like, perhaps, a coincidental killing. It was deer season, after all, when he was slain. Maybe a stray shot killed him."

"Yes, and suicide. Such highly unlikely scenarios are not worth entertaining." She shook her head and reached for another cigarette. He chain lit one for her, and she took a long drag.

"I don't believe in eliminating possibilities out of hand, but I'll agree that a coincidental killing or suicide is unlikely. Was there anything in your private work that might have led to a contract for your father's death?"

"As I implied before, everything about our contract work put us at risk. We tried to keep our work secret, but our customers knew what we were doing. They wrote the agreements and sent the money to our numbered accounts. How could they not know? I was targeted for death, but I was lucky enough to kill my would-be assailants. I lost a customer."

"Some customer. Hyacinth, did you have the impression that your customer was working alone? I mean, did he seem to be working for someone else for whom he was a subcontractor?"

"If Dad told you the story, you know already that my customer was female, not male. She might have been a cut-out. I didn't have any indication of that."

"After you killed her and the others, were you pursued?"

"I took precautions not to return to my place in the US. I took a clandestine route to Venezuela. Since I've been here, I haven't been threatened."

"Could your father have been killed to settle a score with you?"

"I see what you mean. Of course, that might have happened. They may have killed him because they could not kill me."

"Maybe they could drive you out of hiding by killing your father?"

"That's highly unlikely."

"Did you know all the assassination work your father was doing?"

"What are you driving at?"

"Let's suppose your father wanted to be sure that the people who tried to assassinate you were all terminated. He knew what you had done. What if he discovered that others were involved in that plan?"

"He would have killed anyone who tried to kill me. I would have done the same to anyone who tried to kill him."

"It would benefit whoever killed your father to have you hunt the hired gun so he or she could kill you in the attempt."

"Am I supposed to sit idly by on my island cowering in fear?"

"You wouldn't do that, but you wouldn't run headlong into danger either."

"You're right. I'd need a spotter like you to identify my prey. Then I'd be able to take revenge. So will you work for me to help me get revenge?"

"I'll work with you to identify the killer of your father. If I do that, what happens afterward is up to you. If you can live with that, I'll work under the terms you mentioned earlier."

Hyacinth looked at Fulghum and then extended her right hand. He shook it. They had a deal. Their conversation turned to address what was happening in the tumultuous world of Venezuelan politics, and the frightful economic situation that hyperinflation brought to the country. Fulghum mentioned he had brought extra rolls of toilet paper with him. The woman laughed out loud when he said he'd share some with her. He was serious, and she accepted his gift. Now that they had a deal, Fulghum told Hyacinth he wanted to take the earliest flight back to the States.

"We'll book two rooms at the airport hotel and have some dinner together. I'll make the money transfer for your retainer. You can fly home tomorrow morning."

"That sounds like a plan. Hyacinth, are the streets here always this crowded?"

"You call this crowded? You should be here during the festivals or demonstrations. The whole city seems to be one large press of people and vehicles. It's always colorful and full of life." She shook her auburn hair and laughed.

"Yes, and I've read the murder rate is climbing," Fulghum countered grimly.

"It is. Pretty soon assassinations will be so cheap we professionals will be out of business."

"Somehow I don't think so. Was it Juvenal who said that no one dies of natural causes anymore?"

"As it was in old Rome, so it is in every city in the world today."

"Hyacinth, have you ever considered finding the perfect man and settling down, perhaps raising a family. You would make beautiful children."

"You're talking like my father now. Actually, I've found very few men attractive in that way. I'm almost forty years old. I'm used to the single life. Imagine me as a married woman telling my stay-at-home husband that I'm going out for a week on a murderous escapade. Somehow I can't picture that working out very well."

"At the risk of sounding like your father, you are a beautiful woman. You are spirited, independent and intelligent. You'd make someone a tremendous match if he were worthy of you."

"Is this a proposal of marriage, Mr. Fulghum?"

"No, Hyacinth, it is not. We're booking two rooms at the hotel so there will be no ambiguity."

"I've learned that it is best not to mix business and pleasure."

"Did you learn that from your mother?"

"My mother died when I was fourteen, Mr. Fulghum. I wasn't the ideal daughter for her. After she had passed, my father raised me as if I were his only son. I became his protégé." She said this proudly and wistfully at the same time.

"I'd like to return to this person Brutus Higard. Can you tell me any more about him than you already have?"

"I can send you a picture. I can tell you he was left-handed, like me. I can say that when he was in a room at the Agency, everyone avoided him because he was always in such a foul mood. He barked at people who spoke to him. He was always spring loaded for violence. I heard rumors that he liked to lure agents into friendly fire positions. He was a viper in the nest. I don't know why they kept him in the Agency. I'm very glad they never put him in charge of teams. He was an operator and a loner. At last report, he was working in Dar es, Salaam. That was three years ago."

That evening after checking into their separate rooms and refreshing themselves, the assassin and the detective enjoyed a sumptuous meal at the hotel restaurant followed by the brown nectar of Jack Daniels whiskey, coincidentally their favorite drink. Fulghum found Hyacinth's company enchanting. He also discovered that she was a shrewd businesswoman who wanted weekly reports on his progress with expenses itemized. She told him that he would get a large bonus for earlier deliverables and that their contract would terminate in one month whether he delivered the name of her father's killer or not. Fulghum liked decisiveness, and he sensed that this woman knew the value of a handshake.

The best thing about the woman from Fulghum's perspective was her lifelong interest in horseracing. She still placed off-track bets, and she was current on the bloodlines of the frontrunners. Fulghum, himself an expert in this arena, took a few notes on what she said. She did the same when he mentioned his favorite sugar foot and the new Kentucky breeding stables built by the sheik of Dubai. When dinner was over, Hyacinth told Fulghum she would not see him again before his departure. She also said she would email him the picture of agent Brutus Higard as soon as she arrived back on the Isla de Margarita. Fulghum went to his room and fetched the toilet paper he had promised her. She laughed but accepted his gift. They went to their separate rooms, and Fulghum slept soundly. The next morning, he climbed aboard his scheduled flight to Boston.

At Logan International, Fulghum texted Ken Mander that he was back from his trip and desirous of talking about a shadowy operator whose name and picture would be provided shortly. By the time the detective had reached his office, he had received the promised picture of Brutus Higard as an attachment to an email from Hyacinth. He forwarded the email to Ken Mander. While he awaited the CIA agent's response, Fulghum worked hard on the racing forms to see whether he could profitably use the gleanings from his discussion with the assassin. Not able to find the bets he wanted, he decided to visit the Barnes and Noble computers to surf the Internet about Dar es, Salaam, before he went home to bed. He found the Tanzanian city fascinating and exotic, but he did not have a context by which he could place Brutus Higard in the picture. Mander called to say that he was waiting outside Fulghum's office. He asked the detective to pick up a couple of Dunkin' Donuts regular coffees on his return.

Mander and Fulghum enjoyed their coffees with cigarettes while the detective brought the agent up to date on his discussions with his new client. He focused specifically on Agent Brutus Higard.

"What can you tell me about this pseudonymous agent?"

"There's not much anyone can tell you. His records are Director's-Eyes-Only. Your picture is the only one I've seen, and it may be classified for all I know."

"Do you know whether he is alive? Is he still with the Agency? Do you know whether he is still in Dar es Salaam?"

"Whoa! I'm telling you this man does not exist. If he existed—and I'm not saying he ever did—his work is so secret that no one in the Agency who knew could ever say what it was."

"That's a spooky thought."

"Literally as well as figuratively."

"So let's cut through the bullshit, shall we? You know the work name Brutus Higard—true or false?"

"True. When I searched the Company databases, I received a special window warning about searching any further. I was referred not just to the Seventh Floor but, to the Director himself for any further questions. I was advised in a blurb that a note would be made of my search and forwarded to the Director."

"So we touched a live wire."

"There's more. I had our facial recognition people search our imagery archives for a match. Guess what turned up?"

"The same message as for the name."

"That's right. I put no metadata with the picture, so the correlation was made by the search routine. So, my having twice pulled a forbidden subject will earn me a trip to the Director's office and a warning. Thanks a lot, pal."

"Sorry about that, but I'm going to pursue this matter. Will you be able to help at all?"

"I've already sent the picture to the team that is working on Pinza's murder. I ordered them to add the picture—without adding a name—to the suspect list."

"Tell me - is the relationship of the Agency to the police so cozy that the name and picture will be guarded similarly in all the databases?"

"That's an interesting question. I'd have to guess that with a query that hits any associated data, you would get a null return. For any data that has not been integrated, you might get a hit."

"That gives me one idea. Now we need to talk for a moment about Dar es Salaam."

"What's the angle?"

"That's the last known location for this shadowy figure Brutus Higard."

"The details are classified, John, but nearly everyone knows the importance of Tanzania for our counter-terrorism operations worldwide. Any agents working there are likely to be deeply involved in those operations."

"Naturally, those would include wet operations?"

"Naturally. I would say that Brutus Higard—if he existed—would have been or would be a tough assassin, probably working clandestinely and reporting directly to the Director. The DDO has no knowledge of the name or the picture. I know this because I asked her outside the normal channels. She would not lie to me."

"Unless I can connect a few details, I'm going to be stuck going in circles for a few days while I gather wool."

"I'll check a few other angles for you. I take it you like Hyacinth?"

"She's quite a woman. I do like her a lot. She likes Jack Daniels and playing the horses."

"Are you hooked?"

"Our relationship is purely professional and confirmed with a handshake. We have a rule—no fraternizing."

"That's a shame. There was a day when I'd have gone for the gold with her."

"She's still available, Ken. And she is one beautiful, smart and savvy lady."

"If I did not have another long-term relationship, I'd be sorely tempted, John. As it is, I'll try to help you both. Enzio Pinza was a trusted colleague and friend. I owe it to his memory to find his killer."

"No matter where the quest takes you?"

"We shall see about that. I'll get you as much as I can about Tanzania without breaking all the rules."

"Thanks, Ken, and I'll be talking with our friend Officer Pounce of Boston Homicide. Maybe the police side can provide what has been shuttered within the Agency."

"Share what you find, please, John. I'll do the same."

The two friends decided to have three fingers of Jack Daniels to toast the success of their quest. Then Mander went back to his official work and Fulghum went home to bed. The detective tossed and turned all night thinking how the traces of an erased man could be found in the myriad of collections that were amassed hourly around the world. He wondered, *Could computers have eradicated all traces of Brutus Higard? As a betting man, I'd lay money against that.*

Officer Pounce arrived in Fulghum's office early the next morning on police business. Fulghum was just about to call him when he knocked on the detective's door.

"John, I'm sorry I didn't call you first, but I'm under the gun at the station and I couldn't risk being in touch about an active case."

"I presume you mean the killing of Enzio Pinza?"

"Yes. How did you guess?"

"I had finished lunch with Pinza at Dalia's minutes before he went out to receive the bullet to his brain."

"No shit! Did you make a statement?"

"I was in the john at the time of the hit. By the time I went into the sunlight, the emergency vehicles had arrived and the police had the area cordoned off. At the time, I had nothing of substance to contribute."

"I'm having a lot of trouble with this case. Everywhere I turn, I hit brick walls. The Agency is all over me trying to glean my data without giving me anything in return. The man was a war hero, but he was also an enigma. He was an Agency man once upon a time, but he was a freelancer at the time of his death. His next of kin cannot be found. We know nothing about the circumstances of his life or his work. To top it all off, the police chief wants a prime suspect yesterday and the D.A. is being inundated with a plethora of irrelevant data. You wouldn't believe the crackpots lining up to claim they took out the Afghanistan sniper with a taste of his own medicine."

"I know how you feel. How about a couple of fingers of Jack Daniels?"

"John, it's much too early for me. I just dropped by to see whether you could help with this Pinza case."

"As a matter of fact, you've come just in time. I'm on the case for a client, the deceased man's daughter. I also have a prime suspect for you, but you'll have to handle the data carefully since it's sensitive. I received a picture and a name of the one known mortal enemy from the daughter. He may have killed Pinza. He may have ordered Pinza killed. If we can find any evidence that the man was in the Greater Boston area at the time of the assassination, we have most of the mystery solved. I'm forwarding the data to your email now."

"John, this is great news."

"It would be if the Agency were not desperate to keep this man under wraps. He is the epitome of a secret agent. My question to you is this—can you run the picture without the name through your databases of facial images throughout New England for any possible hits within three days either side of the murder?"

"I can do that."

"Can you do it without arousing the suspicion of the Agency?"

"That might be difficult."

"What would make it easier?"

"We could give the image a metadata descriptor with little interest to the Agency. For example, 'sex offender.'"

"Perfect. When will you have results?"

"If I get right back to the station to order the search, by mid-afternoon at the earliest."

"I'll ride with you and fill you in on the daughter and the victim as best I can what with client privilege. I'll take a cab back from the station."

"Don't worry about your return trip. I'll have a black and white bring you back here."

"That's what I call service. I hope the family is well."

"Couldn't be better. Let's go."

Fulghum told Officer Pounce what he needed to know on the drive to the station. Then Pounce asked Officer Clancy to drop the detective off at Joe's Malt Shop. Clancy knew Fulghum from other cases and liked the horses as much as Fulghum did, so they shared tips on the way back. Fulghum invited Clancy up to discuss some of the racing forms, but the officer got an all call radio message. Clancy took a rain check, and Fulghum told him Jack Daniels would be present at their future meeting.

Late that afternoon Fulghum was smoking a Marlboro and scanning his racing forms when a harried Pounce visited his office.

"I just dropped by to give you a quick update. My people found six hits on the photo you provided with 98% validity. They found numerous other hits with partials. The man was definitely in the area during the time interval you suggested. We can put him on Route 4 within fifteen minutes of the murder. In fact, we can put him here in Boston as of yesterday afternoon. John, he may still be in the area."

"I recommend you apprehend him as a person of interest rather than a suspect at this stage. Assume he is dangerous whether armed or not. He may throw up smoke and get the Agency involved. In that case, all bets are off. Is there any way you can hold him without his having a chance at a phone call?"

"No can do, John."

"Well, do what you have to. I've got to make a call. Thanks for the information. We may be close to a solution. Let's not have it slip through our fingers."

Officer Pounce bounded down the stairs two at a time. Fulghum texted Mander about the presence of Brutus Higard in the Boston area.

He then called Hyacinth and left a message on her cell phone voicemail. "Hyacinth, this is Fulghum. The man in your picture was in the Boston area at the time of your father's murder. He is still in the area now. Please call when you've heard this message."

As an afterthought, the detective called Officer Pounce and asked the last known position of the man in the picture. Pounce told him the man was photographed walking the diagonal path across the Boston Common. On a hunch, Fulghum ran down to his car and drove to the Common. He searched the whole area. Not finding Brutus Higard, he sat on a park bench and surveyed the colorful scene before him. It stood in stark contrast to what he had seen in Caracas. Boston was a civilized, well-to-do city with a genteel populace. It treated all people with the same warmth and humanity. It was open to a fault and, as major metropolitan areas go, friendly.

While he sat on the bench, his first caller was Hyacinth.

"Mr. Fulghum, what is the situation?"

"Hi, Hyacinth, police imagery shows that the man shown in your picture was in the Boston area during the time of the murder. In fact, he was photographed on the same highway that runs by the restaurant within fifteen minutes of the shooting. That man was still in the area as of yesterday. I'm now sitting on a park bench within twenty yards of where he was photographed walking. The police are now in the process of apprehending the man as a person of interest in the murder."

"I see. I don't have to remind you of the lethality of this man. He is also well connected in the Agency. Be careful in any event."

"Where are you now?"

"I'm on the island waiting for news."

"I'll call when I have more for you." Fulghum terminated the call and went back to watching the people on the Common.

The second call he received as soon as he hung up on Hyacinth was from Ken Mander.

"We're putting a team on the ground in Boston as we speak. We're going to try to pick up our man before the police apprehend him." Mander's voice sounded urgent and strained.

"Ken—the police are expediting this matter. You may not be in time. What we don't want is a shootout between the police and the Agency."

"Relax, pal. We know what we're doing. By the way, somehow the Agency knows that the man who doesn't exist is in the Greater Boston area. In some quarters, folks are going ballistic. The DDO is personally involved. Expect a denouement imminently. Later." With that, Mander terminated the call.

With the police and the Agency in pursuit of Brutus Higard, Fulghum began to wonder what he was doing sitting in Boston Common. He had no evidence that, aside from one cameo appearance, the man was a regular ambulatory citizen here. Fulghum ran his eyes over the many people who surrounded him. He focused on one person in particular, an apparently elderly man, bent over with age and perhaps homeless with a large, clear plastic bag over his shoulder. The bag was full of collected bottles and cans. The detective was fascinated by the contradictions in the figure. The brand new Adidas on his feet were worth two hundred dollars. The walking stick he leaned on was high tech. While he observed, the man straightened up and seemed to be getting his bearings. He was now not hunched over at all. He was scanning the area with keen interest. He focused on Fulghum with intensity. The detective was now fully alert. He stood up at the park bench and stretched while keeping the man under observation. He then walked across the lawn, avoiding the paved walk on which the man stood.

The man's eyes followed the detective. Then he moved much too quickly for the ancient pedestrian he appeared to be. His bag with the bottles and cans hit the walk and spilled its contents in all directions. The man raised his walking stick from the ground and began to direct it towards Fulghum. The detective began moving swiftly, executing a forward shoulder roll and landing in a crouched position behind the shrubbery. He saw the man's eyes scanning as he came forward with his stick pointed towards the bushes. A policeman had taken notice of the littering, and he was advancing towards the old man from his rear. He called out, and the man turned and dropped his staff. Fulghum saw his opportunity and arose. He ran straight at the man and tackled him causing his staff to fly from his hand. The man was extraordinarily strong and tried to throw Fulghum off, but the detective held on, slipped his arms through the man's arms and locked them behind the man's head. The policeman was confused by what he saw. With his weapon drawn, he ordered Fulghum and the man to stop fighting and lie down on the ground.

"Officer, I am Detective John Fulghum. Officer Nigel Pounce of Homicide will vouch for me. This man is a person of interest in the murder that was committed on Route 4 in Bedford a few days ago. He is dangerous. If I let him go, I can't be responsible for what happens next."

"Stay where you are while I call this in." Apparently, the name Nigel Pounce carried weight among the Boston Police. "Did you say your name was John Fulghum?"

'That's right. The person I'm detaining here goes by the name Brutus Higard. He is a known assassin."

The patrolman was now in contact with his station. "Officer Riley, this is Patrolman Jones in Boston Common. I have a man who says he is John Fulghum, a detective. He is restraining an older person he says is an assassin. Request instructions." The radio was silent while the watch personnel digested what they had heard. Finally, the return radio keyed.

"Jones, please assist Fulghum in every way possible. A team is on the way. Do not—repeat, do not—let the man Fulghum is restraining escape."

Patrolman Jones examined the intertwined bodies and determined that the only help he could render was to handcuff the old man to himself. There the three men stood in a strange tableau, the policeman handcuffed to the assassin and the detective set with a double arm lock around the assassin's back. The policeman had the presence of mind to order the people in the Common to stand clear and proceed with their business.

Fulghum and the assassin said nothing. Finally, the six-person police team arrived in a wagon. Three policemen grabbed the free arm and two legs of the assassin. Then, carefully Fulghum released his grip. That was the chance for the assassin to make his move.

In a flash, he tore away from the three new arrivals and jerked so hard on the handcuffs that Jones's arm snapped. Like a wild beast, he spun around looking for an escape path, but now all the police team surrounded him with weapons drawn. One policeman raised a tranquilizer gun and shot the man in the chest. He writhed and went down. Then the police placed restraints on him and went to fetch a gurney from their wagon. They secured the man to their gurney after which Patrolman Jones took his handcuffs off the man's wrist and gingerly nursed his broken arm. The police team rolled the gurney to the open van, inserted it and locked it down.

Fulghum shook his arms and moved his neck from side to side. He then walked over to the assassin's staff that lay on the ground. He took out his handkerchief, picked up the staff with it and examined the high-tech implement carefully. He nodded and took it over to the police team.

"Take this along, but handle it with care for the chain of custody. It may be a murder weapon."

"Sir, we'll need your statement."

"Why don't we use the recorder? I'll be glad to sign the transcription at the station later."

Fulghum's statement was short and succinct. He said he was sitting on a park bench in Boston Common when he observed a man who looked out of place. The man transformed before his eyes from a homeless man into an assassin whose picture he had been shown in confidence. The man advanced to attack him, but he evaded the attack. Fortunately, the alert response of Patrolman Jones helped him restrain the assassin until the police team arrived to take custody of the man. The staff that the assassin used was some kind of weapon. He had given it to the arresting team for strict custody as evidence. Fulghum gave his name, profession, and permit number.

That statement satisfied the arresting officers, who drove off with their prisoner. Fulghum observed that the litter was being picked over by real homeless wanderers now. One was shoving another to grab a pristine Coke can. Fulghum had seen enough on the Common for one day. He went to his car and drove to the sanctity of his grimy second-story office to make a few calls on his cell phone.

To Mander's voicemail he said, "Ken, this is John. The police have custody of the man called Brutus Higard. I'll fill you in on the details later."

To Ms. Pinza's voicemail, he said, "Hyacinth this is Fulghum. We have the man in your picture in custody. I'll let you know how things go, but I'm going to guess that the clock stops here for my services. I'll send you a bill via email."

To Officer Pounce's voicemail, he said, "Nigel this is John, the police did commendable work today in Boston Common. I think the murderer of Enzio Pinza may be in your capable hands. I'll drop by the station to sign my statement. If you can manage it, a letter of commendation should be given to Patrolman Jones, who was the arresting officer injured by the prisoner in an attempt to escape."

Fulghum then took out a Marlboro and lit it. He sat back in the late afternoon light streaming through the grimy window high up on the wall behind his desk. He watched the smoke curl up into the orange light. He thought about the hunch that had placed him in the Common. He had no idea why the assassin had remained in the area after the murder. He had no clear idea why the assassin took an interest in him. While a thousand thoughts coursed through his fertile mind, the return calls came in order. Rather than answering the calls, he allowed them to be recorded on his voicemail.

"John, this is Ken. Thanks for the word. Good work. Later."

"Mr. Fulghum, you earned the highest bonus. Congratulations. Thanks again for helping and for your priceless gift. Goodbye." He could envision her expression while saying the words in her husky voice. She was not surprised at the outcome or the speed with which he had delivered on his promise. She was talking as one world-class expert to another. Fulghum thought he might have to fly another shipment of toilet paper to Venezuela when the dust settled on this case.

"Detective Fulghum, I'll drop by for an urgent meeting with you and Jack Daniels. You saved my ass today, friend. Don't try to escape. The fun has only just begun."

The detective had a flash of insight, and he scrambled to find the connecting reference in his racing forms. Memory had served him well, for there she was, listed as Hyacinth Rose. She was great horseflesh and a worthy bet to show in Saturday's races. He felt that his discovery was worth a celebration.

He lifted his bottle of Jack Daniels whiskey from the second drawer to the right of his desk. He took out two dusty glasses as well and polished them with his handkerchief. He set the bottle and the two glasses on the desk's surface. Into one of the glasses, he poured three fingers of the brown, viscous elixir of the gods.

He raised a silent toast to his client Hyacinth Pinza as he had done at the hotel restaurant in Venezuela. He drank, savoring the heady flavor all the way down. He left the second glass empty for now in its place. Officer Nigel Pounce would receive Jack Daniels' largesse when he came to the office later after his overly long workday.

"What are friends for?" he asked his friend Jack Daniels out loud. "We've been together all these years. Why, you even came to my meeting in Venezuela, you old dog. She was beautiful, wasn't she? Yes, sir. The sparkle in her eyes was worth the whole damn trip."

Headshots III

Officer Nigel Pounce of Boston Homicide informed his friend John Fulghum, PI, that the Boston Police Department freed the CIA assassin whose work name was Brutus Higard. His release from police custody was accomplished on the grounds of critical national security issues raised by the Director of the Central Intelligence Agency with the Governor of Massachusetts and the Mayor of Boston. Fulghum was outraged because the high tech staff that Higard was carrying at the time of his apprehension turned out to be the weapon used to kill Enzio Pinza in the parking lot of Dalia's Restaurant on Route 4 in Bedford.

The detective telephoned his former client Hyacinth Pinza, daughter of his deceased friend and former warrior, with the latest news.

"Hyacinth, Brutus Higard has been released from jail. I'm very sorry to have to tell you this. There was nothing the police could do but free Higard. Their case against him was airtight on forensic grounds alone. However, as we suspected, the powers that be claimed there were national security issues at risk. All that evidence means nothing now since your father's case has gone cold."

"It means something to me, Mr. Fulghum. Now that I have the facts, I can work independently to terminate this man. Again, I thank you for all that you've done. It's up to me to finish the job of revenge."

"I have heard from a reliable source within the Agency that the CIA is planning independent action to take care of your problem."

"I've heard all that before. In my experience what you do yourself is always more efficient and reliable than anything systems and organizations can do at their best. Goodbye, for now, I'll call if I need your services further."

"Good hunting, Hyacinth. Goodbye."

Fulghum terminated the call and immediately phoned his friend Agent Kenneth Mander of the CIA. The agent was almost always unavailable, so the detective left a voicemail message. "Ken, this is John, Hyacinth is going hunting. Please call me when you can."

Of the many scenarios that John Fulghum played out in his mind, the most attractive from his point of view was Brutus Higard coming to kill him. The prospect of killing the monster in self-defense appealed to the detective's sense of justice.

In all likelihood, though, if he designed a kill, Higard would take a long-shot approach and leave the detective's atomized head as his signature. Fulghum knew that he did not have a chance against a trained professional CIA assassin with a long rifle. He had been lucky on Boston Common to recognize the man through his disguise and help bring him down. The more he replayed the critical events of that day, the more he became convinced Higard's intention was to kill him. He was still unsure how Higard had recognized him as a mortal threat.

Fulghum chain smoked his Marlboros and wondered, "Did someone in the CIA tell Higard I was pursuing him? Had someone shown him a recent picture of me? Was a third party in the Common spotting me for Higard?" The detective was convinced that no one could have predicted his movements on that day. He had acted spontaneously. He had told no one where he was going when he left his office and did not know what he intended to do when he got to the Common. Pure instinct drove him to the place. Chance put him on the park bench from which he identified Higard. He made the identification by rapid ratiocination. His brain, not technology, made the identification possible. Intuitive integration had caused him to evade the assassin rather than to rush him when he raised the staff in his direction.

It was highly unlikely he would ever know what was going through Higard's mind that day. Fulghum thought it was equally unlikely that he would know what was going through his own mind. His actions just seemed to be good ideas at the time. They had served his tactical purposes, but a deus ex machina had intervened at the strategic level. The detective wondered aloud, "What hold on the Director of the CIA could a man like Higard have?" He resolved he would never have the need to know to discover the answer. The sound of his cell phone ring tone broke his chain of thought.

"John, it's Ken. You rang?"

"The prisoner has been released. We're almost back to the starting gate."

"How so?"

"We have forensic evidence that Higard killed Pinza. We have the motive, the placement, and the murder weapon. All those things came together because of my talk with the victim's daughter in Venezuela. She's satisfied I've identified the man who killed her father. You don't have to have a vivid imagination to foresee what comes next."

"We're working the situation, John. We're gaming the scenarios. Our problem is we have so many possibilities."

"You'd have no problem if the man was dead. Do you have any idea why the Seventh Floor of your organization's headquarters at Langley is enamored enough of this fiend to have set him free?"

"I only know the bastard has cards we can't see from our vantage. I've been over this ground with the DDO. The Director has stonewalled her and forbidden anyone's access to the archived, his-eyes-only files. To breach that protocol means an instant, sanctioned death sentence."

"That would have to mean that favors go higher than the Director."

"To obtain an assured Presidential Finding, yes it would mean that."

"And if a rogue or private contractor should take the monster down?"

"Good riddance to Higard, woe to the rogue. Killing him is a no win for the shooter."

"This man will continue to kill until he dies. Until then he can kill anyone he wants with impunity."

"That's precisely someone's intention."

"The man was raising his weapon to kill me right on the Common in broad daylight. Do you know who might have spotted me for him?"

"I've no idea about that, John. I didn't know you were going fishing in the park. None of my team knew anything about it. We were off searching in other pastures. You got lucky."

"Yes, I got lucky—in more ways than one. While you keep nosing around inside the Agency, please let me know if anything useful turns up."

"I thought your work on this was over."

"Officially, it is. I no longer have a client because I delivered her a definitive answer."

"So you're bound and determined to keep hunting without a client?"

"For me, it's now a matter of self-preservation. The man tried to kill me once. Chances are he'll try again. If it comes down to him against me, I want to have an edge. All of your confusing Agency protocols don't mean a thing to me. If I see a man coming to kill me, I won't stop to think of hurting some desk jockey's feelings. I'll just kill the bastard. The police will be on my side after the fact."

"Be careful, friend. 'There are more things in heaven and earth, than are dreamt of in your philosophy.'"

"Goodnight, sweet Prince."

"I'm not dead yet, shamus. I hope you aren't brain-dead yet either."

"We'll see how it goes. In any event, Jack Daniels is waiting here for you whenever."

"Tempting, John, but another game's afoot. The Company never sleeps. I gotta go. Talk with you later." The CIA agent terminated the call and left John Fulghum to ruminate on the little he had just learned. The detective lit another cigarette. His cell phone rang, but he let the caller go to voicemail rather than answering. He heard a mature female voice in a Boston accent that sounded under stress.

"Mr. Fulghum, this is Darcy Figlear, I'm an investigative reporter for the Boston Globe. I need to talk with you right away. It's urgent. It's about a murder. Please call me to arrange an appointment in your office."

Though Fulghum wanted to stay focused on the Pinza case and he normally did not entertain reporters, he was a professional. Perhaps, he thought, he could refer the woman to another private investigator. He returned the call but was redirected straight to the woman's voicemail.

"This is John Fulghum answering your call. My hours are seven am until seven pm weekdays and weekends by appointment. I'm extremely busy now, but I might be able to refer you to another private detective if you require instant service. You know where to call me." He wondered how many phone conversations were held with voicemail messages serving as filters.

Having satisfied his professional duty to respond to the call, Fulghum vainly tried to return to thinking about the Pinza case. Frustrated, he decided to tidy up the heaps of racing forms that lined the left wall of his office. He chain-smoked while he culled and straightened his stacks. He heard steps ascending the stairwell then a knock on his door.

Ordinarily he would have called out to his visitor to turn the knob and enter, but this time, he went to the door and opened it. There stood a young geeky twenty-something girl with braids and granny glasses holding a spiral notepad in one hand and a cell phone in the other. She put the cell phone in her coat pocket and stuck out her hand.

"Mr. Fulghum, I'm Darcy Figlear of the Boston Globe. I left a message on your voicemail earlier today. Since I was in the vicinity, I thought I'd drop by to see if you were available. Do you have time to talk with me about the release of the assassin Mr. Brutus Higard from jail?" The woman seemed so earnest and innocent. Fulghum did not summarily tell her to take a hike.

"Do you smoke?"

"No, if you mean pot. Yes, if you mean Marlboros. Do you mind if I come in and join you for a smoke? Golly, your office is messy. Can I sit in this chair?" She pointed to the captain's chair Fulghum reserved for potential clients and real friends.

"Darcy, be my guest. Have a cigarette. Make yourself at home. It's the maid's day off and coincidentally the receptionist's day off too so we are on our own. Do you mind if I close the door for privacy's sake? No? Well, I'll close it just the same." He closed the door and retreated behind his desk while she lit a cigarette.

"Let me guess. You were born in Boston. You attended Radcliffe on early admittance. You are a fan of Thirties movies about fast-talking female reporters. You wear those goggles because you don't care if men find you brainy. You carry that top-bound spiral notebook to make people think you need reminders when you have a phonographic and photographic memory. You smoke because you're bored silly when you aren't thinking at the speed of light. Oh, yes, you wear your nouveau geek outfit as a flag of your independence. Did I get any of that right?"

"Sylvia told me you'd be like this, but I'll not play a role reversal. Why don't you bring out your friend from the second drawer on the left and two glasses? Pour us each three fingers so we can confab though I'll settle for the beverage without the food, thank you. We'll chain light your Marlboros. If we finish them before we stop talking, we'll start using mine. Okay?" She smiled brightly, took another long drag on her cigarette, laid her pad on the desk and waited for him to pour.

Fulghum liked the reporter's brassy style. He brought out Jack Daniels to join the discussion and poured the brown elixir into two glasses while she opened her purse, pulled out her Tennessee Squires card and pushed it towards him.

"The lady does know how to impress a man," he said as he clinked his glass against hers before sliding hers across the desk. She raised the glass to admire the brown potion and took a sip. Then she set the glass down, pulled out her cell phone and indicated that she was recording their conversation. Fulghum shrugged his acquiescence.

"What do you think about the assassin of Enzio Pinza being set free from jail?"

"It is an outrage against justice. The man probably killed Mr. Pinza. He definitely tried to aim his weapon at me."

"Why do you think he was released?"

"Someone far above in the political establishment made phone calls to the high and mighty and engineered his release. Being a Cliffie, you are doubtless aware of the power of realpolitik?"

"Both Enzio Pinza and Brutus Higard were once assassins for the CIA."

"That doesn't sound like a question."

"Both performed black operations for the Agency for many years, and they diverged from the norm in different ways. Pinza went private along with his daughter. Higard, if we may continue with the charade by using his work name, went deep black into illegal assassinations under the direction of the CIA Director himself."

"I still don't hear a question."

"I don't hear a denial either. I'll continue." She did not continue at once. Figlear crossed and re-crossed her legs provocatively as if she were taking the interview to another level. She took another drag on her cigarette along with a sip of JD. She took off her frog's eyes and laid them on the desk. It was clear to Fulghum that they were just props—she could see perfectly well without them. She had the most marvelous hazel eyes, full of intelligence, wit, and wisdom.

The detective thought her skin was like peaches and cream as well as perfect teeth. As she straightened up in her chair, Fulghum could see that she was very well built. He originally thought her clothing might be a deflection, and it was. Under her layers of garments was one smashingly beautiful girl. She was not wearing a ring on her ring finger, but she did have a ring on the solid gold chain that hugged near her throat. She saw from his expression that he was warming to her charms. She smiled and looked directly into his eyes to show she appreciated his admiration.

"So, Mr. Fulghum, why did you fly to Venezuela in the days following the murder of the man with whom you had lunch minutes before he was assassinated?"

"I went to see a woman who became my client on urgent business."

"And was that client, a woman called Adrienne Poirot, whose real name is Hyacinth Pinza, daughter of the slain sniper Enzio Pinza?"

"Yes."

"So within the space of five days, you saw both the murder victim and his daughter, both of whom were at one time renowned assassins for the CIA."

"That is not a question."

"You returned from Venezuela and almost immediately you appeared in Boston Common on a park bench and just happened to see through the disguise of Brutus Higard. At risk, you helped the police apprehend the assassin. You even identified the staff that the man left on the grass as a possible murder weapon."

"Your monologue is intriguing."

"Is that a denial of the truth of it?"

"I didn't say that. Please have another cigarette. Would you like some more whiskey?"

"Thank you to both. Mr. Fulghum, have you considered why someone might want to kill Enzio Pinza?"

"Yes."

"Did Brutus Higard have a motive for murdering him?"

"Yes."

"Brutus Higard was in the Boston area during the time of the murder. He had a compelling motive for killing Enzio Pinza. He had in his possession the actual murder weapon, as police forensics proved without a shadow of a doubt. The Boston D.A. should have been satisfied that he had an open and shut case for murder one."

"Ms. Figlear, your logic is impeccable. Brava. Not one question in all those declarative statements. I feel like the straight man in a vaudeville show, only the substance is not comedic."

"No, Mr. Fulghum, it is anything but comedic."

"Go on. It's your interview. Do you mind if I refresh my glass? No?" He poured himself another two fingers of whiskey and looked directly at his interrogator as if to emphasize that this was her show.

"The Governor of this state. The Mayor of this city. The Chief of Police. I have interviewed all of them. Uniformly they have no comments on everything I've just told you. What do you say to that?"

"I must agree."

"What? Please clarify."

"I would expect them to have no comment when the evidence is clear and cogent."

"Mr. Fulghum, you know what I mean."

"Ms. Figlear, please explain what you mean in no uncertain terms."

"I mean that a known killer has been set free because the political system was corrupted at a higher level for reasons of national security. What do you say to that?"

"No comment." Fulghum smiled and shrugged.

"You can't mean that!"

"But I do mean it. If something is true, it needs no gloss."

"I'll come at this from another direction. A man who kills for a living, and who killed a man in Bedford, was apprehended and then freed on purely political grounds."

"Go on."

"This is an injustice on the level of a Greek tragedy."

"Enzio Pinza's daughter thinks so. You think so. I think so. So what?"

"What if I could tell you precisely why Brutus Higard has such a powerful hold on the powers that be that he can walk with impunity from the most heinous crimes?"

"I'd say it's time to turn off your recorder and mine as well so that we can discuss this matter with only the CIA's bugs left to record our cabal."

Figlear reddened and turned off her cell phone recorder. Fulghum did the same.

"You really were recording us as well?"

"And why shouldn't I have an identical record to yours? Who knows what you might allege?"

"Do you think your office is bugged?"

"I've no reason to think otherwise. I let almost anyone in here, ply them with smokes and the best whiskey to plunder their soul's secrets, beautiful women like yourself chiefly. Why I've had murderesses sit in that captain's chair and lie. I've had people come to let their weapons talk right through my door. This office is not what it seems at first sight any more than you are, my dear. I wouldn't be surprised if you stripped off all your clothes and stood before me as Superwoman. Please don't be offended. I admire you as much for your brains as for your beauty. You are gifted and I'm not patronizing you though I'm old enough to be your father."

"So where does this leave us."

"It leaves you with a story that your editor will never print. It leaves me with six fewer cigarettes and eleven-odd inches of JD. It makes me wonder why the people who run this country make good, well-meaning people like you and me go stark raving mad to set things right."

"I'm beginning to like you, Mr. Fulghum."

"Liking me, Ms. Figlear, would be a terrible mistake."

"And why is that, Mr. Fulghum?"

"You're sure your cell phone recorder is shut down? Please turn your phone off completely. Thank you. I'll do the same. There. Now put on your fake frog's eyes and pull on your jacket. I'll get mine. We'll take a stroll and talk outside."

On the street, Fulghum was careful to walk on the traffic side sheltering Darcy Figlear. He was now fully alert and watching for danger from all directions. Figlear seemed oblivious to his anxiety. When they came to Fulghum's car, he asked her to climb into the passenger side. He drove while they talked. Rather, she talked while he listened, interjecting his thoughts only occasionally so as not to break the flow of her monologue. Her story was factual, but it sounded like a fantasy or worse—a conspiracy theory. The more she talked, the more convincing her arguments sounded to Fulghum.

She spoke almost nonstop for two full hours while he drove in a meandering fashion, always looking through the rear view mirror for suspicious vehicles and through the windshield for dubious pedestrians or work crews. Fulghum felt as he did when working his brilliant, young and beautiful female agents in the Afghanistan war zone.

As Figlear talked, the detective relived those dangerous days when he served in the Special Forces. He reflected on how alike were the treacherous landlocked nation on the top of the world and this seemingly somnolent, sedimentary, green land leading down to the blue ocean. His heart leaped as he listened to the undercurrents of her story—her longing for companionship and her thirst to know all the truth at all costs. If he had been a lesser man, he might have taken advantage of the woman. She was willing, and he was aroused. Yet he knew that the journey they had begun together had nothing physical about it. It was a virtual labyrinth as intricate as the physical Greek original, only there was no Ariadne to provide the thread to lead them out of it. He knew the minotaur, Brutus Higard, well enough. Yet the labyrinth itself was their target, not the beast within it.

As they approached Fulghum's office on their return journey, Figlear asked a question that startled the detective because it was so pointedly literary and apt.

"What do the names Adrienne Poirot and Brutus Higard mean? I know they are work names, and they aren't supposed to have any particular meanings. In these cases, though, they do. Adrienne Rich the female poet and Hercule Poirot the detective come together as you and I do. Brutus was both the first and last of the Republican Romans and Higard seems to have meaning, but I can't yet fathom it."

"Hyacinth told me that her work name had precisely the derivations you suggest. As for Brutus Higard, you are right about the first name. I'd like to suggest that the second can be interpreted as something like 'high guard,' coming from the well-known Latin motto, 'quis custodiet ipsos custodies.'"

"Of course. That's brilliant."

"I have inside information. That is the motto of the Pinza family business."

"The what?"

"The Pinza's, father and daughter, started a business when they parted ways with the Agency. It's called The Shooters' Society. It's an assassination business, work for hire.

It has something to do with what's been happening. I just haven't been smart enough to figure it out."

"Keep trying, John. You'll figure it out. Meanwhile, you've now got help."

"Meaning?"

"Meaning me."

"Here we are again where we started. I'm mentally exhausted and you need to be getting home. We'll call it a day. I'll watch you as you go to your car. Check that your tires are still intact before you get into the vehicle."

"Mr. Fulghum, you really do know how to show a girl a good time."

"Don't make a habit of seeing me. If you have a breakthrough, just call. If you find that you're being shadowed or threatened, please let me know. I'll be there for you. Let's shake on a great start." He extended his hand, but she was not having anything so formal. She rushed at him and threw her arms around him, hugging him. He put his arms around her and pulled her close. He squeezed her, and then held her at arm's length.

They smiled at each other until Figlear blinked and backed away. She fumbled in her coat pocket for her keys. Then she turned away and walked to her car where she checked her tires. Evidently, her tires showed no signs of sabotage because she shrugged at Fulghum. She unlocked the car, hesitated for a moment as if she remembered she had something else to say. Then she clambered into her car and started it up. She waved and drove off. Fulghum already missed her when she passed from his view.

The detective walked up the stairs to his empty, smoky office, lit another cigarette and sat down in his captain's chair. Now he had to make sense of what he had heard from a most remarkable girl. It was going to take him all night to do that.

Fortunately, he thought, Jack Daniels was standing by to help. "Some things never change," he said out loud. Then he opened the top left drawer of his desk and took out a fresh, legal-sized yellow pad and a Bic pen. He hesitated with the pen above the yellow paper. Then he reasoned that he needed companionship in his quest. He poured three fingers of JD and set it by his right hand. Now that he was truly ready, he began to describe the maze that Darcy Figlear had outlined during their drive.

At the center of the sheet of yellow paper, Fulghum drew a square box. He then drew lines outward from each side of the box. At the end of each line, he drew an oval. In block letters, he wrote "OPP" in the square and in the ovals he wrote "CIA," "NSA," "SF," and "PRIVATE." He then wrote names Figlear had provided by each of the ovals, for example, Enzio Pinza correlated with "PRIVATE." Each name was a person who had been murdered during the last eighteen months. Fulghum's classification was not precise. Pinza, for example, fit in three categories of the four. Fulghum opted to identify him by the last category that applied to him. What mattered most was the association of all the names with the Office for the Protection of the Presidency, the OPP that lay at the center of the detective's diagram.

Fulghum knew that the OPP was an organization whose mission was to protect the office, not the person, of the President of the USA. Cloaked in secrecy, the OPP undertook its duties quietly. It was independent of the many governmental organizations and of the many functional bodies that comprised the Office of the President. For American democracy to work respect for the office of the President had to be maintained. Presidents came and went, but the executive power lived on independent of them.

Darcy had stumbled upon the OPP while researching a story about the strange death of a former Director of the CIA. The investigative reporter had picked up the threads of evidence and built a story that might have earned her a Pulitzer. Her editor at the Globe had been excited by her findings and analysis, but when the planned publication date neared, he had second thoughts. Darcy was told to cease and desist working on the story. Shortly afterward, she had been contacted by a man whose credential was an official OPP identification card. The man had informed her that her story about the death would not be published in America, and consequences would follow its publication elsewhere in the world.

The net effect of this clear violation of Figlear's First Amendment rights was to focus the investigative reporter on the OPP. Darcy admitted that much of her spiked article was speculative and its findings inconclusive. She combed the article for evidence that might have impinged on the presidency but found none. She asked herself, "What gives this shadowy organization the power to override the editor of a major newspaper and silence a reporter?" She decided she would find out even if her research met the same fate as her spiked story.

Early in her research on the OPP, she had a radical insight that spawned a major question. How did the OPP do its enforcement? She understood it was a watchdog organization, but what were its teeth? As she explained to Fulghum in his car, she began to look for evidence of the OPP's methods. She soon found that she was not alone asking questions about the OPP. Two other investigative reporters, from the New York Times and the San Francisco Bee, respectively, had been victims of OPP's censorship, and both had made the same decision as Darcy. Those two had joined forces to do their research, and when they learned of Figlear's quest, they asked her to join them.

Figlear liked to work alone, so she demurred. Her friend and mentor Sylvia, the savvy archivist at the Globe, congratulated her protégé on remaining independent of the others. Sylvia told the young reporter to interview John Fulghum at her earliest opportunity but to have a good reason for seeing him. The Enzio Pinza murder case was the opportunity Figlear had been looking for because it connected both to her OPP investigation and to her desire to meet the infamous, hard-boiled detective. When he learned of the OPP connection, Fulghum was fascinated.

He had asked Figlear at the time, "Why would a world-class sniper's activities be a concern of the OPP?" She explained that within the OPP, or working for it, was an enforcement team that eliminated anyone knowledgeable about illegal black operations perpetrated by the President or in the President's name. Figlear theorized that Pinza had been doing illegal black operations directly for the President. Fulghum was not so sure. He resolved to ask Hyacinth Pinza what she knew about her father's assassinations, but he would not do it over an open line. If Pinza was in a red sector before he was killed, Fulghum figured he was included in that red sector because from the OPP's point of view Pinza might have said anything during their lunch. The investigator told Figlear he did not know why Brutus Higard was going to kill him in the Common, but he suspected it had to do with his contact with Enzio Pinza.

Fulghum chain lit a cigarette as he examined the design he had drawn. Figlear had included three names of victims in each of the four categories. The most interesting name in each category for Fulghum was the index name discovered by the investigative reporter. First among the index names was that of the former CIA Director, the circumstances of whose death remained a mystery. Second on the list was Enzio Pinza. Third in line was a former Special Forces general officer who had been shot to death by a pizza deliveryman in North Carolina. Fourth was a cryptanalyst at the NSA; he had been found drowned in his own bathtub in a suburb of Laurel, Maryland. Fulghum wondered what evidence and logic connected the dots between these diverse figures. He also brooded on the problems of investigating forbidden knowledge.

Is Darcy Figlear chasing phantoms? Or is she on to something large? he asked himself. Since Figlear had volunteered to show him all her research on the death of the CIA Director, Fulghum figured he was going to be able to sift and winnow her material for an answer. Now that he had written down all the details he remembered from Figlear's facts and deductions, the detective decided he had done what he could for now. He was ready to go home and get some sleep as it was nearly midnight. He locked up, went down to his car and saw that all four tires were flat. While he considered what he was going to do, a man in a trench coat came up behind him.

"Bad luck, Fulghum. You'll have to call a garage, but it's late. I can give you a lift if you like." The man extended his identification. Fulghum used his cell phone light to read it.

"The trouble with you OPP folks is that you're sloppy. You have no sense of finesse."

"Hahaha. We get results. If you don't want a ride, perhaps we could go up to your office to talk."

Fulghum shrugged and then gestured for the man to lead the way.

They proceeded up the stairs to the detective's office where they sat across Fulghum's desk from each other. They did not take off their coats.

"It's your nickel, Mr. Arthur, if that's your real name."

"Fulghum, I had no idea you were an artist. May I look at your diagram on that yellow sheet?"

"Be my guest. I figured you'd already know what I drew from one of your mind readers."

"You flatter my organization. We don't know all and see all. We like to remain discreet about what we know. Your drawing has merit, I think. Perhaps it should be exhibited in a prominent place?"

"I don't think so. It's just a sketch. Perhaps the Technicolor painting that follows can be shown at the Museum of Contemporary Art, though. Let's cut the crap. Why did you spike my tires? What do you have to say for yourself?"

"Enzio Pinza's murder was not sanctioned by the OPP. He knew things that he should not have known. It was not his fault that he had the knowledge. What did you and he discuss over lunch at Dalia's?"

"If you didn't order Pinza killed, who did? Do you even know?"

"We know. You're aware that the man called Brutus Higard did the actual assassination."

"All the evidence points to that."

"Higard gets his orders from only one man."

"The Director of the CIA?"

"I will neither confirm nor deny that."

"What is the connection of the OPP to the names on that chart you're holding?"

"Ms. Figlear has been extremely visible in her research. She's done well considering that she has no security clearance and no history of the agencies."

"You'd have done better if you'd let her publish her article on the OPP rather than censoring it. You've created an extremely intelligent and determined adversary."

"So far she's not touched any live wires with her research."

"Then why are you here tonight?"

"Like I said, I want to know about your lunch conversation with Pinza—and a few other matters."

"I'm afraid I can't tell you much of interest to the OPP. Your organization never came up in our discussions. None of Pinza's operational missions were discussed."

"Why did you meet?"

"Pinza wanted to hire my services to find out who was trying to frame him for assassinations he did not commit."

"Did he hire you as he planned to do?"

"We hadn't resolved that before he was shot dead. We were comrades in arms in Afghanistan during the long war. He told me a few war stories. He gave me his business card. End of the matter. Now if you'll excuse me ..."

"Why did you fly to Caracas shortly after the murder? To us, that seemed awfully suspicious."

"Providing that information would violate a client relationship."

"We know that you flew there to talk with Hyacinth Pinza, the deceased's daughter. What we want to know is why you did that."

"I paid my condolences to the bereaved. If you check your records, you'll find I wasn't in Venezuela more than twenty-four hours."

"Is that where you got the picture of Brutus Higard?"

"That's privileged information."

"I'll take that as a yes. I'll also hazard a guess that the name Brutus Higard also came from the same source."

Fulghum sat deadpan. He wondered whether his visitor had a gun under his trench coat.

"Is Higard part of your organization?"

"No, Mr. Fulghum, he is not. He's far too unstable for us. His boss is not a friend."

"Do you have all you want from me?"

"For now, yes. I don't suppose it would do any good to ask that you stand down on your quest for answers about OPP's role and activities?"

Fulghum ignored the OPP man's question. Instead, he asked a question of his own. "What was the relationship of Brutus Higard and Enzio Pinza?"

"We knew they were mortal enemies."

"Do you know why they were mortal enemies?"

"Long ago Higard did not want Pinza to do a particular assassination. He threatened to kill Pinza if he did not back down and renounce his contract for hire. Pinza killed his target. Higard bided his time. Finally, Higard killed Pinza. You coincidentally had lunch just before that happened."

"Who did Pinza assassinate to inspire Higard's vendetta?"

"Why, Mr. Fulghum, the man is on your chart. It's the one with the asterisk here."

"I see. And that man's death had nothing to do with the OPP?"

"It had everything to do with the OPP, but Higard's allegiance was also to an office."

"And he has always worked directly for only one man in that office. Why?"

"In the intelligence world, information is wealth. Let's say that Higard, in those terms, is an extremely wealthy man."

"That would make him hated—and vulnerable."

"Yes, and no. In fact, he may be the most invulnerable man in this country. Recent events prove that. Mr. Fulghum, do you have any wish that Ms. Pinza remain alive?"

"Are you threatening her?"

"No, we are not, but, we happen to know that Brutus Higard has been ordered to terminate her with extreme prejudice. As far as we know he has only once failed in a mission."

"And when was that?"

"Funny you should ask. Actually, he failed twice on the same mission before the order was rescinded. He was ordered to kill you along with Pinza in the parking lot of that restaurant. He then was sent to Boston Common, and you know the rest of that story."

"You're telling me that Higard had intelligence about where I was on both occasions."

"No comment."

"Why was he called off finally after his second failed attempt to kill me?"

"We don't know the answer to that. Given the personality of this dangerous assassin, he may continue his attempts to kill you if only for pride's sake. He, not I, slashed your tires. For all I know, he's out there waiting for you."

"I'll take my chances. Speaking of chances, will you tell me the information Pinza knew that caused your office concern?"

"Since you don't know it already, I can confidently say that you won't be on our list. If Pinza did not tell you, you'll never know. I've taken too much of your time. As I told you down on the street, I'll be happy to drive you home if you like. It's chilly, and few taxis are running this late."

"No thanks. I like my office. I've slept here often after working late. Goodbye now, I hope we don't meet again."

"I don't think you have to worry about that. Ms. Figlear is another matter entirely."

"If you don't stand down on her immediately, I will be your enemy. If she is harmed in any way whatsoever, I will hunt you down and take retribution."

"I understand you, Mr. Fulghum, but my office will have to make that determination. As for your threats, we get them all the time. We don't often get them from persons with your patriotism and documented heroism in battle. At all risks, our allegiance is to protecting the office of the presidency. Nothing else matters. Goodbye."

With that, the OPP representative walked out of Fulghum's office door and down the stairs. The gunshot that followed the man's entry onto the sidewalk brought Fulghum out of his chair grabbing for his weapon. He hit the floor on the landing outside his door and covered the stairs. After bounding down the stairs two at a time, he cautiously peered out the door. There on the street was the OPP man's body on the ground with its head a bloody mass. He had taken a head shot from a high-caliber weapon. Blood and brains were scattered on the pavement. Fulghum thought the gunman was likely to be waiting for him to appear. Instead of exiting the door, the detective called 911 on his cell phone and reported the murder. A black and white arrived within ten minutes and the police did what they were paid to do. When requested, Fulghum dictated the little that he knew to the recorder. He said police forensics would have to discover the facts.

"Wow, you were serious about checking the tires! I'm on my way. I'll probably be there in twenty-five minutes."

Figlear picked up Fulghum. For a change, he did the talking. He explained what the OPP man had told him and she did not interrupt him. When he finished the tale, she brooded for a moment before she plunged right in.

"I suppose you've warned Hyacinth Pinza that Brutus Higard might be calling."

"I did. I'm convinced, though, that the OPP is not involved in a plot against her."

"You didn't get the name of the man Higard works for?"

"No, I didn't. I'm assuming it's the Director of the CIA."

"What's your logic?"

"The data is sensitive, in fact, classified so highly that I'll put you at risk to tell you. Suffice it to say that the OPP man told me as much last night before he left my office."

"So on the one hand, we have the OPP taking care of business with no qualms about the methods they have to use to protect the presidency. On the other hand, we have Brutus Higard performing hits for the Director of the CIA."

"Yes and yes. From what the OPP man told me, Higard was the man who slashed my tires. He is the most likely suspect in this recent assassination."

"What would have been Higard's motive for killing him?"

"That's an excellent question. I think he was trying his luck with his third attempt on my life, but he mistook the OPP man for me."

"I thought you said that the order to Brutus Higard to assassinate you had been rescinded."

"Yes, but the deceased also told me to watch my back because Higard might make another attempt out of pride."

"Where does all this leave us?"

"The key to our mysteries is still Brutus Higard. He is untouchable and on the rampage."

"Do you think he'll hang around for a fourth attempt on your life?"

"I just don't know. By now, he'll realize he shot the wrong man—assuming he really was gunning for me. While we're wool-gathering, we have to leave open the slight possibility that Higard was targeting the OPP man on orders."

"That's a creepy thought. You said the OPP was tracking me closely."

"That's right, Darcy. They're watching you and following your research. As long as you don't find anything you could use against them, they'll probably leave you alone."

"I'll find everything there is, eventually."

"Then we have a problem."

"Fulghum, I have a problem. Except for Brutus Higard, you're in the clear."

"Not so. The OPP man never got the chance to report our discussion to his group. That means my answers to his questions are not in their database. I'm still a question mark to the OPP."

"If we could take Higard out of the equation, we'd be way ahead of where we are now."

"Yes. Our primary target is Higard. My bet is he's gone to ground for a while."

"I'll wager he's gone to Venezuela."

"If he goes there and attempts to assassinate Hyacinth, she'll recognize him and take him out."

"Who's watching her back?"

"Are you game for a flight to sunny Venezuela?"

"I never thought you'd ask. Are you paying?"

"Let's drop by your place so you can pack and pick up your passport. Yes, I'm paying. Do you have extra rolls of toilet paper?"

"As a matter of fact, I do."

"Pack as many rolls as you can."

"You're not kidding, are you?"

"Definitely not, it's a kind of currency down there, interchangeable with the local fiat money."

"Hahaha. Are we going as man and wife?"

"Don't get any ideas along that line, Darcy. We'll be booking separate rooms."

"Sylvia said you'd be like this." Figlear smiled at Fulghum and shook her head.

"She should know. By the way, how is she?"

"This morning she said she was glad the man who was shot outside Joe's Malt Shop was not John Fulghum."

"So was I, Darcy. So was I."

After Figlear had packed, she drove Fulghum to his office where he kept his traveling bag and passport. She saw the condition of the detective's car and whistled. Fulghum called his garage and told the mechanic what he needed done. He left his car key in the exhaust pipe for the tow truck operator. The detective called Hyacinth and told her that the cavalry would meet her in Caracas. Figlear seemed intensely interested in the detective's familiar tone with the female assassin. Then Figlear drove them to Logan International where they took the next flight to Caracas. They arrived in Venezuela's capital city early the next morning.

Just outside the baggage area, Fulghum and Figlear found Hyacinth dressed in her signature black pants suit holding the sign that read "H'ya." The two women looked each over as if they were rivals. Hyacinth immediately took on the role of big sister and smiled sweetly when she told Darcy to sit in the back seat of her Mercedes.

"Don't get too settled. We're going to drive around for a while. After that, we're flying to the Isla de Margarita in three hours. I'm paying for your travel. You'll stay at my estate. That's where Brutus Higard will try to do his dirty work and that's where we'll put an end to his aura of invulnerability."

"Have you seen any signs of him or his spotters yet?"

"None as yet. Tell me what you've discovered since we last talked."

"Darcy has the best perspective on the big picture. Darcy, review the bidding for all of us. Start where you found out the story you wrote was spiked by your editor."

Figlear was glad to have the opportunity to be superior to Hyacinth for a few minutes. From the back seat, she launched into the results of her research to date and integrated the latest information she had heard from Fulghum. Hyacinth listened carefully and nodded her understanding at each stage of the narrative. Fulghum had the impression that the female assassin was impressed with the investigative reporter's intelligence and clarity of expression. When she had completed her ad hoc presentation, she deferred to Fulghum to tell her about the shooting outside his office.

Fulghum nodded and gave Hyacinth a succinct digest of events surrounding the murder of the OPP man. Hyacinth took a moment to digest what he said while she weaved around pedestrians in the crowded streets.

"So Brutus Higard is the key."

"We think so, yes. He works alone and takes his orders from one person, presumed to be the Director of the CIA. We are not certain of the substance of his enduring hold on the

Agency. We are fairly sure, based on what the OPP man told me before he was slaughtered, he was not working for the OPP when he killed your father. In sum, the man is an Agency man doing dirty, unsanctioned wet work for a living. Since he tried three times to kill me and failed and since his new orders are to kill you, we figured he'd show up at your estate to complete his latest mission."

"I'm glad for the update, and I'm glad you came. I intend to reimburse you for your support. I'm afraid I cannot take away the risk that you'll be caught in the crossfire if and when Higard shows up. Some things can't be guaranteed. I can provide everything you'll need at my estate including weapons. Now let me tell you about my security."

For the next twenty minutes, Hyacinth gave a professional's view of the security systems her estate afforded. The vulnerabilities she had exploited to kill the former owner and his concubine had been eliminated. New cameras and seismic sensors made it highly unlikely that anyone approaching the main house would go undetected. She had installed underground quarters in case of attack by air, heavy weapons or gangs of humans. In the case of siege, she had water and provisions for a week or more for five people. The only thing she did not have was toilet paper.

Fulghum told her that he had brought four rolls in his bag and Figlear had brought five. Hyacinth laughed appreciatively. She said it was time to get back to the airport for their flight. She turned in her Mercedes rental, and the assassin, the detective, and the investigative reporter progressed to their boarding area. The threesome encountered a slight delay in their flight, but they arrived on the island before dinnertime. Hyacinth's Jeep was waiting at the airport. She invited Darcy to sit in the passenger seat and let Fulghum sit in the rear. She took a Glock from the glove compartment and handed it to Fulghum. He checked the weapon, safed it, then put it under his belt. After that, the women talked while Fulghum watched for signs of trouble. It took twenty minutes to reach Pinza's estate. The automatic gate swung open when Hyacinth entered the security code. The Jeep went through the middle of a long double line of palm trees and stopped in the circular driveway in the front entrance to the main house.

Hyacinth showed her guests to their rooms and told them she would give them a guided tour of her security measures as soon as they felt ready. Once they were established, she arrived wearing a holster with a .375 Magnum pistol in it. She handed Darcy a belted holster with a similar weapon in it. To Fulghum, she gave a scoped, 30-06 hunting rifle. Touring the outside of the building, the assassin pointed out the cameras and showed how their fields of view overlapped each other. She indicated where seismic sensing arrays were located all around the periphery. She explained how the visual sensors were installed on the double walls around the perimeter of the grounds.

"Well, Mr. Fulghum, how would you penetrate these defenses?" Hyacinth asked him, one professional to another.

"I'd come in from the air in a one-seat microlite aircraft and drop on the roof of the main building. I'd try to do this when you were out and position to shoot you in the main drive upon your arrival. If you were in the residence, I'd drop in at night after providing a diversion, a flash bang or grenade. I might even hire a decoy to provide the diversion before I dropped."

"I like the idea of a decoy," Hyacinth said. "So how would you disperse our forces to have the best chance of fending off the attack and killing the attacker?"

center flashed red. Other red warning lights turned on as the investigative reporter proceeded down the long tunnel. Finally, she reached the end of the tunnel. Satisfied by what she saw, she turned and walked back towards the command center. A warning light indicated a problem in the vestibule above the command center. Hyacinth punched a few buttons to locate the trigger for the warning. Gunfire erupted in the space above them. Fulghum hit the floor and aimed his weapon in the direction of the stairwell leading from the ground floor level to the command center. Hyacinth continued to swing her remaining interior cameras to view the attacker. She displayed a figure dressed in black setting a charge on the wall and running back to be free of the blast effects. A huge explosion tore a hole in the area of the stairwell. Fulghum and Pinza now aimed their weapons at the area of the blast hole where smoke and debris obscured their view. Fulghum saw objects being dropped through the hole.

He yelled, "Flash bangs and grenades! Run for the tunnel door."

Hyacinth wasted no time racing for the tunnel door. When she reached it, the deafening sound and blinding light of the flash bangs worked their infernal magic. The female assassin was thrown into the tunnel by the blast effects. Now Fulghum was alone in the command center, still on the floor with his weapon aimed at the black hole where he thought the threat was going to emerge.

A voice descended from above, "Surrender Hyacinth Pinza and live. We've come to do to her what Mr. Higard did to her father. That is our mission. We don't want any collateral damage."

Fulghum remained absolutely still. He said nothing. His senses were still recovering from the intense flash effects and the sounds of the explosions. He hoped that Hyacinth was now making her way down the tunnel to safety. He hyperventilated and strained to see through the dissipating smoke. He remained calm. He had lain in wait in Afghanistan many times. His weapon was unsafed. He thought he might need only one shot with his 30-06, and he began thinking through what he would do to eject a shell and fire a second. Then a black line fell through the opening and a body rappelled to the floor immediately afterward and landed on its feet. Fulghum pulled the trigger, worked the bolt and held his rifle steady to fire the second round. He waited patiently to see any signs of life.

"Your game is over. Put down your weapon and stand up straight."

Fulghum waited after he spoke for what seemed four minutes. Then another line dropped through the hole and a second figure in black stood before him. The former Special Forces officer pulled the trigger and ejected the shell, ready to fire a third time if necessary.

"Fulghum, for a soldier, you don't perform badly. Too bad, that while this diversion has been playing a farce, at the other end of the tunnel, the real action has been playing a tragedy. Hahaha. Maybe it's going to be fourth time lucky. We'll see."

Down the tunnel came the sound of two pistol shots. He heard a female cry of anguish.

The detective did not react. He did not speak. His finger lay against his hair trigger. The third line dropped through the hole and the third figure landed on its feet. Simultaneously Fulghum pulled the trigger. The third body fell as the former two bodies had done. A noise from the tunnel door made Fulghum avert his eyes from the blasted hole. There in the door was Darcy supporting Hyacinth, who walked with a limp. Darcy held her pistol at the ready as she pushed through the door into what was left of the command center. She eased Hyacinth into a chair.

Then the investigative reporter coolly walked to the place where three black lines hung into the room. She knelt and felt for signs of life in the three corpses but found none. She then pulled out her cell phone and activated its light to shine on what might have been three faces once. Fulghum had risen to his knees and abandoned his firing position with the rifle in his hand. He saw what Darcy saw—the horrible result of three headshots with a high-powered rifle. He knew what she was feeling, so he walked behind her and slowly eased her pistol from her hand. She turned and threw up all over his midriff. She grabbed him desperately with her arms as if he were a life buoy in a stormy sea. He held her tight with her gun and his rifle in his two hands behind her back. She began to sob uncontrollably and as she wept and convulsed, she tried to say something but could not get it out.

"What she's trying to tell you, shamus, is that she shot him. Brutus Higard is down in the tunnel, dead, shot right between the eyes. He got a shot off before he hit the ground. The bullet hit me in the thigh. It's a flesh wound, I think. I'll live but I'm in shock. When you can manage it, please go up there and find a blanket and a large towel and bring them down to me. Right now, I'm sorry, but I'm going to have to pass out." Hyacinth was as good as her word. She fainted from pain and stress.

Fortunately, for Hyacinth, the former Special Forces soldier could field dress a wound plus treat shock and trauma. Emergency medical personnel were on the scene within ten minutes, and Hyacinth was taken to an emergency clinic, which offered the best medical services Cuban doctors could provide to a wounded woman of means. The corpses, their weapons, microlites, and equipment were taken away by the local police who accepted Fulghum's account of the battle verbatim. In that account, he took full credit for all four kills. He thus deflected attention from the newshound who had shot an attacking assassin with a Magnum handgun as if she were Annie Oakley. Fulghum and Figlear stood by Pinza in the hospital in shifts. They used their precious toilet paper supply to bribe the attending staff to treat her well, and they helped her make the transition back to her blasted estate.

Hyacinth made good on her promise to pay her two protectors richly for their service.

"You deserve the money. I'll wire the full sum with a generous bonus immediately to your bank account, Detective Fulghum. Please see that Darcy gets one-half of that amount. I'm glad that this nightmare is over, my father's death is avenged. When I have recovered fully, I'll get back to work, but maybe I'll need to change my venue. We shall see."

"If you're sure you can handle things if we depart, then so be it," Fulghum told his client. "Watch for further threats, and let me know if you need help."

"Darcy, where ever did you learn to shoot so well?" Figlear winced, and Fulghum saw his cue.

"As I should have known from the start, our investigative reporter is actually a CIA assassin. The way she handled that big gun was the final piece of the puzzle I've been trying to assemble since she walked into my life."

"Darcy, say it's not so," Hyacinth said with a laugh. Darcy joined her laughter good-naturedly.

"Goodbye, Hyacinth. It's been a pleasure working with one of the greats in our business. Who knows, when I go freelance, I might be looking for a position with The Shooters' Society."

"I didn't hear that, Darcy. That is your real name, isn't it?"

"As much as Hyacinth is Adrienne Poirot's real name." Then she picked up her bag and headed for the door. "The taxi is here to take us to the airport. Are you coming, John?"

"Go ahead, Figlear, I'll be right behind you. Hyacinth, I'm going to leave you with the last rolls of toilet paper but one. I'd leave you that one too, but I don't know how long it will take us to get out of this country. Stay well and keep in touch."

"Kiss me, shamus."

Fulghum obliged the lady and she smiled wistfully.

"You might just consider Darcy a keeper, John. I wish I could compete."

"Hyacinth, there is no contest. This time, everyone who counts came up a winner. At least in our final battle, only the losers failed. We were lucky. I hope my luck continues at the track. Speaking of which, I've got a ream of racing forms to catch up on. Later then."

John and Darcy pulled up to the airport and made all their flights plus transfers as they had planned. They seemed to be a good looking, January-May couple having a fine time on holiday. They laughed as if they were in a separate world with the kind of knowledge only lovers share. At Logan International, they climbed into Darcy's car and drove directly to Joe's Malt Shop where Fulghum's car waited with all its new tires intact.

"Well, John, I've said it before. You sure know how to show a girl a good time."

"Will I see you again now that your mission is over?"

"I'll go back to Langley tomorrow morning. Then who can say where I'll be vectored?"

"It's goodbye then."

"Au revoir, my love." He smiled at the prospect.

She sped away, and Fulghum breathed deeply. He already missed her though she was not yet out of sight. He leaned over and checked the exhaust pipe of his car. His key was there, so he fetched it out and put it in his pocket.

The detective walked up the stairs to his office landing and saw outside his door a box. He thought for a moment about calling the bomb squad. Then he examined the box carefully on the top and four visible sides. The name and address were correct. The sender was a Tennessee gentleman named Jack Daniels.

John Fulghum unlocked and opened his office door, shuffled through the piles of new mail that lay on the floor, set his traveling case by his desk and brought in the box of whiskey. He situated the box close by the right side of his desk so that he could transfer the bottles to the second drawer eventually with ease. He thought the divine elixir the perfect ending to a case well accomplished. He scooped up the mail from his office floor, placed it in a pile on the desk and sat in his captain's chair.

Just then, his cell phone jangled its texting tone. It was from Hyacinth, a long string of positive emojis ending with a number and the text, "Transfer complete." He thought for a moment before replying with a simple smiley face.

"That about sums it up on my end," he said out loud.

Then he took out the bottle that was in his second drawer and one glass, which he filled with three fingers of the brown, velvety potion. He was about to raise a toast to the races but had second thoughts. He rummaged through his desk to find the new racing forms and began scouring them for any name that clicked with "Darcy." He sipped the JD and felt it course all the way down to his stomach. It was going to be a long, lonely night, but the answer lay in the sheets on the desk before him. He would bet on that.

Acronyms and Glossary

A Capella - Italian expression meaning "in the manner of the chapel" or singing without instrumental accompaniment
ATF - Bureau of Alcohol, Tobacco, Firearms and Explosives
Burqa - an enveloping outer garment worn by women in some Islamic traditions to cover their bodies when in public
Chavista - A follower of Venezuelan socialist Hugo Rafael Chávez Frías (1954-2013)
CIA - Central Intelligence Agency [aka The Agency]
Cliffie - student or Graduate of Radcliffe College
CONUS - Continental United States
D. A. - District Attorney
DEA - Drug Enforcement Agency
Deus ex-machine - Latin for "god from the machine" [translated from a Greek expression] an unexpected power or event saving a seemingly hopeless situation
DDO - Deputy Director of Operations [of the CIA]
DNA - DeoxyriboNucleic Acid
DoD - Department of Defense
EA - Executive Assistant
Emoji - ideograms and smileys used in electronic messages and webpages
ESD - Emergency Shut Down [Procedure for Oil and Gas Pipeline Closure]
FBI - Federal Bureau of Investigation
FEMA - Federal Emergency Management Agency
HR - Human Resources

Imam - Islamic leadership position associated with a worship leader of a mosque
IP - Internet Protocol [Internet address]
ISIL - Islamic State of Iraq and the Levant
ISIS - Islamic State of Iraq and al-Sham [aka ISIL and Daish]
JTAC - Joint Terminal Attack Controller
KL - Kuala Lumpur [City in Malaysia]
LGBT - Lesbian, Gay, Bisexual, and Transgender
NSA - National Security Agency
OPP - Office for the Protection of the Presidency [A secret organization often confused with the Office of Presidential Personnel]
OSS - Office of Strategic Services, active during World War II
PRC - People's Republic of China
Quis custodiet ipsos custodies? Latin for "Who will guard the guards?"
SCIF - Sensitive Compartmented Information Facility
SF - Special Forces
SOP - Standard Operating Procedure
TACP - Tactical Air Control Party [Air Force Ground Mobile Air Control Unit]

E.W. Farnsworth

E.W. Farnsworth is a former military officer, contractor, and a current consultant to law enforcement and intelligence agencies. He lives and writes in sunny Arizona.

Farnsworth's first volume of *John Fulghum Mysteries* and *Engaging Rachel* appeared from Zimbell House Publishing LLC in 2015. Also published are *Bitcoin Fandango,* Farnsworth's picaresque novel about global intrigue in crypto-currency enforcement, and *Desert Sun, Red Blood,* stories about cowboys and Indians in the Arizona Territory during the Apache Wars of the mid-Nineteenth Century.

To date, eighty-three stories are published in numerous anthologies in the U.S. and the U.K., including many in Zimbell House Publishing LLC anthologies.

The author's *Pirate Tales* will appear from Zimbell House in March 2016. *DarkFire at the Edge of Time,* his collected science fiction stories will appear from Audio Arcadia in England in July 2016. His spy stories, *The Secret Adventures of Agents Salamander and Crow* are expected to be published in twenty-six monthly installments in 2016 and 2017.

Future works include his *Love in the Time of Baro Xaimos*: The Gypsy Holocaust in the next few months. This novel brings to light the gypsies' struggle to survive in Europe during the Nazi period. In addition, E.W. Farnsworth is working on an epic poem, *The Voyage of the Spaceship Arcturus,* about the future of humankind when humans, avatars, and artificial intelligence must work together to instantiate a second Eden after the Chaos Wars bring an end to life on Earth.

An interview with E.W. Farnsworth is featured on the Zimbell House LLC website, http://zimbellhousepublishing.com/author-spotlight/e-w-farnsworth//

For continuous updates on the current and forthcoming works of E.W. Farnsworth, please see his website www.ewfarnsworth.com.

Reading Group Guide

1. Is John Fulghum's character convincing as a present day private investigator?
2. In *Gypsy Traveler,* John Fulghum is introduced to the gypsy culture and alludes to their assistance to the US Government through various wars and events. Do you think they are helping today in some way?
3. Do you think May Bell is the unacknowledged daughter of Roberto Rapello and Maria Strong?
4. The gypsy culture and way of life is unlike a typical American's. Is it a lifestyle you could accept?
5. Throughout *Hacker I,* the relationship between Jonathan and Cynthia grows. Despite their attraction for each other, would Jonathan and Cynthia's marriage actually survive the constant work interruptions to their plans?
6. In *Bloody End of the Line,* we learn of Alia's ongoing assignments infiltrating local Middle Eastern communities. Should she have considered leaving with Marty or is the mission the only important thing to accomplish?
7. John Fulghum's life is complex yet seems to be without current personal relationships. Is Alia the one who got away?
8. In *Headshots I and II,* a glimpse into the life and training of professional assassins is provided. Do you think the internal conflict in taking a life becomes easier over time?
9. Have you read John Fulghum Mysteries Volume I or any other works by E.W. Farnsworth?
10. If you were to talk with the author, what would you want to know?

A Note from the Publisher

Dear Reader,

Thank you for reading E.W. Farnsworth's second novel in the John Fulghum Mysteries series.

We feel the best way to show appreciation for an author is by leaving a review. You may do so on our website: www.ZimbellHousePublishing.com, Goodreads.com, Amazon.com, or Kindle.com.

Made in the USA
San Bernardino, CA
26 March 2016